ESCAPE TO THE WEST
BOOK ONE

NO ONE'S Bride

NERYS LEIGH

Prologue

February, 1870

"But that money is rightfully mine!"

Franklin Courtney leaned back into the green leather upholstery of his chair, one side of his thin lips twisting up. "Is it? And you have that in writing, do you?"

Realisation opened a void in Amy's gut. How could she have been so naive? "There was a contract."

"Really? And where is this alleged contract now?"

"I... you and Mrs Courtney said you would keep it safe for me." Even as she said the words, she knew they were futile.

Mr Courtney's mouth curled further. "Funny, I don't recall that. In fact, I don't recall a contract at all."

A heated belt of anger coiled around Amy's chest. He couldn't do this to her, not now, when she was so close. "You said I would be paid once I reached twenty-one. I trusted you. I was only fourteen."

"And that was seven years ago," he said. "You were just a child. I wouldn't expect you to remember the events surrounding your employment accurately. My felicitations on your birthday, by the way."

"You can't do this! I'll..."

"You'll what? Go to the authorities? With what proof?" He leaned forward, resting his elbows on the polished surface

1

of the expansive mahogany desk in front of him. "I have many friends in the higher echelons of the police, not to mention the judiciary. Who do you think they'll believe? A well-respected member of New York's highest society?" His eyes travelled down her body, his smile becoming a sneer. "Or a kitchen maid?"

She shook her head slowly, hardly believing what was happening. How could he steal her dreams from her without the slightest hint of remorse?

"However," he continued, "I am not unsympathetic to your plight."

He pushed back from the desk and sauntered around the huge piece of furniture. Amy took a step back, a lifetime of having to watch over her shoulder making her wary.

"There is no money for you," he said. "Your wages covered your bed and board, nothing more. But I'm sure we could come to an arrangement so that when you do eventually leave my employ you won't be left completely destitute."

She backed away as he advanced, looking beyond him to the door he'd somehow cut her off from. How could she have been so stupid, coming to him alone? But she'd been so eager to collect the seven years of wages she was owed. So eager to start her life.

Her back hit the wall beside one of the tall bookcases in the office.

Courtney continued his advance. "As you are aware, my wife spends much of her time on long visits away from home. I don't begrudge her the opportunity to spend time with her family and friends, but a man has certain... needs that must be fulfilled."

The staff of Staveley House were well aware of Courtney's reputation. Amy had no doubt his "needs" were being met regularly in any number of the city's houses of ill repute. Not that it had stopped him from ogling her at every opportunity.

Fear skittered up her spine. Since she was sixteen she'd known better than to allow herself to be caught alone with Mr Courtney. Why did she come here?

He was only three feet away now. "My proposition is that you come to my bed every day for two years. After that, you may leave with a generous donation towards your future." He smirked, clearly anticipating her agreement.

Stunned at his brazenness, Amy glared at him, fury fuelling her words. "I am not one of your whores. I will never let you touch me."

The smirk melted from his face, replaced by anger. "Foolish girl. Perhaps you will change your priorities when you don't think yourself so pure."

He lunged forward, his hands grasping Amy's arms. Pinned into the corner, she struggled to push him back. Despite being more than twice her age and rotund from lack of exercise, his strength still outclassed hers.

Help me, Lord!

She turned her head away as the alcoholic fumes of his breath puffed around her face.

"Don't struggle, my dear," he rasped, his hands tugging at her skirts. "You might even enjoy this. I know I will."

"No," she gasped, her voice barely audible as she frantically strained against his bulk. "Let me go!"

A knock sounded on the door.

Courtney clamped one hand over Amy's mouth and shoved her back, his bulbous gut pinning her in place, and barked, *"What?"*

"Sir, Mrs Courtney has arrived home," Mr Rand replied from outside the closed door.

Courtney's jaw clenched, a vein throbbing in his temple. "I'll be right there."

"Yes, Sir." The butler's footsteps receded along the wooden floor of the hallway outside Courtney's office.

He leaned forward until his nose was almost touching Amy's. "No one will believe you if you say anything about this."

He released her and she ran for the door, pulling it open and fleeing along the hallway. She didn't stop running until she reached the bedroom she shared with three other women in the servant's quarters. No one else was there and she threw herself onto her narrow bed, burying her face into the thin pillow and sobbing.

How could this happen? This morning she'd woken up filled with joy that her hopes and dreams were about to be realised. How could everything have gone so badly wrong?

"Amy? Amy, what is it?"

The mattress dipped and hands touched Amy's shoulders. Amy sat up and collapsed into her friend's embrace.

"What happened?" Katherine said, rocking her slowly.

Between sobs, Amy told her about the meeting with Courtney.

"That... that... that..." Katherine sputtered. "I can't even think of a word bad enough for him!"

"What am I going to do, Kate?" Amy wiped at her eyes with her sleeve. "You'll be married in two months and gone to live with Edward and I'll still be here with him. I have to get away."

Katherine dug into her pocket, pulled out a handkerchief and handed it to her. She always was more organised than Amy. "You can come and live with us."

Amy dabbed at her eyes. "It's kind of you to offer, but Edward's home is barely big enough for the two of you. Marrying him is your dream and I won't spoil it for you."

"Well, isn't there anyone you would want to marry? You

4

know how happy I am with Edward. I know you could be just as happy if you found the right man."

Amy knew Katherine meant well and that she was truly happy, but Amy knew the devastation that came when everything you loved was lost. Love would never blind her. "I'm not going to marry. I won't be dependent on any man. The only person I will ever rely on is myself. Too many things can go wrong."

"You can rely on me," Katherine said softly.

"Oh, Kate, you know that's not what I meant. I know you would never let me down."

Katherine took her hand and squeezed it. "God will help you. He'll provide a way out, I know He will. And in the meantime, none of us will leave you alone, I promise. Mr Courtney will never get the chance to hurt you. We stick together, us kitchen girls."

Amy managed a small smile. "I know."

She reached beneath her pillow and pulled out a crumpled piece of paper, its edges worn from years of handling. She unfolded it to reveal a page from a magazine with a photo of a building eight storeys tall that took up a whole block, with white painted walls, flags fluttering on the roof, and so many windows she couldn't even imagine how many rooms were inside.

"I have to go here," she said, her determination stronger than ever. "Whatever it takes, I have to get to San Francisco somehow."

Chapter 1

Three months later.

Amy peered through the train window as it chugged into the station, staring past the dust and grime that had accumulated during the long journey.

Around her, chattering voices grew excited.

"Can you see them?"

"There are so many people, how do we know..."

"Over there! That must be them!"

"Oohhhh, they're all so handsome. I can't even decide which I want to be mine."

A series of sighs followed, but Amy was barely listening. She didn't even glance in the direction of the group of men her companions were so fascinated by. Instead, she scanned the station, first finding the ticket office and the exit and then identifying possible escape routes and places to hide.

Going on the amount of time the train had spent at previous stations, she wouldn't have much time. But if she missed her window of opportunity there was always the backup plan, such as it was.

It wasn't a very big town, Green Hill Creek. Population six hundred and thirty-four, according to Mrs Wright at the Western Sunset Marriage Service. About to increase to six hundred and thirty-nine.

Six hundred and thirty-eight, Amy corrected herself. She wouldn't be staying.

She tightened her grip on her small carpet bag as the train slowly came to a halt. Those around her got to their feet and men, women and children began filing down the aisle between the seats. From previous stops when she'd done the same, Amy knew they weren't all getting off here. On a long journey any opportunity to stretch one's legs in the fresh air, or as fresh as it got around the steam train, was welcome.

Her companions rose, smoothing their clothing and hair, asking each other how they looked.

"Amy? Aren't you coming?"

She moved her gaze from the window to look up at Sara. The strawberry blonde young woman was smiling down at her. Sara was two years older than Amy and during their week long journey from New York they had struck up a friendship that made Amy sorry she wouldn't be staying. She hoped the man Sara had come for treated her as well as she deserved.

"I'll be right there," Amy said. "You go on."

"You don't have to be nervous," Sara said, sitting down next to her. "They look like fine men. I'm sure we'll all be very happy here. Are you sure you don't want to borrow one of my dresses? We could find somewhere for you to change before we get off. It's not too late."

Amy smiled and shook her head. "No, I'm fine, thank you. But you're very kind. I hope you'll be happy here."

"We'll both be happy," Sara said, "you'll see." She took Amy's hand and stood. "Come on, let's go and meet our husbands." She laughed. "Doesn't that sound strange?"

Amy followed her to the door, swallowing the lump in her throat. She desperately wished she could say goodbye, but she couldn't risk it. As soon as she was off the train she would sneak away, buy another ticket, and find somewhere to hide until the train left again. It was the only thing she could do.

7

Outside, she was relieved to see many of the passengers still milling around the station. Slipping away into the crowd should be easy. She pulled her hat onto her head and took a step towards the ticket office.

Sara grasped her hand. "Oh Amy, I'm a little nervous myself now." She pulled Amy after their three other travelling companions, in the direction of a group of men standing a little way back from the train. "If you feel me starting to swoon, pinch me hard. The last thing I want is Daniel thinking I'm a feeble woman who isn't able to cope with life in the west."

Panicked, Amy glanced over her shoulder towards the ticket office as Sara tugged her along. She had to get away.

"Ladies, welcome to Green Hill Creek."

A man with a round belly and greying hair was smiling at the little cluster of women Amy was now trying to hide behind. A plump, kind looking lady was at his side. Beyond them stood a group of four young men looking more nervous than if they'd been caught in the middle of a stampede of bison. Or whatever it was they had out here. A fifth, older man stood a little off to one side.

Amy tugged her wide-brimmed hat lower, glad she was behind everyone else. She focused on the man who had spoken and the woman beside him, purposely not looking at the young men. The last thing she wanted was to see him. If she saw the man she was doing such a terrible thing to, she might lose her nerve.

"I'm Pastor Simon Jones," the man said, "and this is my wife, Irene."

The woman next to him grinned. "We're so thrilled to welcome you all. I'm sure you will be happy in our little town."

"That we are," Pastor Jones said, matching her smile. "Now, I'm sure you are all tired from your journey, so I'll

8

make this quick. I will read out each of your names in turn and your intended will introduce himself, then we'll all go to the church and perform the ceremonies. Don't worry, no long sermons." He grinned and his audience laughed. "And then you can all go to your new homes and get settled in."

Please Lord, don't let me be first, Amy prayed, glancing back at the ticket office again. She subtly tried to extricate her hand from Sara's, but her grip was like iron.

"All right," the pastor said, looking at a piece of paper in his hand. "First, Elizabeth Cotton."

Lizzy bounced forward, her curly dark hair doing its best to escape from the ribbons holding her topknot in place. During their long journey, Lizzy had always been the one who wanted to see and do everything, her boundless enthusiasm infectious. Amy hoped her new husband loved her for it.

A tall man with short brown hair and a neatly trimmed moustache stepped forward.

"Miss Cotton," Pastor Jones said, "may I introduce Richard Shand."

Richard held out his hand. "Ma'am."

Lizzy squealed and launched herself at the shocked man, throwing her arms around his neck and almost knocking him over. There were scattered gasps around the group. Mrs Jones put one hand to her mouth, chuckling behind it.

Regaining his balance, Richard held his hands out without touching the woman wrapped around him, looking uncertain what to do.

Lizzy let go and smiled up at him. "I'm so pleased to meet you, Richard. You're very handsome."

He appeared slightly stunned as he looked down at his enthused bride. "I'm pleased to meet you too, Ma'am. And thank you."

She giggled and slipped her arm through his as they

9

stepped back.

"He's going to have his hands full," Sara muttered to Amy.

Amy couldn't help but smile. "He certainly is."

"Well, um, yes," the pastor said, rallying. "So far so good." He looked at his piece of paper again. "Louisa Wood?"

Louisa stepped forward, pushing a non-existent stray strand of auburn hair under her bonnet with a white lace gloved hand.

"Louisa, this is Peter Johnson."

The older man stepped forward, pulling his hat off to reveal a mop of greying mid-brown hair. Despite his age, which Amy would have judged at late forties, he had a large, muscular build with exceptionally broad shoulders. "Miss Wood, I'm Jesse's father and I'll be taking you to meet him, if that's all right."

"Of course," Louisa said, her impeccable manners shining through her confusion. "I do hope he's not unwell."

"Oh no, Miss. He'll explain when we get there."

She smiled and nodded, moving to stand beside Mr. Johnson as he stepped back.

Please, Amy thought. *Please*.

Pastor Jones consulted his paper again. "Sara Worthing?"

Sara gasped and squeezed Amy's hand.

"Shall I pinch you now?" Amy whispered.

Stifling a laugh, Sara let go of Amy's hand and walked forward.

Amy moved back a little, but didn't leave despite the chance to escape. She badly wanted to see who Sara's future husband was.

"Miss Worthing," Pastor Jones said, "meet Daniel Raine."

A very handsome, dark haired man stepped forward. "I'm very pleased to finally meet you, Sara," he said in a deep, smooth voice, smiling and holding out his hand.

Amy watched Sara practically melt onto the platform. She gazed up at her husband to be, her mouth opening and then closing again. Finally, she took his hand.

"Hi," she said, her voice barely more than a whisper.

Daniel placed her arm around his and led her back into place with the others. Sara's eyes shone as they smiled at each other.

Amy allowed herself a moment to feel happy for her friend. Sara was obviously delighted and Daniel looked like a good man. Saying a silent prayer for their happiness, she took another step back, glancing at the ticket office. She heard the pastor say Josephine Carter's name, introducing her to a Gabriel Silversmith, but she didn't wait to see what happened. Stepping behind a family gathered nearby, she looked for a way to sneak off without being seen.

"And finally, Amy Watts."

Amy froze.

"Amy Watts?"

Don't look, she told herself. *Just go. Don't look back.*

"Amy?" Sara called.

The area around her was emptying. She had to go now, while she still had the chance.

She heard confused voices. The family she was hiding behind began to move.

Run!

She turned to flee, not looking where she was going, and collided with an arm clad in a black jacket sleeve. She looked up. The arm was attached to a man dressed in a black suit who was staring behind her. He glanced down at Amy, a line forming between his close set eyes and his lips pursing beneath his thin moustache.

11

"Excuse me," she muttered, stepping back.

"Amy, there you are!" she heard Sara call.

Screaming at herself not to, she slowly turned towards the group of people she was trying to escape.

Beside Pastor Jones, a young man stood looking around him, twisting his hat nervously in his hands. He was tall and wore a grey suit and shiny black shoes, unlike the other men who were all dressed in plaid shirts and wool trousers and boots. His clean-shaven face was handsome, framed by gently curling dark brown hair down to his collar. He was the complete opposite of what she'd imagined. He looked kind. And utterly terrified.

Guilt pierced Amy's soul. She couldn't do this, not to him, not to anyone. It was a despicable thing to do to another human being. She wished, not for the first time, that her heart was harder.

Cursing herself for looking when she knew she should have run, she threw one last, longing glance at the ticket office and then walked towards the little crowd of people. She would just talk to him, explain, come to an arrangement.

It would work out somehow. She would think of something. She'd come this far, she'd escaped. She could do it again.

Reaching Pastor Jones and the young man, she pushed her hat from her head and let it hang behind her on its thong.

The pastor let out a sigh of relief. "There you are," he said, smiling. "Amy Watts, may I present Adam Emerson."

Adam stared at her with the bluest eyes she'd ever seen, his gaze travelling from her sandy blonde hair caught up in a loose braid, down past her beige shirt and brown linen jacket, to her brown trousers and brown leather shoes. Amy swallowed, suddenly feeling self-conscious. She'd dressed for the possibility of having to ride, not meeting someone she was supposed to marry. She glanced at the other women with

12

their fancy dresses and ribbons in their hair, thinking how strange she must look. And how much of a disappointment she must be to the man who thought he was meeting his wife today.

Except, she hadn't intended to meet him at all. She should have been buying a ticket for the remainder of the journey to San Francisco and getting back on the train by now. Or, failing that, finding the nearest livery to buy a horse to ride there.

Taking a deep breath, she squared her shoulders and held out her hand. At least this way, when she explained how she wasn't going to marry him, he might at least be a little relieved.

"It's a pleasure to meet you, Mr Emerson," she said.

He looked back at her face, a bemused expression lingering on his features. "Uh, yes," he said. He took her hand and shook it. "Pleasure to meet you too, Miss Watts." He smiled slightly.

"Well," Pastor Jones said, "now we're all sorted out, let's get the luggage and head to the church."

"Can I carry your bag?" Adam said as they all headed for the far end of the train.

Amy looked down at her shabby carpet bag. "Oh no, thank you." While she was almost certain he wouldn't run off with it, she felt safer with it in her hands. It held everything she owned.

He nodded and looked at the ground awkwardly. Amy felt instantly sorry for him. How on earth was she going to do this?

The baggage car was being unloaded when they reached it. Amy watched Sara smile up at Daniel. He leaned down to say something to her and she laughed and tightened her hold on his arm. Amy glanced at Adam beside her. He had replaced his hat and was moving stiffly, his hands stuffed in his pockets. She sighed and shifted her grip on her bag.

The men set about sorting out the various trunks and bags and loading everything into their wagons and buggies.

"Which one's yours?" Adam said, looking around at the rapidly dwindling pile of luggage.

"Oh, I don't have anything else," Amy said. She patted her bag. "It's all in here."

He studied the small bag. "Are your things being sent separately?"

This wasn't supposed to be happening. She should have just gone, bought the ticket and got back on the train. Later she could have written to Adam and explained and apologised. Why hadn't she thought of that before?

"Um, no. This is all I have."

His eyes widened. "In the world?"

She nodded.

"Oh." He seemed uncertain what to say at first, then he perked up, smiling. "Don't worry, there's a very good general store in town. They have everything anyone could possibly need. We could go there tomorrow if you like, after you've rested."

Why did he have to be nice? Amy looked at his expression, so eager to please her, and hated herself. "Thank you," she said softly.

With everyone's luggage loaded, they began the short walk to the church. Amy began to panic. She looked desperately back at the train as it pulled away from the station behind them. What was she going to do? Say no at the altar? She searched around her for something, anything, to get her out of the situation.

"Are you all right?" Adam said.

She started at his voice. "Yes. No. I'm..."

And then she fainted.

14

Chapter 2

Shocked voices surrounded her.

"Oh my, is she all right?"

"Give her some air!"

"Amy? Amy, can you hear me?"

She kept her eyes closed and her body relaxed. She'd seen it performed several times before, the fake swoon. Of course, all those times had involved women fainting into the arms of a convenient handsome bachelor, usually with the intention of gaining a husband. She was doing it for the exact opposite reason, but the technique was the same. After counting to sixty, she opened her eyes, fluttering her eyelids as if she was regaining consciousness.

"She's awake!"

"Give her some air!"

The first thing she saw was Adam's face staring down at her, his face filled with distress. His eyes so incredibly blue.

He was kneeling next to her, his hand on her cheek. He snatched it back as soon as she focused on him.

"Are you all right?" he said, helping her to sit up.

She put a hand to her head. "I'm sorry, I don't know what happened." That was the traditional opening line after a feigned swoon and she didn't see any need to change it now.

"You've obviously had a lot of excitement and stress travelling," Pastor Jones said, crouching beside her. The others formed a circle around her semi-prostrate form.

"I'm all right," Amy said, feeling uncomfortable with all

the attention. "Truly, I'm fine."

Adam held her firmly as she stood, putting his arm around her waist to steady her.

Pressed against him, she got the impression of strength. Hoping she wasn't wrong about that, she took a step in the direction of the church and softened her knees. Everyone gasped as Adam grabbed her to stop her from falling, much to her relief. Going down the first time she'd hit her elbow and it hurt.

"Maybe I should just take her home," he said. "Could we possibly have the ceremony tomorrow?"

"Of course we can," Pastor Jones said. "That's a good idea. I'm sure all she needs is some food and a good rest."

Sara untangled her arm from Daniel's and came over to them. "Are you well, Amy? Can I do anything?"

"No, I'll be fine." She lowered her voice to a whisper. "You go and marry your handsome cowboy. I know you want to."

Sara smiled and leaned in close to her. "He's wonderful, isn't he?"

After more refusals of help and some fussing from Mrs Jones, everyone crowded into the white clapboard church and Amy and Adam continued past towards the centre of town.

He had let her go when Sara came to talk to her and now he didn't seem to know what to do. He hovered at her side, looking like he expected her to keel over at any second.

"I'm not going to faint again," she said. "You don't have to worry."

He continued to look concerned, but he did move away a little.

"I'm sorry," she said as they walked.

"What for?"

"For spoiling everything for you. The wedding and

16

everything."

The sound of his laughter caught her by surprise.

"Oh, don't be sorry about that. To tell the truth, I wasn't looking forward to it." He gasped and looked at her. "I mean... I don't mean I wasn't looking forward to marrying you. I just meant the whole idea of a mass wedding was a little... I don't know. Unromantic. Just the two of us will be much nicer." He smiled and looked at the ground, stuffing his hands into his pockets.

Amy couldn't believe he still wanted to marry her, even with her looking like she did and having fainted like one of the pampered princesses she saw in the city. She couldn't imagine what she'd written in her letters to make him so enamoured of her. Maybe she'd tried too hard in her desperation to escape from Mr Courtney. Now she'd met Adam, she wished she hadn't been so... whatever she'd been. This would be so much easier if he was disappointed.

They came to a halt on the wooden walkway in front of one of the shop fronted buildings towards the end of the main street. Lost in her thoughts, Amy hadn't been paying attention to where they were going. She looked up, but with the wooden awning above her she couldn't see any sign to indicate what kind of store it was. It looked closed. Adam produced a key from his pocket and unlocked the door, stepping aside to let her in.

"Just go on through," he said, indicating a door in the back wall as he locked the door behind them.

She looked around as she moved through the room. A whole wall of cubby holes sat behind the counter, filled with letters and parcels. A set of shelves nearby held paper and pens and pencils and other writing related paraphernalia along with brown paper, string and envelopes.

A post office.

Beyond the door was a modest sized parlour with a pale

17

green settee and two brown armchairs. Against the back wall was a kitchen area with a sink and large dresser and a table surrounded by four mismatched chairs. Through the window over the sink, Amy glimpsed a fenced in yard. A door in the far right corner led outside.

"Please, have a seat," Adam said, removing his hat and jacket and hanging them on a coat stand. "May I take your coat?"

He owns the post office, Amy thought as she put down her bag, shrugged off her jacket and handed it to him. He seemed so young to be a postmaster. She wished she'd read his letters, but she hadn't wanted to know about the man she was going to use to get her across the country and then abandon. It occurred to her how selfish that was now. He had paid for her train fare, a significant amount of money, and would be getting nothing but betrayal in return. She should at least have read his letters instead of getting Katherine to read them for her, but she'd been afraid of losing her nerve if she knew anything about him.

"Would you like something to eat?" Adam said, hovering beside her as she sat on the damask settee. "Or drink? Did you eat supper already on the train? Or would you like to clean up? Or maybe take a nap?"

She stared up at him, trying to decide which question to answer first. He seemed so uncertain what to do. It was endearing.

No, it wasn't endearing, because she did not want to be endeared to him. At all.

"Um, yes please, yes, no, if it's not too much trouble, and no, thank you."

He gave a small laugh and sank onto the other end of the settee, rubbing his hand over his face. "I'm sorry, I didn't mean to interrogate you. I'm a little nervous."

She couldn't help smiling. "It's all right. So am I." That

18

was the truth, at least.

His eyes held hers for a long moment before moving away. "Well, this is my home." He gestured vaguely around the room then looked back at her. "I mean your home. Our home." He smiled, his cheeks reddening a little. "It's not very big, but I've tried to make it pleasant and cosy. The outhouse is through that door out the back and there are two bedrooms upstairs. I've made up a separate bedroom for you. I don't expect, I mean, even if we had got married today, I didn't expect us to be sharing a bed straight away. I just wanted you to know that. I'm not the kind of man who would ever pressure you to do anything you're not comfortable with. Just, it will be entirely up to you. That's all." He laughed again, closing his eyes. "And that was entirely too much information all at once when we've hardly even had our first conversation."

Amy couldn't help it, she burst out laughing. Adam froze, staring at her with wide eyes. Then he started to laugh too.

"I'm sorry," she said, "I'm not laughing at you. It's just..."

"I know exactly what you mean." He was smiling at her, his eyes shining. He started to reach out his hand towards her, but then stopped and withdrew it. "Well, how about I show you upstairs and while you're freshening up, I'll make us some supper."

"That would be perfect, thank you."

They both stood and Adam's eyes went to her bag which was sitting on the settee between them. "I can carry it upstairs for you," he said, "if you'd like."

She smiled. "Thank you."

He seemed to relax at that as he picked up the bag.

A door opened onto stairs and Amy followed him to the second floor. Two doors led off a small landing, both of them

19

open. Amy glimpsed a double bed with a colourful quilt and a large, oak wardrobe through one door. Adam stood aside to allow her to enter the other door ahead of him.

She stopped inside, her mouth opening in amazement.

A single bed stood opposite the door, topped with a blue quilt, a knitted blanket in shades of pink folded at the foot. Next to it stood a small table with a vase of fresh violets. On the other side of the room was an oak wardrobe that matched the one in the master bedroom, only smaller, a matching chest of three drawers beside it. A washstand against the wall opposite the window held a basin and jug, towel and cloth and a fresh bar of soap. The walls were painted a subtle shade of lavender blue and the curtains at the window were white with embroidered flowers in blue along the bottom edge.

It was the most beautiful room Amy had ever seen and it was all for her. For tonight, anyway. She felt tears stinging her eyes and she blinked rapidly.

Adam walked past her and placed her bag onto the bed. "I know it's not very grand," he said, looking around, "and you must be used to so much more in New York. I did my best, but maybe it needs a woman's touch. If there's anything you'd like to change..." He stopped as he turned to face her. "Amy? What's wrong?"

She sniffed and shook her head rapidly, her fingers covering her mouth. "It's perfect," she managed to whisper. "It's the most perfect room I've ever had."

The truth was she'd never had a room to herself, and even the ones she'd shared with others weren't anywhere near as beautiful as this one. But she couldn't tell him that.

She cleared her throat, silently chiding herself for the outburst of emotion. "Thank you. It's lovely. I know I'll be comfortable here."

The look of relief on Adam's face made her want to cry again. What was wrong with her? She wished he wasn't so

20

eager to please her. It made her feel so much worse.

"I'll leave you to rest or whatever you want to do," he said. "Just come down whenever you're ready. And call if there's anything you need. Anything at all."

He gave her one last smile then walked back out to the landing, pulling the door closed as he left.

Amy sat down on the bed and ran her hand over the quilt. It was soft and beautifully made. She wondered if Adam had already owned it, or if he had bought it especially for her arrival. He seemed to have put so much thought into everything.

For a moment she wondered if it would really be so bad to stay here and marry Adam. From what she could tell, he was a good man. He would be a good husband. She might even be happy here...

She shook her head to dislodge the unwanted thoughts. Her father had been a good man and a good husband and of what use was that to her and her mother when he died? She wouldn't become dependent on any man to look after her. This was her life and she would find a way to live it relying on no one but herself. She would be no one's bride.

No matter how good and handsome and kind Adam Emerson was.

Amy spent a while in the bedroom, cleaning the dust from the journey away with the water and lavender scented soap, unpacking the few meagre belongings she had, then sitting in the comfortable chair by the window and gazing at the scene outside. Directly behind the post office was a yard with two wooden outbuildings and the outhouse in the far corner. Beyond that was another road, with more houses huddled together. The two houses directly behind, however, were single storey, so from her window she could see over the top to the vista beyond. It took her breath away.

She'd spent much of the train journey here staring out

21

the window at the wide open spaces of the country she'd lived in all her life, but never seen. She was used to the city, noise, people everywhere, dirt and rubbish, wealth and squalor side by side. It hadn't ever occurred to her how much empty space there was just beyond her small world. On her way across the country she'd seen prairies and mountains and desert, lakes and great forests. Now she gazed at the fields of gently waving corn interspersed with lines of trees where a creek or river flowed, stretching to the horizon where blue mountains reached for the sky.

It filled her with a deep sense of peace, a feeling she wasn't used to. Tears rose unbidden to her eyes.

"Thank you, Father," she whispered. "Thank you for this moment."

She knew what was to come would be tough, a challenge, and she may not feel this kind of peace again for a while.

But she would remember this moment and this beautiful view and know that God was with her.

Chapter 3

Adam closed the door at the foot of the stairs and leaned back against it, running one hand down his face and groaning softly.

This morning he'd had a plan all worked out. He would meet Amy at the station, they would get married alongside the other new couples, he'd show her the post office, her bedroom, help her get settled, make her supper, they'd get to know each other. It wasn't much of a plan and it certainly wasn't going to sweep her off her feet, but it was something.

The station part had happened, but from that point on he'd felt completely overwhelmed.

Breathing out a long sigh, he pushed himself away from the door and went to the settee, dropping into it. He leaned back, closed his eyes, and tried to relax.

He liked to think he was a fairly calm person, most of the time. Well, some of the time. He ran his own business and had a job, he lived alone and took good care of himself and his home. He was a strong, steadfast man.

It was disturbing how many times he'd had to remind himself of that over the past hour.

It wasn't that Amy had brought so little with her. He knew she'd been a kitchen girl in a big house in New York. He didn't know what they were paid, but it apparently wasn't much. That was probably why she was dressed as she was. But he didn't mind. He wasn't rich and he'd had to save for over a year to get the money for her train fare, but he would do everything he could to give her anything she needed.

It wasn't even the fainting, although that had sent him into a temporary panic. Women didn't faint in Green Hill Creek, apart from Missy Evans that one time in the street outside the post office, but she'd been eight months pregnant at the time and the day had been hot and humid. After she'd had a glass of cool water, she'd waved the doctor away and carried on with her day. Here, the women were as tough as the men. They had to be.

But perhaps it wasn't the same in the east. Once, when Adam was eleven years old, he'd snuck away with one of his mother's dime romance novels to the tree behind their house, climbing into the branches and reading the forbidden pages hidden amongst the leaves. The cover had a red haired woman in a long, pink, scandalously low-cut dress, fanning herself under the gaze of a tall, dashing, dark haired man in white breeches. What he read inside was decidedly less exciting than the cover and he'd become bored after only a few pages. But in those few pages, the heroine swooned twice. And her sister had also been overcome by 'an attack of the vapours'. To this day he wasn't sure what vapours were. He'd assumed it was all nonsense, but maybe there was a smidgeon of truth to it. Although, unlike the heroine in *Bostonian Hearts Aflame*, Adam was fairly sure Amy had *not* been overcome by his intense masculinity.

No, the thing that had thrown him the most about meeting Amy, apparently robbing him of most of his faculties, was that she was so *pretty*.

He was ashamed to admit it, even to himself, but he'd had an idea that any woman who was willing to travel almost across the entire country to find a husband must have been somewhat... homely. He'd told himself it didn't matter what Amy looked like. She'd seemed very nice, if a little

24

unforthcoming, in her letters and that was what mattered, what was inside. Adam wasn't superficial. He was determined to make a life with this woman who was prepared to come all this way for him. And after all the praying he'd been doing about it, he trusted God would bring him the right woman.

But standing on that platform, seeing each of the not at all homely women being introduced to their prospective husbands, he'd had to readjust his ideas. And then *she'd* stepped forward. Amy Watts. With blonde hair the colour of a sunset, filling him with the most distracting thoughts of running his fingers through the silky tresses, and deep blue eyes that seemed to look straight into his soul, and a smile that had sucked every intelligent thought from his head. At first, he'd barely been able to speak.

More than that, she was funny and smart.

He'd dreamed for so long of finding the woman God had in store for him, and although Adam trusted that He would bring the perfect wife for him it was still nerve-wracking to finally meet her. Now he had, he was even more apprehensive. What if she didn't like him? What if she didn't like his home? He'd done his best, trying to make it how he thought a woman would like, and he'd scrubbed every inch of every room in the past couple of days, but maybe that wasn't enough. Now he'd met Amy, he very much wanted her to be happy here, with him.

If he could just stop sounding like he only had half a brain, that would be a good start to making that happen.

He glanced back at the door to the stairs and then closed his eyes. "Father," he whispered, "thank You for bringing Amy here. She's..." a smile crept onto his face, "incredible. Forgive me for doubting that she would be. I know You have things in hand, which is good because I feel like I haven't got any idea what I'm doing. And thank You that she's so pretty.

25

It wasn't essential, but I sure do appreciate it. In the Name of Your Son, Jesus Christ, Amen."

Feeling a little better, if not much more relaxed, he stood and went to light the small stove he used for cooking and warmth. First he'd make them supper, then he'd go back to worrying if Amy liked it here. Liked him.

With the stove warming, he fetched plates from the dresser to take to the table. A knock at the back door almost made him drop them. Rolling his eyes at his jumpiness, he put down the plates and went to the door leading into the back yard.

Mrs Goodwin smiled at him when he opened the door. "Adam, I'm real sorry to disturb you on your first evening as a married man. I know you and your bride must be busy getting to know each other... Oh, and there she is now."

The short, round woman with white hair pulled into a bun and a covered serving dish in her hands stopped in the process of bustling through the door to look past him. Adam turned to see Amy walking into the room. His breath hitched. She didn't actually look any different, and yet she seemed to have got even prettier. How was that even possible?

Mrs Goodwin looked her up and down. Amy hadn't changed from her trousers and shirt and the older woman seemed taken aback for a moment.

Adam smiled at Amy, trying to convey an apology with his eyes. "Mrs Goodwin, please let me take that from you." He reached out to remove the serving dish from her unresisting hands. "Miss Watts, this is Mrs Goodwin. Mrs Goodwin, meet Miss Watts."

Mrs Goodwin snapped out of her surprise and, rallying, put on a smile. "It's lovely to meet you Miss..." She frowned. "Wait, shouldn't that be Mrs Emerson?"

Adam winced internally. He'd hoped there wouldn't be any need for explanations.

Amy hurried forward and shook Mrs Goodwin's right hand which, along with her left, was extended in front of her as if she was still holding the dish.

"It's a pleasure to meet you, Mrs Goodwin," she said. "Mr Emerson and I didn't get married today. I was tired out from the journey and on the way to the church I had a spell of fainting. It was decided it would be best if the wedding was postponed so I could rest." She gave a smile that would surely charm Mrs Goodwin, if the effect it had on Adam was anything to go by.

At the mention of fainting Mrs Goodwin became the soul of distress. "Oh, you poor girl. Yes, of course, you must rest. But..." She glanced at Adam who was setting the dish down onto the table. "That means the two of you will be spending the night in the same house, unwed..."

"Miss Watts and I will be sleeping in separate bedrooms," Adam said, giving his voice a hint of firmness. "And we will be married tomorrow. I promise you, Mrs Goodwin, there will be no impropriety. But I'm sure you wouldn't think otherwise, knowing me as you do."

Mrs Goodwin breathed out. "Yes, of course." She smiled. "Of course."

Amy walked to the table and lifted the cloth on the serving dish. A smell wafted out that made Adam's mouth water.

"Is this for us?" she said. "It smells delicious."

"I figured you wouldn't want to be cooking, this being your first night together." The colour drained from Mrs Goodwin's face. "I mean, I didn't mean..."

Adam had to clamp his teeth together to stop the laugh bubbling up inside him. "Relax, Mrs Goodwin, we know what you mean."

She gave a small laugh. "Mr Goodwin always says I only visit a place twice, and the second time is to say how sorry I am about the first time. Anyway, that there is beef stew and dumplings. I'm taking the same to each couple, so I'd best get going before the others get cold. The two of you have a restful evening and you feel better soon, Miss Watts."

She took Amy's hand and patted it, little wrinkles forming around her pale blue eyes.

"Thank you, Mrs Goodwin," Amy said with another smile that sent shivers up Adam's spine.

Mrs Goodwin nodded and turned to bustle out. In all the years he'd known her, which was just about his entire life, Adam had never seen Mrs Goodwin walk in anything other than a bustle.

Out in the road that ran behind the back yard Mr Goodwin waited in a buggy with the reins in one hand and a pipe in the other. He raised the pipe to Adam. Adam nodded back and closed the door, relieved Mrs Goodwin had left without any further discussion on the unchaperoned night he and Amy would be spending in the house.

"I was about to start supper, but Mrs G does make the best beef stew in the whole town, maybe the whole state. So if you have no objections maybe we can postpone your discovery of my mediocre cooking until *after* we're married."

"I'm sure your cooking is easily the match of mine," Amy said, lifting the cloth over the stew again and taking a deep breath, "but this may be the nicest thing I've ever smelled."

Adam walked over to her, placing two dishes onto the table beside the bowl. "Wait until you taste it. Have a seat."

He indicated one of the four chairs at the small table and she sat as he brought cutlery and napkins and glasses of water.

"Mrs G sometimes brings me food, what with me being single," he said as he walked back and forth. "I think she has an idea men starve without a woman to cook for them." He

28

set two plates of thick sliced bread along with a plate of butter onto the table, then sat opposite Amy. "I must admit, I haven't done anything to fix that notion. She is a *very* good cook."

He reached both arms towards her and smiled. Amy stared at his hands lying open on the table, a confused expression on her face as if she didn't know what they were for.

The smile melted from Adam's face. "Oh, I didn't... we just have a habit around here of holding hands for the blessing." He slid his arms back awkwardly and folded them in his lap. "I didn't think. You probably have different customs back in New York."

She smiled slightly. "This isn't New York."

Adam's stomach did a little flip. Hoping he wasn't misunderstanding her words, he reached his hands out again. When she slipped her hands into them, his heart tried to pound its way out of his chest.

He lowered his head and closed his eyes, willing his voice to be steady. "Dear Father, thank You for this food You have provided. Thank You for Mrs Goodwin and her kindness, and please bless and keep her and Mr G safe as they deliver the rest of the meals." He paused. "And thank You for answering my prayers and bringing Amy here. In the Name of Jesus, Your Son, amen."

"Amen," Amy whispered.

Reluctantly, he let go of her hands and removed the cloth from over Mrs Goodwin's stew, releasing the full force of the aroma. Steam curled up from the dish of moist beef, vegetables and gravy, and plump, white dumplings. Adam took a deep breath in. He loved Mrs Goodwin's cooking so much he'd often thought that if Mr Goodwin hadn't been around he'd have asked the woman who was more than twice his age to marry him himself.

29

"That looks wonderful," Amy breathed. Her stomach rumbled and she pressed one hand to it, blushing. "Pardon me."

Adam smiled as he loaded the two plates with food. "I'm sorry, I should have given you something when you arrived."

She shook her head. "I'm glad I'm hungry. It means I'll have more room for this stew."

"That is very wise of you." He placed the loaded plate in front of her and picked up his knife and fork, waiting for her to start before he took his first bite.

She cut a lump of beef and a piece of dumpling and ate her first mouthful, closing her eyes and murmuring, "Mmmm," as she chewed.

She opened her eyes and Adam quickly dropped his gaze to his own plate, hoping he hadn't been caught staring.

"How was your journey?" he said, spearing a chunk of potato with his fork.

"I never imagined how tiring sitting down could be. I kind of feel like I'm still on the train, like everything's moving a little, and my ears are humming. But it was amazing. I've never been outside New York before." Her face lit up as she spoke, looking out the window as she remembered. "I didn't know how different it was beyond the city. There was so much to see. Even when it got dark the stars and the moon were so beautiful. I hated going to sleep each night in case I missed something. One day we passed a whole herd of buffalo, just grazing next to the tracks." She smiled. "I didn't know what they were, but Sara had seen pictures. That was when we were in the plains. We went past mountains and over huge rivers and through forests that went on for miles and miles. We stopped once near an Indian settlement and some of the women came to the train to sell things they made. I'd never seen an Indian before. They looked so beautiful with their embroidered dresses and jewellery."

"Did you buy anything?" Adam prompted. Maybe he could get some idea of what she liked and buy her a wedding gift. Mr Lamb in the general store traded with the local tribes and he often had Indian-made items for sale.

Her eyes snapped back to him and she shook her head. "No. There was a turquoise and silver necklace... but I didn't have... no. The other girls did though." She took another bite of stew.

"I've never been any farther than Sacramento," Adam said. "I'd love to go further though. My sister is a schoolteacher in San Francisco. She loves the city." He pushed a dumpling around his plate. "Maybe one day we could travel together. If you'd like to." He looked up at her then back at his plate. Was it too early to talk about their future life together? He couldn't stop thinking about it.

Amy studied her own meal. "Maybe."

He busied himself with slicing up his dumpling, trying to hide his disappointment at her less than enthusiastic response. But then again, she had just travelled thousands of miles. Maybe she simply wanted to settle down for the time being.

There was a period of silence that somehow managed to hover between awkward and comfortable as they ate.

"It's beautiful here," Amy said after a while. "The view from the bedroom is amazing."

He smiled, thrilled he'd done something right. It was exactly why he'd given her the room he usually used. "I hoped you'd like it. I can move the double bed back in there when we're..." he swallowed, embarrassed, "well, you know. Both using the same bed. Whenever that happens." He prodded at his food. Maybe he should just stop talking now, before it got any worse.

"Back in?"

31

He looked up at her. "I thought you'd like the view of the mountains so I moved into the front bedroom."

She stared at him for a few seconds. "You didn't have to do that."

"I wanted to. I want you to be happy here." He sighed and set his fork down. "I know this is all such a big change for you, leaving your home and coming all this way to marry someone you've never met, and I want to do anything I can to make it easier for you. To be honest, I can't imagine why you would do this. I'm kind of ashamed to admit this, but I thought you'd be more..." His eyes widened in horror. What on earth was he *saying*? "That is, um, less... I thought only a woman who couldn't find a husband where she was would come all this way for one, even though we have a lot to offer out here. But you're..." *Stop TALKING!* "There must have been no shortage of men competing for your attention in New York, is what I'm trying to say. But I'm grateful that you're giving me a chance. I'm real glad you're here."

He fought the urge to drop his head into his hands and groan. He stared at his food and waited for her to announce she wanted to go right back to New York in the morning. What was wrong with him?

"Thank you," she said. "You're very kind."

He was? He looked up at her and she smiled slightly. He nodded and returned his attention to his food, feeling like he'd just dodged a bullet.

Maybe he should just tie a gag over his mouth when he was finished eating.

Chapter 4

Amy woke up hating herself.

She'd squirmed and fidgeted so much during the night her bedcovers had ended up in a twisted mound at the end of the bed, scrunched up against the metal bedstead. She'd finally fallen asleep as the sun was rising, which felt like five minutes before she woke again. For all Amy knew, it was.

She kept the penknife she'd had since she was eleven under her pillow out of habit, but it wasn't fear that kept her awake, at least not fear of attack. Somehow, she knew she could trust Adam. For the first time since she could remember, she felt completely safe. It was strange. Alien.

Wonderful.

No, it was fear of the morning that made her toss and turn. Fear of having to tell Adam the truth.

When she reached the kitchen, Adam was cooking eggs in a frying pan on the stove. He was humming. With his back to Amy he hadn't noticed her arrive and for a few moments she simply stood and watched and listened. Even his back was handsome, with his gently waving dark hair and tall, strong build.

She'd found out the previous night as they talked that in addition to being the postmaster he worked part time at Green Hill Creek's only bank. With relatively sedentary occupations, she would have expected him to tend towards the plump, as so many of the upper class men did in New York. But Adam was as far away from those tepid fops as it was possible to be.

If only he'd been unattractive. Boring. Dull. A few warts wouldn't have gone amiss. She didn't want to regret she wasn't marrying him. She had a plan and she would rely on no man, even one as handsome and charming and funny and smart as Adam.

Besides, even if she had changed her mind, which she hadn't and wouldn't, there was no way he'd want her after he knew what she'd done. The thought of having to tell him saddened her. He sounded so happy. She wanted the moment to never end, wanted to never have to disappoint him.

But then he turned and saw her and the moment was gone.

For a second he stood still, his eyes flicking down and back up to her face. She'd worn her dress, her only dress. It was blue, with white lace cuffs and a subtle vertical white stripe. It wasn't anywhere near new and a hand-me-down several times over, but it fit her, more or less. And it was all she had.

Now she wished she hadn't worn it. It made her look like she was ready to get married.

"Good morning," Adam said, smiling. "I hope you slept well."

"I did, thank you," she lied.

"I hope you like eggs. I should have asked, but I didn't want to wake you after yesterday. You look like you still need rest." He winced. "I mean, well, I don't mean you look terrible, just that you look, um, tired." He gave a small laugh. "Please take from that mess of a sentence the good things and forget the rest."

She sat at the table, resisting the urge to cover her face with her hands. "I know what you mean. I looked in the mirror in the bedroom." Her pale skin and the dark circles under her eyes had made her wish she could wear a sack over her head.

Adam turned back to the eggs, taking them from the heat and sliding them onto two warmed plates with slices of buttered, toasted bread.

"I didn't mean it how it sounded," he said, his back to her. "You look... very pretty."

Her breath caught in her throat. When he turned around to carry the plates to the table, she lowered her eyes. "Thank you."

Adam said the blessing, again holding her hands as he did so. His hands were smooth and warm and she berated herself for liking the feel of them so much. At her first taste of the food she almost rolled her eyes. Of course the eggs were delicious. Of course he'd be a good cook. Surely there was something bad about him? Something that would make her glad she wasn't staying. She hadn't even heard him snoring during the night. She'd even crept out of her bedroom and pressed her ear to his door during the dark, sleepless hours, hoping to hear snores so loud she'd be thanking the Lord they would never share a bed. But all was silent.

"I thought I'd go and see the pastor after breakfast and find out what time he'll be free to marry us," he said as they ate. "Did you want any of the others to be there? I imagine you had time to get to know the other ladies on your journey."

Her heart started to pound. "I, um, no." She stuffed another forkful of scrambled eggs into her suddenly dry mouth.

"Then we could go over to the church whenever he's free, I guess."

Amy closed her eyes. She had to tell him. It was cruel to go on like this. Placing her knife and fork down onto her half full plate, she took a deep breath.

And held it.

And held it.

When she couldn't hold it any longer, she blurted out, "I lied to you."

Adam's fork paused halfway to his mouth. "About what?"

She stared at her plate, unable to look him in the eye. *Just say it. Just get it over with.*

"Everything." She took another deep breath and spoke rapidly, before she lost her courage. "I tricked you. I never intended to marry you. I didn't even read your letters; my friend read them for me so she could tell me if you'd asked a question I needed to answer. I had to get away from New York and the only way I could was to trick you into paying my fare. I meant to just buy another ticket and get back on the train as soon as we arrived yesterday, to carry on to San Francisco, or if I couldn't do that I was going to buy a horse. Then I was going to send the money to repay you for the fare as soon as I had it. Even the fainting wasn't real. I couldn't think of anything else to do to stop going into the church. I lied about everything." She gasped in another breath, blinking back tears.

The silence was so complete she could hear the blood thumping in her ears. After a few seconds, she risked looking up. Adam was frozen in place, his fork still hanging in midair. Slowly, he lowered it to his plate, his eyes lowering with it.

"I'm sorry," she whispered.

His neck bobbed as he swallowed. "I... um..." His eyes rose to hers. "So you never knew anything about me until yesterday?"

She shook her head. "Not much. I didn't want to know. I was afraid I wouldn't be able to go through with it if I got to know you."

"Why are you telling me this now?"

"Because I can't marry you," she whispered.

He pushed back his chair, the sound of it scraping on the floor sounding so harsh in the silence that Amy jumped. "I... I have to go and cancel the wedding."

Then he left. Seconds later, she heard the front door open and close.

Dropping her head into her hands, Amy burst into tears.

~ ~ ~

Adam stopped beneath the awning outside the post office and took a shuddering breath. It felt like the first air he'd drawn into his lungs since Amy had said...

What had just happened?

Yesterday, his emotions had cycled from fear as he'd waited for the train, through relief that his bride was so pretty coupled with shame at his unintended superficiality, to more relief that she didn't seem disappointed with him, to more fear as she'd fainted, to a growing happiness as they talked and he discovered how much he liked her.

It was enough to make him dizzy, but his worries had all melted away as they'd talked and laughed into the evening and Adam knew without a doubt that Amy was the one for him.

He'd gone to bed feeling like he was riding on a wave of joy, filled with praise and thanks to God as he saw his whole future ahead of him. A future filled with happiness with the wonderful, beautiful Amy. And he'd been so sure she felt the same way he did.

But now...

He was numb. Shocked. How could things have gone so badly wrong? It didn't feel real. He wanted to go back inside where she could tell him that she really was going to marry him today and that it had all been a mistake, a bad joke.

"Why, Lord?" he whispered into the cool morning air. "What did I do wrong?"

Pushing his hands into his pockets, he walked across the street and headed in the direction of the church, his feet dragging over the dry and dusty packed earth. He didn't even know if Pastor Jones would be there this early. The truth was, he'd used cancelling the wedding as an excuse to get out of the house. To get away from the woman who had used him and torn his heart in two.

A flash of anger coursed through him. She hadn't even bothered to find out anything about him. She'd used him, stolen from him, and didn't even care who he was. He glanced back at the post office, half expecting to see her leaving now that she had the chance. She'd seemed like such a caring, considerate woman last night. Maybe she was going to San Francisco to become an actress on the stage. She was certainly good at fooling others she was someone she wasn't.

He wiped at a tear rolling down his cheek, ashamed. How could he have been so gullible?

When he reached the church building Pastor Jones was walking through the front door. Adam stopped. He wasn't sure he wanted to tell anyone what had just happened. But he did need to cancel the wedding. Now he was here, he might as well do that, then he could go for a walk and try to clear his mind. Or maybe he'd go and get Stride from the livery. Riding always helped calm him.

"Good morning, Adam," Pastor Jones said, looking up from the altar as he walked in. "Aren't you a little early? Or are you that eager to be married?" He grinned.

It was as if someone had reached into Adam's chest and squeezed. He sank onto a chair, dropping his head into his hands. Seconds later, the pastor was beside him.

"Adam, what's wrong?"

"I... she... Amy lied. She tricked me into paying her train fare so she could get to San Francisco. She never intended to marry me."

The pastor's eyes widened. "She *what*?"

In faltering words, Adam related everything that Amy had told him. He burned with humiliation as he broke down, but he couldn't hold back the tears. At the end, he wiped at his eyes with his sleeve, ashamed of himself. He shouldn't have allowed himself to have such high hopes. Even if Amy *had* come to marry him, there were any number of other things that could have gone wrong. Maybe he'd mistaken his own desire for an end to his loneliness for God's prompting. He'd obviously been very wrong about Amy.

"Oh, Adam, I'm so sorry," Pastor Jones said, putting a hand on his shoulder. "I feel like this was somehow my fault, as involved as I was in arranging with the agency to bring her here. And that poor girl."

He raised his head. "Poor girl? Are you talking about Amy?"

The pastor nodded. "What kind of terrible situation must she have been in that forced her to do such a thing?"

Adam's jaw dropped. He hadn't even considered that. "I... I didn't think to ask."

"I know you may not want to hear this now," Pastor Jones said, "but bad things happen to us for different reasons. Sometimes it's to teach us something, sometimes to make us stronger, sometimes because we live in an imperfect world where many people don't follow God's will, and sometimes they just happen and we may never know why until we can ask God when we get up there to Heaven. But sometimes they may happen to us so we can help someone else." He squeezed Adam's shoulder. "I know how much you've been praying for the right woman to come into your life. I don't believe God could have got it so badly wrong."

Adam drew in a breath and straightened, grasping at the tiny glimmer of hope. "Maybe you're right. I should have asked before I thought the worst of her. It was just such a shock."

"I'll make sure everyone who was going to come knows the wedding isn't happening. You can work out what to tell them later. If you want to stay for a while, you can. Irene won't be here for another hour. I warn you though, if you're still here when she arrives you'll find yourself cleaning windows before you know what's happening and you won't be able to work out how she made you do it."

Despite his sour mood, Adam smiled. He knew just how persuasive Mrs Jones could be. "No, I should go back. I at least want to know why Amy did it. Thank you, Pastor. You've helped."

He left the church feeling much better, but as he walked back to the post office his trepidation grew again. What if he got in there and Amy didn't have a good reason for destroying his dreams? He tried to focus on what Pastor Jones had said. Even if he never knew the reason this had happened, God was still with him.

And if Amy wasn't the one for him, he'd just save up for another year for the train fare and find the woman who was.

Adam's heart was racing as he walked into the parlour behind the post office. He tried to ignore it. Amy was where he'd left her, her head resting on her crossed arms on the table, face hidden.

Guilt stabbed at him. He didn't know what to do with it. He could almost hear his father saying to him, *She's the one who used you, boy. Why are you the one feeling guilty?* He hated it when he started thinking like his father.

"Amy?"

She lifted her head and wiped the back of her hand across her puffy, red eyes. Wordlessly, she pushed an

40

envelope across the surface of the table towards him. Inside were banknotes totalling sixty-five dollars.

"It's all I have," she said. "It's the money I was going to use to buy a ticket and get a room once I got to San Francisco. I know it's not even half what you paid to get me here, but I'll find a job and pay back the rest as quickly as I can, I promise. I always intended to pay you back. I've packed my things. I'll go to the boarding house."

Her bag was on the chair next to her. She didn't have much to pack.

Adam stared at the envelope. "Can you tell me why you did it?"

She looked down at her lap. "There was a... situation in New York I had to get away from. Far away. I didn't know what else to do." Her eyes lifted to meet his. "I didn't mean to hurt you. You have to believe me."

He hated himself for not answering, but he wasn't sure if he did believe her. He'd gone from being certain she was the most wonderful woman in the world to not knowing her at all. But maybe that was the problem. How could he possibly know her in less than a day? His desire for someone to love had clouded his judgement.

She stood and picked up her bag. "I'm sorry, Ad... Mr Emerson."

As she turned, the handle of the bag caught on the top of the chair, causing it to jerk from her grasp and fall to the floor. Something tumbled onto the wood, bouncing a couple of times before coming to a halt against Adam's shoe. He bent to pick it up, a shudder going through him as he did so. Pulling at the groove in the metal, he watched the blade slide free from the handle of the folding knife.

Had she meant to harm him?

But then he saw the fear in her eyes, her shoulders trembling, and realisation dawned. "Amy, were you in

41

danger in New York? Did someone hurt you?"

She shook her head, not meeting his eyes.

"Did someone *try* to hurt you?"

She didn't answer, but a tear caught the light as it fell from her chin to the floor. In an instant, all his anger drained away. He took a step towards her, reaching out a hand before thinking better of it and folding the knife back into its handle and holding that out instead. She took it from his hand and looked up at him. The fear and vulnerability he saw in her eyes almost knocked him flat.

"I won't let anyone hurt you." The words came out before he even knew what he was saying, but he meant them, maybe more than he'd ever meant anything in his life.

She wiped her eyes again and sighed. "You don't have to do anything. I meant what I said, I'll get the money to pay you back, I swear." She picked her bag up from the floor. "Which way is the boarding house? I don't remember seeing it yesterday."

Suddenly, the thought of Amy staying in Trenchard's Room & Board terrified him. Mrs Trenchard, the widow who ran it, wasn't a bad person, but she did have a tendency to overindulge with the wine in the evenings. In addition, the boarding house wasn't far from the saloon with its drunken patrons and noise and other activities that went on upstairs. It wasn't a safe place for a woman on her own.

"You can stay here," he blurted, before he could think it through.

She looked up at him, startled.

"I mean in the room you stayed in last night. The boarding house, it's not... What I mean to say is, it's near the saloon and the noise could be... distracting." He breathed out, trying to unscramble his mind. "I don't want you to feel afraid anymore."

She stared at him for a few seconds before lowering her

42

gaze. "What do you want?"

He frowned, confused. "What do I want?"

"In exchange for me staying here. I can't pay you straight away, until I find a job. I can clean and cook, but if you want more than that..." She swallowed, still not looking at him. Her trembling fingers clutched the knife against her stomach.

Adam still didn't know what she meant. "More than...?" And then understanding came like a punch to the chest. He took a step back, stumbled against one of the chairs, and dropped onto it with a thud. "You think I would... No! I would *never*... I meant you can stay here for free. I don't expect anything from you, and certainly not... I just want to help."

Her eyes were wide as she looked down at him. "Why would you do that? After what I did to you?"

He was about to answer it was because he was a good man, unlike whoever had tried to hurt her, when he remembered something. He chuckled, rubbing one hand across his eyes.

"Why are you laughing?" Amy said. She looked as if she was undecided if she should run.

"Last night I picked up my Bible to read, like I do every night, and I dropped it and my bookmark fell out. I couldn't remember exactly where I was, just that it was somewhere near the start of 1 Peter. But instead I ended up in James, on the verse where it says if there is a brother or sister in need it's no good to just wish them well without doing anything to help them. I've read that verse so many times before, but last night it seemed to stick in my mind." He smiled, shaking his head. "It seems God was making me clumsy to teach me something for today."

Amy moved back to the table, taking a seat opposite him. "Sometimes I think God speaks to me. Not out loud, like

43

I hear you now, but in my mind. Do you ever get that?"

The only voice he ever heard in his head telling him what to do was his father's. "Not that I can recall."

"But you think He made you drop your Bible?"

He shrugged and smiled. "Maybe He knows I don't listen hard enough and so He has to do things I can't ignore."

She smiled back at him. For a moment, Adam could only stare. She had such a beautiful smile.

"So will you stay?" he said. He really wanted her to stay.

She lowered her eyes to the tablecloth, took a shaking breath and let it out slowly. Adam waited, holding his breath.

"If you truly don't mind after what I've done." Her eyes found his, fear mingling with hope in their depths.

He breathed out. "I can't say I don't feel hurt, but what kind of man would I be if I turned you away when you need my help?"

She looked down at the knife still clutched in her hand. "You'd be like most other men, at least the ones I've met."

What had happened to her? Adam wanted to ask, but it wasn't his business. Maybe one day she would trust him enough to tell him.

"Well then I don't want to be like other men," he said firmly. "So will you stay?"

She nodded and smiled a little. "But I'll find a job and pay you back for the fare and my board. And I'll do everything I can for you here. I'll cook and clean, not that your home isn't clean, it's beautiful, but I promise you won't have to lift a finger. I'll do everything."

He laughed, relief making him feel like a weight had lifted from him. "You'll spoil me."

She grinned. "Rotten."

Adam couldn't stop smiling. Even if she wasn't going to marry him, it could work. They'd spend time together, get to know each other, become friends.

And maybe, for a while, he wouldn't be so lonely.

Chapter 5

"I have the mailbag to sort that came on the train yesterday and then I have to open the post office for a few hours this morning for people to collect their mail, but I'm free this afternoon. Are you sure I can't do anything?"

Amy glanced back at Adam on the settee and waved a wet hand. "You stay right there. Relax. Drink your coffee."

"You're going to have to let me do something. I can almost feel my mother's disapproving stare on me."

"Does she live here, in town?" She tried to keep her tone light, but the mention of Adam's mother had her stomach clenching. What would Mrs Emerson think of a woman staying with him who'd tricked her son into paying for her to cross the country? It was a meeting she most definitely didn't want to have.

"No, my parents live on my grandparents' farm. Well, it's their farm too."

Keep it casual. "Is that far away?"

"An hour and a half's ride, more or less. I don't see them very often."

Amy breathed a surreptitious sigh of relief.

"Ma taught us all to look after ourselves, even the boys. She says folks should marry for love, not cooking and cleaning. I'm not used to other people doing everything for me."

"What were you going to do once you were married?" she said, carefully not looking at him.

"I supposed we'd work it out together, somehow. I was kind of looking forward to all that, to getting to know each other and adjusting to living in the same house. I knew it wasn't going to be easy, but I was looking forward to doing it together, as a couple." He laughed softly. "I think I have a bit of an overly romantic view of marriage."

Amy's stomach sidled down to her feet. She set the plate she was washing on the drainer, dried her hands and went to sit on the other end of the settee from Adam. "I'm sorry. I didn't mean to ruin it all for you. You must hate me now."

"I don't hate you. I understand why you did it. You had no choice." One side of his mouth curled up. "Besides, how can I hate someone who just washed all my dishes and is insisting on spoiling me rotten?"

She couldn't help smiling back. "I'd better get right on that then. I'll dry up and start on the cleaning. Then I can go out and look for a job." She started to rise.

He leaned forward and grasped her wrist. "You don't..."

Panic flashed through Amy's chest. She jerked her arm away with a cry, scrambling to her feet before she was even aware of what she was doing.

Adam gasped, pressing back away from her, his face filled with horror. "I'm sorry, I'm sorry! I didn't mean to..." He lifted both hands, palms out towards her. "Please, I wasn't... I'm sorry."

She squeezed her burning eyes shut, embarrassed. What was wrong with her? She knew Adam wouldn't harm her. "I'm sorry, I don't know why I did that."

Sinking back down onto the settee, she tried to calm her pounding heart.

Adam lowered his hands and held them against him, looking like he was trying not to move too much in case she spooked again.

She sighed. "It's not you. I'm not afraid of you."

He seemed to relax a little, moving his body forward from where he'd been pressed into the corner of the settee. "I shouldn't have touched you. It wasn't my right."

She drew in a deep breath and let it out slowly. The last thing she wanted was for Adam, after everything he was doing for her, to feel like he had to be careful what he did in his own home.

"If I'm going to live here, we need to make some rules," she said.

He nodded slowly. "All right."

After a moment's hesitation, she reached out and took his hand. "Rule one; you don't have to be afraid of touching me."

He looked at their hands resting together on his thigh and gently threaded his fingers between hers. "All right."

Amy tried to ignore her stuttering heart which now had nothing to do with fear. If she could have taken it out and slapped it, she would have. "Rule two; this is your home and you can do whatever you want in it. Although I will do my best to get in as much spoiling as I can."

The corners of his mouth twitched. "All right."

"Rule three; if you change your mind about me being here, you have to tell me and I will move right out. I don't want you to regret doing this."

He stared at her for a few long seconds before nodding. "All right."

His fingers were still entwined with hers and she found herself desperately trying to think of more rules so he wouldn't let go. "Rule four; you get to make any rules you want and I will stick to them."

"All right."

To her regret, she couldn't think of anything else. "Do you have any rules?"

His eyes dropped to their hands. "Just one. If you ever

feel afraid or threatened in any way, tell me. I'll protect you, you have my word. You should feel safe here."

Safe. Could she truly feel safe anywhere? Was it possible to live life with no fear of harm whatsoever? Amy couldn't imagine such a thing, but as she looked at Adam she got the feeling that if it would happen anywhere, it would be with him.

"All right."

His gaze held hers, his thumb tracing a slow circle on the back of her hand and sending small tingles of sensation into her skin. Maybe she was wrong. Maybe she could stay and marry...

No.

She slid her hand away and clutched it in her lap. It didn't make any difference how good a man Adam was or how safe she felt with him; she wouldn't depend on him or anyone else.

He cleared his throat and sat back.

Feeling awkward, Amy stood. "I'll finish up the dishes." She walked to the sink and resumed washing up.

Behind her she heard the settee squeak a little then Adam appeared at her side, taking a towel from a hook and picking up one of the clean, still wet plates.

Before she could object he said, "Rule number two, remember?"

She smiled and returned her attention to the pan she was scrubbing. "Do you know of anywhere they might be hiring?"

"Not that I've heard, but that doesn't mean much since I haven't been looking."

She finished scrubbing and rinsed the pan. "I can go and take a look around town when we're finished."

He held out the towel for it. "I can show you around a little before I open up the post office. I would have liked to

49

have kept it closed, it being the day after you arrived, but Saturdays are always my busiest day and I figured you'd want to rest and settle in after your long journey. You can still do that though. You could look for work on Monday."

Rest sounded good after the night she'd had, but she needed to find a job as soon as possible. "I'm OK. Now I'm on solid, not moving ground I feel so much better. I would like to go out today, if that's all right."

"You can do whatever you want to, you don't ever have to ask my permission. I want you to be comfortable here. While you're staying here, this is your home." He smiled. "I could make that my rule number two if it would help."

She laughed. "I'll do my best with it being a suggestion rather than a rule."

He nodded and placed the pan into the dresser cupboard. "Just let me know if you need me to make it official."

~ ~ ~

It was after nine by the time they left the house, and the main street of Green Hill Creek, while not exactly bustling, still had a smattering of people going about their daily business.

"Mornin', Adam." A man sat in a rocker outside a store two doors down from Adam's post office, tilting slowly back and forth. He raised the pipe held in one weathered hand in greeting.

"Morning, Isaiah."

Isaiah moved his gaze to Amy, a network of wrinkles forming in the dark skin at the corners of his eyes. "And a good mornin' to you, missy."

"This is Amy Watts," Adam said. "Amy, meet Isaiah Smith. He's the town's best cobbler." He indicated the building at Isaiah's back with its sign depicting two pairs of shoes, one men's and one women's, either side of the words 'SMITH'S QUALITY FOOTWEAR'.

"I also happen to be the town's *only* cobbler," Isaiah said, his eyes twinkling, "but that don't make me any less the best."

Amy stepped forward, holding out her hand. "It's a pleasure to meet you, Mr Smith."

Isaiah's smile grew as he grasped her hand and shook it. "Just call me Isaiah. Everybody does. So, you two off to get hitched?"

Amy glanced at Adam, her smile disappearing. Caught up in the emotional whirlwind of the last couple of hours as she'd been, she hadn't given much thought to how they were going to explain the situation to his neighbours and friends.

Adam looked like he was trying to think of something to say. "The truth is..." he began.

"The truth is," Amy said, "I didn't come here to marry Adam. I needed to get out of New York and he is kindly allowing me to rent his spare bedroom for the time being until I can pay him back for the train fare and get together enough money to continue my journey to San Francisco."

One of Isaiah's eyebrows raised slightly and he nodded. "Well now, that explains all the fuss."

Adam grimaced. "Fuss? What fuss?"

"'Bout an hour ago, Matilda Vernon comes out of the church," he waved his pipe towards the cross just visible above the roofs of the buildings along the road, "and runs over to Violet Winters across the street. They have a talk, are joined by two more of the upstanding ladies of our community in the meantime, then all four of them rush down here and stand right there," he used the pipe to point at a spot directly opposite the post office, "staring at your place and whisperin' to each other for 'bout ten minutes. Then they all hurried back up the road like somethin' was on fire."

Adam groaned, pinching the bridge of his nose.

"What's wrong?" Amy said, touching his arm. She looked around nervously.

He heaved a sigh. "Nothing. It's just, Mrs Vernon can move faster than a jack rabbit when she has some gossip to spread. And I imagine the news that a young woman I'm not wed to is staying in my house unchaperoned made her day. Possibly her year. It'll be all over the town by now, and probably not in any form approaching the truth. I'm sorry, I should have thought of this."

Her stomach curled in on itself. "Do you want me to move out? I'll ruin your reputation."

His eyes widened. "*My* reputation? Oh no, I don't care what they say about me. Besides, I'm a man, it's very hard to ruin a man's reputation. It's you I'm worried about. I don't want you to have to be bothered with all that."

Amy considered it for a moment. She wasn't staying here so it didn't matter what people said about her. Her only concern was Adam, but if he wasn't worried, then should she be? "Well, I don't care what people think of me. Gossip's everywhere in New York and I was never in the kind of social circle where it mattered. Doesn't it say somewhere in the Bible about gossiping being bad? And if God thinks that about it then so do I. As long as it doesn't hurt you, it doesn't matter one bit to me."

Isaiah removed the pipe from his mouth and burst into laughter. "Miss Amy Watts, I like your style."

"That makes two of us," Adam said, grinning. "Do you know of anyone who's looking to hire?" he said to Isaiah. "Amy wants to find a job today. Maybe in one of the stores or the hotel?"

"Haven't heard nothing," Isaiah said, replacing his pipe. "'Part from George is lookin' for someone for the livery, but mucking out horses ain't no job for a lady. But that don't mean there ain't nothing to be had. There are some things that go on in this town even I don't know about."

"I'm not sure that's true, Isaiah," Adam said, smiling.

Isaiah grinned back. "Maybe."

They left Isaiah to his pipe and people watching and continued along the road, Adam pointing out the local landmarks as they walked.

"Down that road is Green Hill Creek Emmanuel Church where we'll be going tomorrow. I don't know if you remember the way from yesterday."

"Where I performed my fake swoon, yes."

He chuckled. "It was very convincing. Scared me half to death."

"I'm sorry," Amy said with a sigh. "It was the only thing I could think to do."

He stopped and turned to face her. "You don't need to apologise, for any of it. I understand you were desperate. To be truthful, I think you were very brave to do it."

"You do?" she said in disbelief.

He resumed walking and she fell into step beside him. "Not many people, man or woman, who would have the courage to come all this way across the country to this wild place with no real idea of what was going to happen once they got here."

She looked around at the slightly rough around the edges, but otherwise pleasant seeming town. "Doesn't look very wild to me."

He smiled. "Well, no. It is pretty peaceful in these parts nowadays, but there are some places where it's still dangerous, with bandits and the fighting with the Indians and such. Marshal Cade is good for the town too. He's been here just over a year. Fought in the war. He keeps everyone in line." He pointed to a one storey brick building ahead of them, a sign next to the door saying 'MARSHAL'S OFFICE'

53

swinging slowly in the breeze. "That's his place there, but I hope you never have cause to need his services."

Further on they passed a three storey wooden clapboard building painted in a faded green with red trim. A big sign on the front of the second floor balcony proclaimed it to be the saloon. From the scantily clad women lounging in chairs on the balcony, Amy guessed it was more than just a drinking establishment.

"If you were thinking... and I'm not saying you were because I'm sure you weren't, but just in case, that place isn't safe for women, even just to walk into. Not that I'm suggesting you would want to work as a... I meant if you were thinking of working in the saloon itself, not upstairs." Adam ran one hand down his face and groaned. "I think I'll stop talking now."

Amy put one hand over her mouth to stifle her laughter. Adam was so adorable when he was flustered. "I understand. No going into the saloon. Got it."

He gave a rueful chuckle. "Believe it or not, there are times when I do actually sound like I have a brain in my head." He dug a watch from his pocket, worry on his face as he checked it. "I really need to go and open the post office, but with Mrs Vernon spreading rumours I don't want to leave you alone. Are you sure you don't want to wait to do this? I could come with you this afternoon."

"No, I'll be fine, I promise. You go and I'll be back with a job before you know it." She wasn't at all sure of that, but she tried to sound positive. She didn't want Adam worrying about her. He'd done so much already.

He scanned the people around them, finally sighing and returning his attention to her. "All right. But if you change your mind, just come home and I'll go with you later. I truly don't mind."

"I know you don't, but you don't have to worry about

me. I can look after myself."

A small smile touched his lips. "I have no doubt of that. I'll see you later."

Despite her words, as she watched Adam walk away she suddenly felt very alone.

Chapter 6

With a deep sigh, Amy pulled her gaze from Adam's retreating form and looked around. Her eyes came to rest on the hotel at the top of the street. It was as good a place to start as any.

The four storey building occupied a prime position at the very head of the road where it curved off to the north, giving everyone on the street a view of the hotel and everyone in the hotel a view along the street. It was constructed of brick, unlike most of the other buildings in the town apart from the bank and the marshal's office, and looked to Amy altogether too fancy for a small town such as Green Hill Creek. Although with its tall windows and decorative columns flanking the entrance, it wouldn't have been out of place in New York. Not the upper class, wealthy centre, but in the not quite so affluent areas it could have easily passed for a city establishment. Perhaps whoever had invested in it was expecting the new railroad to bring in clientele.

An image of her dream hotel in San Francisco came to mind. Perhaps if she could work here it wouldn't feel quite so far away.

Reaching the door, Amy smoothed her hair and her skirts and walked inside. Other than a bored looking, red-headed young man behind the reception desk, the velvet draped and wood panelled lobby was deserted.

She walked up to the man and smiled. "I was wondering

if I could speak to someone about employment in the hotel?"

He snorted a laugh. "You must be new around here."

"Uh, yes?"

He swept one hand around the sumptuous room. "See all these guests?"

Amy looked round in case there'd been an influx of people while her back was turned. There hadn't. "Uh, no?"

"Exactly. No guests, no jobs. If it wasn't for folks who won't go into the saloon using the restaurant and just keeping the place above water, I wouldn't even be here."

Amy lowered her eyes to the polished surface of the oak reception desk. "Oh."

The man sighed. "I'm sorry, Miss, I didn't mean to be sharp. Saturdays are usually my day off. I'm much nicer Monday through Friday."

Despite her disappointment, Amy laughed. "Maybe I should come back Monday."

"You should," he said, smiling. "There still won't be any jobs, but I'll be here to brighten your day. Truth is, if there were any jobs and it was up to me, I'd hire you in a second."

"Without even knowing anything about me?"

A mischievous smile tugged at his lips. "Having a pretty woman on the staff couldn't hurt business, if there was any business to be had. I'm Zach, by the way. Welcome to Green Hill Creek, I guess."

"Amy."

"It's a pleasure to meet you, Amy.... wait." He frowned. "Not the Amy who came in on the train to marry Adam and now isn't Amy?"

"I, um, suppose. How do you know all that?"

He rolled his eyes. "Mrs Vernon. By now everyone knows who you are. She didn't come in to tell me, but I overheard her talking to Mrs Sanchez, the cook here." He chewed his lip. "Is it true you and Adam are living together?"

57

Amy pursed her lips, frowning. This gossip thing might turn out to be more trouble than she thought. "If by living together you mean in the same house, yes. If you mean in the same bed, *no.*"

He held up both hands in a gesture of surrender. "Hey, I didn't mean to suggest anything. It's just what Mrs Vernon said. So you and he aren't...?"

He left it hanging, but they both knew what he meant.

"Absolutely not," she said, a little more forcefully than she'd intended.

He nodded slowly. "Oh. Well, in that case, would you care to have dinner with me sometime?"

She raised her eyebrows. "You work fast."

"Not many women out here that aren't taken," he said, shrugging, "and certainly none as pretty as you. You've got to get ahead of the game."

Amy couldn't help laughing. "You're sweet, Zach, but I have to say no. I'm only staying in Green Hill Creek until I can make enough money to pay Adam back. Then I'll be leaving for San Francisco."

He sighed, placing a hand over his heart. "Can't blame a man for trying."

"Why don't you try one of the agencies that matches women back east with men out here? It works for a lot of people. Handsome man like you, I'm sure you'd get lots of interest."

He leaned one elbow on the desk and looked across the lobby to the door, running a hand through his red hair. "I would, but the pay here barely keeps me fed. If it weren't for working part time for my pa, I'd be homeless too. I'd have no chance of paying for a girl's train fare all the way from the east coast."

Amy patted his hand in sympathy. "My mama always used to say that with God all things are possible. You never know what's around the next corner."

He smiled sadly. "I think God's got more important things to be concerned about than getting me a girl."

"God is big enough and loving enough to do everything. Besides, it's important to you. Just keep praying."

"You think so?"

"He got me here," she said, stepping back from the desk. "I'd better get looking for that job. It was nice to meet you, Zach."

"Likewise," he said. "Good luck. If you change your mind about that dinner, you know where to find me."

Laughing, she walked back to the door and out into the morning sunshine. Even though her first try hadn't worked, her conversation with Zach had lifted her spirits. Feeling a little more optimistic, she headed for the store on the other side of the road.

The Green Hill Creek General Store, proprietor G. L. Lamb, was a wooden single storey building fronted by a covered porch crammed with heaps of boxes and barrels. Two wide, grubby windows flanked an open door. Movement caught Amy's eye as she approached and she watched a large brown rat scurry beneath the raised porch. Maybe she could get a job cleaning the place.

Inside, the building was bigger than it looked, deeper than its width at the front suggested. The walls were lined with shelves and merchandise was stacked every which way on the floor. Thanks to the ineffectual windows, which were the only source of light, it was gloomy. Even in the poorer parts of New York it would have struggled to attract customers, but Amy supposed presentation wasn't a priority when you were the only general store for miles around.

Two women were inspecting brightly coloured bolts of fabric stacked on a table to Amy's right as she entered and they watched her wend her way through the store. As soon as her back was turned, one of them whispered to the other and they both giggled. Amy did her best to ignore them as she walked up to a plump middle aged man with a balding head standing behind a counter which doubled as a half wood, half glass display case.

"Mornin', Miss," he said, a cheerful smile making his red cheeks bulge. "How can I help you?"

Amy glanced back at the women. They were making a show of studying the fabric, but it was obvious they were listening. She stifled a sigh and turned back to the man.

"I'm new here and I'm looking for a job. I was wondering if you had anything? I'm trustworthy and very hardworking."

His expression turned to sympathetic regret. "I'm sorry, Miss, but I have all the help I can afford. I'd take you on if I could."

Amy nodded, trying not to show her disappointment. "Well, thank you anyway." She pointed to a display of candy a little further along the wall shelves. "If you put one of those jars here, by the register, you'll sell more of them. In New York they do it all the time. The children beg their parents for a piece when they're paying."

He looked at the candy and then the cash register. "Hmm, I never thought of that. I'll give it a try. I'm Grover Lamb, proprietor of this here store. If I hear of anyone hiring, I'll let you know, but things are slow around here right now. Town's still waiting for that magic railroad touch to kick in." He smiled and held out his hand.

Amy took it, trying not to wince at his crushing handshake. "I'm Amy Watts, and thank you, Mr Lamb."

She turned, not failing to notice the two women looking rapidly down at the fabric display as her eyes fell on them. Squaring her shoulders, she walked past towards the door. Whispers followed her. She tried to ignore them, she really did, but by the time she'd reached the door she'd had enough. Stopping abruptly, she turned around and marched back into the store.

The two women's eyes widened as she walked up to them.

"Good morning, I'm Amy Watts, although I'm guessing you already know that. As you are so effective at spreading news, I'd be grateful if you could let everyone know that I'm looking for work. I can cook, clean, sew or anything else anyone might need. I can be contacted at the post office, but I'm guessing you know that too. Thank you so much, your help is very much appreciated."

She caught a glimpse of Mr Lamb as she turned away from the shocked women. He was laughing quietly behind one hand.

When she got back outside, Amy took a deep breath and grimaced. "Sorry, Lord," she muttered. "I'll try to be more gracious next time."

~ ~ ~

Amy spent more than three hours working her way up and down Green Hill Creek's streets, trying every store and business she could find. In every place it was the same, they were very sorry but they had no work available. It seemed everyone thought that the arrival of the railroad six months previously would bring new prosperity to the small town, but it hadn't happened yet. She even tried the train station.

Eventually she ended up back at the saloon, staring at the large three storey building across the street with the peeling green paint and weathered sign. It was just about the only place she hadn't tried, but after Adam's warning it made her nervous.

A narrow balcony spanned the building on the second

floor. As Amy watched a window opened and a young woman wearing a shawl over little more than her undergarments climbed out onto the balcony and took a deep breath, hands on her hips as she lifted her painted face to the sun. Seeing Amy, she waved and smiled. Feeling a pang of sympathy, Amy waved back. No, she wasn't so desperate that she was ready to work in a place like that. She hoped she never would be.

She turned away and wandered along the street, tired and dejected, not really caring where she was going.

What do I do now, Lord?

There was nowhere left to try, no one who would give her employment. No way to pay back Adam. The only thing left was to go with her original plan, somehow get to San Francisco, get a job there and send Adam the money. The thought of leaving now made her feel sick to her stomach, but what else was she to do? And she wouldn't be able to tell him either. She knew Adam would just tell her it didn't matter and ask her to stay, and if he asked her to stay she didn't think she'd be strong enough to say no.

A frown creased her brow as she thought about that. She'd known Adam for less than twenty-four hours and already she'd grown fond of the idea of being around him. That wasn't in her plan. Admittedly, though, her plan was on shaky ground right now.

At the sound of men's voices Amy looked up from the ground. Without realising, she'd wandered right to the very edge of town. A large, barn-like structure stood ahead of her, a sign above the door identifying it as Parson's Livery. She didn't know if this was the place he meant, but she remembered Isaiah mentioning the person who owned the livery was looking for help. Working with horses wouldn't be so bad. Even though she'd never ridden one, she liked horses.

Perking up, she increased her speed.

"Not sure as I can pay more'n six dollars a week. I know people would be more likely to want the job if there were more hours, but that's stretching it for me as it is."

"Well, George, I'll ask around, but I don't know who'll be interested. But I'll ask."

An older man emerged from the livery entrance, lifting his hat and nodding a greeting as he passed her. Amy walked up to the large double doors and peered in. A man was close to the entrance, his back to her. He was shorter than Adam, but with a larger build, probably from years of hard physical labour. His dark hair was greying and unkempt, falling below his collar.

She stepped forward and looked around the interior of the large building. Stalls lined the walls, all of them empty. A set of double doors stood directly opposite her and she could see a glimpse of fences, grass and blue sky. Riding equipment and saddles hung from hooks dotted around the walls.

The whole place smelled of horse and manure. Mostly manure.

"Can I help you, Miss?"

Amy jumped, startled. She hadn't realised the man had turned around. His face was what could only be described as craggy, the bottom half hidden by facial hair that looked less like an intentional beard and more like he simply hadn't shaved in a few days. It was hard to judge his age, but she guessed at somewhere around fifty. As his brown eyes studied her, she couldn't help feeling she was being judged in some way.

"Um, yes, Sir." She stood up straight, offering up a quick prayer for strength. "I heard you were looking to hire someone. May I ask what the job is?"

He folded his arms and leaned his hip against an old, battered table standing next to the door. Pieces of paper and a leather-bound ledger were scattered across the top.

"Well, it's for general help in the livery here, looking after the horses, mucking out the stalls, cleaning, that sort of thing. You know anyone who might be interested? Pays six dollars a week for eight hours work a day, Saturdays and Sundays off."

Amy smiled, trying to exude confidence she didn't feel. "Yes. I would like to apply for the job."

The man looked confused. "You want to apply on someone's behalf?"

"No, I want to apply for myself. I want to do the job."

The man stared at her for a few seconds. Then he burst into laughter, holding his hands to his stomach as if to contain his guffaws.

Amy frowned. "What's so funny?"

His laughter petered out and he wiped one hand across his eyes. "What's so funny? You asking me to hire a girl, and a slip of a girl at that, to do man's work, that's what's funny. Go and try the general store or the laundry or the bakery, little girl."

Amy put her hands on her hips. "I may not be as strong as a man, but I can work hard. And I can certainly muck out horses and clean this place." She gave an exaggerated sniff. "And from what I can smell, it is sorely in need of it."

His smile disappeared and he shook his head. "Go away, girl. I don't have time for games." He turned away.

Amy stared at his back, tears of frustration burning her eyes. She whirled round and strode away, shame and humiliation driving her steps.

Stop.

The word flashed into her mind. She came to such an abrupt halt her feet almost tripped over themselves. Unsure what to do, she looked back at the livery. The man had taken a chair at the table and was studying the ledger on it, lines creasing his forehead.

Sighing, Amy wiped her eyes on her sleeve and walked back to the door.

The man looked up as she approached. "You can't take a hint, can you?"

"I need a job. I've tried everywhere else in town, but no one is hiring, only you. You need someone to help you here and I can do that. Just give me a chance and I'll show you. What can it hurt, just letting me try?"

He pressed his lips together, frowning. "If I hired you to work here I'd be a laughing stock."

"That's what you're worried about? What people will think? I'd have thought a man like you wouldn't care what other people thought."

"I have to care. This is a business."

"So you're worried I'll hurt your business?"

"No. Yes. I don't know." He huffed out a breath. "You're confusing me, girl."

"What if I can improve your business?" It was worth a try even if she had no idea how she could.

He leaned back, looking amused. "And how are you going to do that?"

"I'll show you once I've started work." She smiled and stuck out her hand. "Deal?"

His frown returned. "Now hold on, I never said..."

"When would you like me to start?"

"You don't give up, do you?" Lips pursed, he shook his head. "I'm going to regret this. Be here at nine Monday morning." He looked her up and down. "And wear something more suited to hard work than that dress."

Amy grinned. "I'll be here. You won't regret this."

"I already do, girl."

"My name's Amy. Amy Watts."

"George Parsons."

"Well, thank you for the job, Mr Parsons." She turned to

go.

"And by the way," he called after her, "job pays four dollars a week."

Amy spun back. "But you said..."

"It would be six dollars if you was a man, but you ain't, so it's four."

She opened her mouth and then closed it again. It was a job. She didn't want to lose it before she'd even started.

Turning away again, she headed back towards the post office.

Chapter 7

When Amy reached the post office there was a sizeable queue of people waiting to be served.

The moment she walked in the door the conversation stilled, each and every one of the eleven men and women turning to stare at her. Her heart sank. Why hadn't she gone around to the back door? She'd been so eager to tell Adam she had found employment that she hadn't considered he could have customers.

She took a step back, wondering if she should leave.

At the counter, Adam looked up and gave her a smile that made her stomach flutter, although that was undoubtedly just indigestion.

At one end of the sales counter was a hinged section allowing access. Lifting it, he nodded for her to join him. It appeared there was nothing else for her to do. Stifling a sigh, she walked along the length of the waiting line of people, eleven pairs of eyes silently following her progress. It was only when she was with Adam behind the counter that she relaxed a little.

He turned to address their audience. "Well, ladies and gentlemen, looks like you've won the jackpot. Of the unusually high number of customers I've had today, you have managed to be here at just the right time to catch sight of my infamous houseguest. Congratulations. I'd like all of you to meet Miss Amy Watts."

Every person in the room suddenly seemed to want to

look at anything but her. There were a few mumbled greetings and "Ma'am"s.

When Adam winked at her Amy had to cover her mouth to stop herself from laughing.

"I'll be closing in about half an hour," he said quietly.

"Do you need any help?"

"No, I'm fine. I'm guessing you had a harder morning than I did. You go and relax."

She didn't want to say anything, but it was true that her feet were aching from all the walking she'd done. "Thank you."

She was certain she felt the customers' eyes on her as she walked to the door leading to the parlour, but she didn't dare look back.

~ ~ ~

Half an hour later Adam walked into the parlour and flopped down onto the armchair by the settee, letting out an explosive breath.

Amy looked up from her book.

"I must say, I never saw that coming. I think I served every resident of Green Hill Creek today." He grinned and pointed at her. "You are incredibly good for business."

She replaced her bookmark. "They really all came to see me? I thought from all the surreptitious glances I got while I was out that everyone already *had* got a good look at me."

"Maybe they wanted to see us together in our sordid den of sin." He grimaced and rubbed his hand across his eyes. "I'm sorry, I didn't mean that to sound the way it did. All morning I haven't known whether to be amused, exasperated, or just plain angry. I just don't understand how people I've known in some cases my whole life can be so judgemental and self-righteous when they don't even know

68

what's going on." He shook his head and stretched his long legs out in front of him, crossing his ankles. "Anyway, how did your morning go? Any luck?"

She'd almost forgotten about her news. "Oh, yes, I got a job at the livery. Are you sure my being here isn't going to hurt your business?"

He chuckled. "Well not so far. Don't worry, it's not like they can go somewhere else to post their letters. The nearest post office other than here is miles away." His smile disappeared. "Wait, did you say you've got a job at the livery?"

"Yes."

"Doing what?"

"Just general duties, cleaning, looking after the horses, that sort of thing."

"You're going to be mucking out horses?" He looked horrified.

"What's wrong with mucking out horses? You like horses. You have one."

"Well, yes, but mucking out horses is so..." His nose wrinkled. It was cute. "...dirty. It's not a job for a woman."

She couldn't help smiling. "I used to scrub the range in the kitchen at Staveley House. It couldn't possibly be any worse than that, believe me."

"But, but..." He huffed out a breath. "Surely there was something else? *Anything* else."

"Not unless you wanted me to apply at the saloon. I imagine they'd have openings."

His eyes widened in horror. It made her want to laugh. Instead, she leaned forward and patted his arm. "It'll be fine, you'll see."

He shook his head. "I don't know how you managed to convince George to hire you. He can be a bit... ornery."

"I noticed that. But I'll win him over."

A smile slid onto Adam's face. "Well, if anyone can, it's you."

A thrill shivered through Amy's stomach at his words. She silently told it to go away, swivelling her stockinged feet out from under her and into her shoes. "I'll start lunch. You stay here and relax." She saw a protest coming as he opened his mouth to speak. "And if you are completely set on not allowing me to spoil you rotten, you can wash the dishes afterwards."

The protest turned to a smile. "I can live with that."

He stood from the chair and pivoted onto the settee she'd just vacated, lying on his back and draping his legs over the arm. He'd unfastened the top few buttons of his shirt and rolled his sleeves up to his elbows and the way he smiled up at her from beneath his dark lashes made her heart thud. She dragged her eyes away before her staring became unseemly and went to light the stove and start the food.

Her apparent attraction to Adam wasn't at all helping with her determination to leave for San Francisco as soon as possible. She'd been here less than twenty-four hours and already annoying little doubts were creeping in.

She shook her head, trying to dislodge the unwanted musings. As soon as she had paid him back and had enough money to continue her journey, she would be leaving. No matter how kind and funny and charming and handsome and handsome and handsome and...

She jerked her traitorous eyes from his relaxed form, turned her back on him, and chopped the potato she was holding with renewed vigour.

Chapter 8

"The first thing I'm going to buy with my wages is some material for a new dress," Amy said as she walked into the parlour, smoothing down her skirt. "I haven't met enough people yet for it to show, but sooner or later someone is going to notice this is the only one I have... what are you doing?"

Adam was sipping from a coffee cup as he toasted bread. He turned to look at her, eyebrows raised. "Making breakfast?"

She sighed loudly and joined him at the stove. "How am I supposed to spoil you if you keep cooking?"

"I'm almost done now. I promise I'll let you cook later."

"You'd better." She tried to look stern, but his amused expression made it impossible to do with any conviction. Instead she began setting out the cutlery and dishes, hiding her smile.

Adam finished the last slice, closed the oven and brought the plate of warm toast to the table. They sat down to eat, Adam saying the blessing as they held hands. Amy didn't like to admit it, but she was beginning to look forward to thanking God for the food before every meal, for all the wrong reasons.

He pushed one hand into his pocket and pulled out two dollar bills, holding them out to her. "Here. You can buy whatever you need tomorrow."

She opened her mouth to object.

"And you can pay me back at the end of the week," he

71

said, before she could speak.

She didn't want to take more of his money, but she did need some clothes. "Thank you."

"If you need more, just ask." He stopped buttering his toast and raised a finger. "Actually, I think I'll make that rule number two. If you need anything at all, ask me. There, it's official. You have to do it."

"I'm going to regret the whole rules thing, aren't I?"

"It was your idea," he said. "You can't take it back now."

"How big is the congregation?" She took a bite of toast with butter and honey and closed her eyes in bliss. "This is delicious."

"Daniel keeps bees on his farm. He sells the honey at the market on Wednesdays. The Emmanuel Church building is always pretty full Sunday mornings, but I don't know how many that is."

"Is that the same Daniel who married Sara, who arrived with me?"

"That's him."

Amy nodded and looked at her toast.

Adam ducked his head to look into her eyes. "Is something wrong?"

"No. Not really. It's just..." She placed the toast back onto her plate as melted butter began to drip from the edges. "Yesterday when I was in the general store there were two ladies and they were, well, they were watching me and whispering. And the other people on the street who were looking at me. And then the thing with your customers. It's silly, I know, and I'm trying not to think about it, but it bothers me that they're talking about us like that and spreading rumours that aren't true. You've been nothing but kind to me and I'm bringing all this down on you. It's just wrong. I'm just a bit nervous about seeing them in church, is all."

72

"Mrs Vernon," he said, a frown darkening his face. "I'd give her a piece of my mind if she wasn't my boss' wife. Don't worry about me, there's nothing they can do that'll hurt me. But it isn't right that you should feel nervous about anything and especially not about going to praise our Lord. " He reached out and took her hand. "It's going to be all right. I promise."

She couldn't imagine how he was going to fulfil that promise, but with his shining blue eyes gazing into her face and the feel of his fingers wrapped around hers, he could have told her he was going to sprout wings and fly to the top of the nearest mountain and she would have believed him.

She smiled and squeezed his hand. "I know."

~ ~ ~

Green Hill Creek Emmanuel Church was a simple wooden building with plain arched windows and a large wooden cross fixed to the top of the gable at the front. The whitewashed walls glowed in the morning sunshine and troughs of bright flowers either side of the door made it look cheery and welcoming.

A steady stream of people in their Sunday best were entering as Amy and Adam approached and Amy looked down at her hand-me-down dress, self-consciously patting at the scarf she'd tied over her hair in the absence of a bonnet.

She'd been telling herself all the way from the post office that it didn't matter what these people thought of her. Mostly she'd convinced herself it was true.

Mostly.

"You look beautiful," Adam said in a voice meant only for her.

Amy's heart leaped, spun in mid air and collapsed, gasping for breath, somewhere near her navel. She

73

swallowed and muttered, "Thank you," without looking up at him, in case he saw her undoubtedly crimson cheeks.

Mr and Mrs Goodwin stood to either side just inside the doors of the church; the welcoming committee. To Amy's surprise, Mrs Goodwin gave her a warm hug when she walked in.

"I was so sorry to hear you won't be staying in our town, Miss Watts," she said quietly, "but while you're here, you are very welcome. And if you need anything, just ask."

She drew back and gave Amy a cheerful smile.

"Thank you, that means a lot to me," Amy said with conviction. "And thank you again for the meal. Your stew and dumplings were the most delicious I've ever eaten."

"Why, thank you so much for saying so," Mrs Goodwin said, beaming. "I'll give you the recipe. Maybe you could make it for Adam while you're staying with him. He needs a good woman to look after him." The smile dropped from her face. "I mean, well, I didn't mean to suggest..."

"We know what you meant, Mrs Goodwin," Adam said, giving Amy an amused look.

Amy clamped her mouth shut against her laughter and nodded.

Mr Goodwin nodded to her with a smile, removed his pipe briefly to say "Miss," and handed Adam a hymnal.

They left Mr and Mrs Goodwin and Adam led Amy to an empty row of seats near the back, leaning down to her as she sat. "Will you be all right on your own for a minute? I just need to see Pastor Jones about something."

"I'll be fine," she said. "I'm a big girl, I can look after myself."

He glanced around the church for a moment with a worried expression, but when he looked back at her he was smiling. "I know. I'll be back soon."

She watched him make his way down the centre aisle,

circumventing groups of chatting men, women and children. When he was almost to the platform a young woman wearing a black mourning dress stopped him. They smiled at each other and she leaned forward to speak to him, placing one hand onto his arm.

A thick feeling developed at the base of Amy's throat as she watched them. From the way they spoke and the woman's hand lingering on his arm, they knew each other well. But why should that bother Amy? Adam was entitled to do whatever he wanted, with whoever he wanted. Swallowing the lump of what she suspected was jealousy, she looked away. She would not be jealous, had no reason to be jealous. You couldn't be jealous for a man you barely knew and had no intention of staying with. That was that.

Sweeping her gaze around the large interior of the church, she became aware of glances in her direction, people looking away quickly as her eyes landed on them. She suddenly felt very alone.

"Amy!"

She looked up to see Sara making her way along the row towards her. The sight of her friend filled her with relief and she smiled as Sara sat beside her and gave her a hug.

"I'm so happy to see you," Amy said. "How are you? How are things going with Daniel?"

Sara's face stretched into the biggest smile Amy thought she'd ever seen. "Everything's wonderful. His house..." She laughed. "I mean *our* house is lovely. And the farm is beautiful, all trees and fields and so much more peaceful than the city." She glanced at her husband who was standing at the end of the row, talking to another man. "And Daniel is the most amazing man. He's everything I ever wished for. Oh, Amy, I think I'm falling in love and we've only known each other less than two days. Am I being foolish?"

Amy glanced at Adam where he was now standing on

the platform at the front of the church, talking with Pastor Jones. "No, I don't think you're being foolish at all." She returned her attention to Sara and smiled. "I'm so happy for you."

A squeal interrupted them as Lizzy edged along the next row forward and sat, twisting to face them. She grasped their hands. "Amy, Sara, how are you both? Isn't this place wonderful? It's so beautiful around here I could die!"

Amy couldn't help laughing at Lizzy's ever-present exuberance. "It is wonderful."

"It certainly is," Sara said. "How are things with Richard? Are you madly in love yet?"

Lizzy's smile slipped, just a little. "It's good. The house is nice and it has a lovely garden and the farm is so much fun. Richard is... well, we're still getting to know each other. But I'm happy I'm here. It's so exciting to have a whole new life. Have you seen Louisa and Jo?"

"Louisa is at the front with Jesse," Sara said, pointing to where Amy could just see Louisa's blue bonnet over perfectly coiffed hair. "I saw Gabriel on the way in. I asked him about Jo and he said she's not feeling well this morning so she stayed at home."

"I do hope she's all right," Lizzy said. She looked at Amy. "Are you all right? I heard about... well..."

"What did you hear?" Amy said. She wasn't sure she wanted to know what rumours were going around about her and Adam, but sticking her head in the sand wasn't going to help either.

Lizzy winced and looked at Sara.

"You might be happier not knowing," Sara said.

"Just tell me. It can't be any worse than I'm imagining."

"Well, no one's said anything directly to me, for obvious reasons, but I overheard someone say that they'd heard you tricked Adam into paying for your train ticket. And that you

76

were now sharing his bed as payment in kind. I'm not sure they'd really thought it through."

Amy sighed. "The first part's true, but I was desperate. I didn't know how else to get away."

"You don't have to explain to us," Lizzy said. "We know that you would never do something like that without a very good reason."

"I'm sorry I lied to you all," Amy said. "I wanted to tell you I wouldn't be staying, but..."

Sara took the hand Lizzy wasn't holding. "I understand completely."

"But the part about sharing a bed is absolutely not true," Amy continued. "He's letting me stay in his spare bedroom. He's been so kind and understanding. He's a good man."

"But you don't want to marry him?" Sara said. "You don't think you could be happy here?"

Amy let out a long breath. "It's not about being happy. It's hard to explain."

Sara sat back. "You know what? You don't have to explain. You should do what is right for you. And if you need anything, I'm here for you."

"We both are," Lizzy added. "And I'm sure Louisa and Jo are too."

Tears burned Amy's eyes. "Thank you both. You're such good friends."

Lizzy squeezed their hands and lifted them up. "We have to stick together, us mail order brides and not yet brides. We will conquer the west, blaze a trail for women everywhere, and follow our dreams. Are you with me?"

Amy and Sara chorused, "We're with you!" as the three of them dissolved into giggles.

"Good morning, ladies."

Amy looked up to see Adam approaching along the row. He sat beside her, on the other side from Sara.

"Adam, this is Sara and Lizzy. They arrived on Friday with me."

"I remember. Lizzy, you married Richard Shand, didn't you?"

"Sure did." She grinned. "Listen to me, I already sound like I'm from round these parts. Ha! I can't stop! It's so nice to meet you, Adam. Oh, everyone's sitting down. I'd better go and find Richard. I'll see you all afterwards."

She swept off, greeting Daniel as he made his way along the row to sit next to Sara.

He leaned forward and smiled at Amy around his wife. "We didn't get a chance to meet on Friday, Miss Watts. Sara's told me all about your journey together."

"It's nice to meet you." Amy couldn't blame Sara for falling for him so fast. He was certainly handsome. Not as handsome as Adam, but very attractive.

All around them people were taking their seats and the murmur of conversation died as Pastor Jones stood and walked to a lectern at the front of the platform.

"Good morning," he said, "and welcome to this morning's service on this glorious Lord's day. I'd like to extend a special welcome to the five young ladies who arrived on Friday. I hope you are all settling into your new homes and that you will feel welcome here in our little town. Gabriel, please convey our welcome to your wife and that we will be praying for her to feel better. And on that note, Adam Emerson has asked to speak to you all before we start the service. You all know Adam and his family. He grew up here and has been a great asset to our town since he took over as Postmaster two years ago from his uncle after he sadly became ill and passed away. He has also been an unwavering support to this church and is a good Christian man, so I know you will all give him the respect he deserves." He looked towards them. "Adam?"

Amy looked at him, confused.

He smiled, patted her hand and said, "Don't worry." Then he stood and made his way to the front of the church.

Standing on the platform looking out over the gathered people, he looked a little nervous. "Um, thank you for letting me speak. I won't be long and I'll hand you right back to Pastor Jones."

"Take as long as you need. I'm sure they're happy to not be listening to my voice," the pastor said, to laughter from the congregation.

"I'll be quick anyway," Adam said. He took a deep breath. "I'm sure most, if not all of you are aware by now that Amy Watts and I didn't get married as I had planned. And I know that there are some rumours going around town about our living arrangements. So I wanted to tell you all the truth about what has happened."

His eyes flicked to Amy and she couldn't help feeling a flash of apprehension. She trusted Adam, but she wished he'd told her beforehand what he was going to say.

"When Amy arrived on Friday I found out that she didn't come here in need of a husband, she came here needing a friend. She also didn't come here to be judged or blamed or gossiped about. She needed my help and the Lord Jesus never turned away anyone in need, so neither will I. She needed a place to stay and until she moves on from Green Hill Creek she is living in my home. I'm sure I don't need to tell you that we are sleeping in separate bedrooms and nothing improper is going on. She is a kind, respectable, good Christian woman who loves the Lord. I love this town and I'd like to think that those who are in need are welcome here, so I'm asking that you accept Amy as part of our community, that you help her to feel like she belongs here, and that you don't give heed to any untrue gossip and rumours you may hear about us. That's all. Thank you."

"I'd like to add that I was fully aware of the situation with Amy and Adam," Pastor Jones said as Adam made his way back to his seat, "and I completely endorse his actions. He has shown commendable understanding, compassion and integrity. And Amy, we hope that you will feel right at home here, for however long you stay."

Many among the congregation turned to look at her, giving her smiles and nods. Adam sat back down next to her and gave her a small smile and for a moment she so badly wanted to throw her arms around him that she had to sit on her hands to stop herself.

Then the pastor announced the first hymn, Adam moved his attention to finding it in the hymnal, and Amy focused on her lap, silently thanking God for the man sitting next to her.

Sara leaned in close and whispered, "You're right, he is a good man."

~ ~ ~

Following the service, the congregation lingered at the church for a while to socialise. Some of them had likely come in from the farms scattered outside the town and so this was their only opportunity to see their friends and neighbours.

Amy talked with Sara and Lizzy and Louisa and met a few more of the townsfolk. She saw George from a distance, but didn't speak to him, not wanting to provide him with any opportunity to change his mind about employing her.

Not everyone had been swayed by Adam's heartfelt speech and she noticed a few disapproving looks sent her way, but it no longer bothered her. Adam believed in her enough to risk the condemnation of his neighbours; she didn't need any more than that.

Outside, he introduced her to the owner of the bank, Mr Vernon, and his wife. Both of them were polite and friendly, on the surface. Amy decided to ignore the lemon-sucking expression she glimpsed on Mrs Vernon's face when she thought Amy wasn't looking. Maybe that was her normal resting expression.

As they walked away from the Vernons, Zach waved to Amy across the crowd. She smiled and waved back.

"How do you know Zach?" Adam said.

"We met when I went into the hotel looking for work yesterday. He was very nice even though he'd heard the rumours about me already." She laughed. "He invited me to dinner when I told him you and I weren't... you know."

Adam glanced at Zach then back at Amy. "He, uh, he did?"

"I declined and told him I wouldn't be staying. He was very sweet though. Do you know him well?"

"We grew up together. He's a couple of years younger than me. Small town and it was even smaller back then. All the kids knew each other." From the way he was looking at Zach, Amy wondered if they didn't get along.

"Adam!"

She turned at the sound of his name being called to see the woman in black from before the service approaching. A few of the other women gathered frowned at her, probably at her loud use of his Christian name in public, but she didn't seem to mind.

She arrived slightly breathless, a smile on her face. "You must be Amy. I wanted to welcome you before you left. You've created quite a stir around here so I like you already. I'm Daisy, a friend of Adam's."

"It's a pleasure to meet you, Daisy."

"If you need anything, you just let me know. Any friend of Adam's is a friend of mine." She grinned at him and nudged his arm with her own.

For reasons she didn't want to dwell upon, Amy very

81

much wanted to dislike Daisy. It would have been so much easier if the woman wasn't so friendly. "That's very kind of you. Thank you."

Daisy nodded, smiled at Adam while touching his arm again, and disappeared back into the crowd.

"So, are you ready to go?" Adam said.

Amy studied his face for any clue as to the extent of his relationship with Daisy, but found nothing. Not that it was any of her business. "Yes, I think so."

As they left the dwindling crowd outside the church and started in the direction of the post office, Sara and Daniel passed in a buggy drawn by a sleek, dark brown horse.

Sara and Amy waved to each other.

"I'm glad Sara's so happy. She and Daniel seem like a good match."

"Dan's over the moon," Adam said. "He couldn't stop talking about her. I probably shouldn't tell you this, but before you arrived we had a small wager on whose bride would be the prettiest. Can you believe today he tried to claim he'd won? I guess you really can be blinded by love." He was staring at the ground ahead of him, his hands in his pockets.

Amy's heart did a little flip. "You don't agree he won?"

"Well, Sara's pretty, but compared to you..." He glanced at her, smiled, and looked back down at the ground. "We agreed to disagree. He was completely wrong though."

They walked in silence for a while as Amy tried to wrestle into submission the smile doing its best to take over her face.

"What do you say to a picnic lunch?" Adam said as they approached the post office. "The weather's so good and I thought maybe you'd like to see that view you have from your bedroom up close."

The day just kept getting better and better and it wasn't

even midday yet. "I'd love to."

"If you don't mind starting the food, I can go and saddle up Stride." He dug into his pocket for the key to the back door. "Tomorrow I'll get a new key made so you can have your own."

"You don't have to do that. I can just..."

"I want to." He handed her the key. "It's your home too."

Amy swallowed the lump that had suddenly invaded her throat. "Thank you."

As Adam headed off in the direction of the livery, Amy circled around to the rear of the post office. Her home.

She looked around the parlour as she walked inside. She hadn't had a home of her own for so long she barely even remembered what it was like. The orphanage didn't count and certainly not anywhere else she'd been since she was six. Standing in the middle of the modest room, she felt tears sting at her eyes. She hadn't realised how much she wanted a home of her own. Somewhere she was safe. Somewhere she could be happy. Somewhere she could share with a man who cared about her...

She wiped at her eyes in annoyance and went to the dresser to begin her preparations for the picnic.

Dreams like that didn't last.

No one knew that better than her.

Chapter 9

"Stride's ready and waiting," Adam said as he walked through the back door.

Amy looked up from the sandwiches she was wrapping in a napkin. "Should I pack the food into a bag? I wasn't sure how we would carry it on a horse."

"I brought saddlebags." He picked up a napkin parcel, sniffed it and grinned. "Cheese, my favourite. Let's get these out and packed. It's such a beautiful day, I want to spend as much of it outside as possible. You're going to love the country around here."

He piled himself up with food, grabbed a blanket from the couch, and headed out the back door. Amy couldn't help smiling at his enthusiasm. He seemed almost like a child showing off his favourite toy. Gathering up the rest of the picnic, she followed him into the back yard. And stopped.

Adam turned from where he was packing the food he'd taken out. A smile spread across his face at her expression. Amy stared, awestruck.

"Amy," Adam said, taking the food from her hands, "meet Stride."

She didn't think she'd ever seen a more magnificent creature than the sleek black stallion standing patiently in the middle of the yard. Stepping forward, she held out one hand. Stride lowered his nose to her fingers, sniffing her and then snorting softly. She touched the side of his neck gently and, when he didn't shy away, slid her hand down his jet black, silky mane.

"He's beautiful," she whispered in wonder.

She lowered her hand and Stride followed it with his nose, nudging at her arm and making her laugh. When she stroked his forehead, he pushed into her touch. Glancing at Adam, Amy found him watching her, half a smile curving his lips.

"He likes you," he said. "And if you give him this, he'll love you forever." He held out one of the apples she'd packed.

She took it and held it out on her palm and Stride gently plucked it from her hand. Dipping his head almost as if he was thanking her, he munched in contentment.

Adam patted his shoulder. "Are you used to riding?"

"No," she answered, stroking Stride's mane again. It was so soft. "I used to go to the stables at the house where I worked whenever I could, but I never got to ride. I just liked being with the horses."

"Well, we'll have to fix that." He placed his right foot into the stirrup and swung effortlessly into the saddle. Then he held out his hand to her.

She stared up at him. The back of a horse seemed suddenly so high. "I... uh..."

Adam leaned down towards her, looking into her eyes. "Trust me."

For a few seconds she couldn't tear herself from his gaze. How were eyes that blue even possible? Almost of its own volition, her hand rose to meet his.

His smile widened and he grasped her arm. "Hold on."

Afterwards, she had no idea how it happened, but somehow she was swinging into the air and onto Stride's back behind Adam. She gave a little yelp of surprise.

"You OK?" he said.

She looked down at the ground which was very, very far

85

away. "Mm hmm."

"I'll keep it slow to begin with, but if you're not used to it riding can feel unsteady. So you're going to need to hold on."

She looked around. "What to?"

He glanced back at her. "Me."

Her stomach shivered a little. "Oh. Yes." Trying not to slide off, she shifted her position so she was directly facing his back and tentatively slid her arms around his waist. "Is this OK?"

"You might want to hold on a bit tighter, but yes, that's OK."

She didn't want to hold on tighter. Her heart was already trying to pound its way out of her chest at Adam's proximity, she certainly didn't want to be any closer. Although with the limited room on Stride's back, she wasn't sure how much closer she could get. She kept her arms loose.

Adam clucked his tongue to Stride and pulled on the rein to turn him towards the gate. Everything lurched beneath her. Heart jumping into her throat, Amy immediately tightened her hold around Adam's waist. She wasn't certain, but she may have felt him shaking with suppressed laughter.

"I have a question," Adam said as they rode towards the edge of the town. "If you've never been on a horse, how were you planning to ride all the way to San Francisco if you couldn't go by train?"

Embarrassment burned Amy's cheeks and she was glad he couldn't see her. "I thought I could pick it up as I went along. Well, more hoped, really. I didn't know what else to do."

He was quiet for a few seconds. "You must have been real desperate to leave."

"I was," she said softly.

His silence went on for even longer this time. "Well,

horses can be dangerous if you're not used to them so maybe it's a good thing you're staying for now."

Bumping around on Stride's back and holding onto Adam as if her life depended on it, Amy couldn't help agreeing with him. "It is much more... wobbly than I thought it would be. And a lot further off the ground."

He laughed and touched her hands at his waist. "Don't worry, Stride would never let you fall and neither will I. I could teach you to ride, if you'd like."

Amy smiled at the back of his head. "I'd like that very much."

After a few minutes they left the outskirts of the town and joined a tree-lined track that ran along the edge of a field of gently waving wheat. Or barley. Or whatever crop it was. Amy had no idea.

"How are you doing back there?" Adam said. "Do you think you're up to going a little faster?"

She looked nervously down at the ground. "How much faster?"

"Not galloping or anything," he answered. "Just a faster walk."

A faster walk didn't sound so bad. "All right, I think I can live with that."

Adam did something with his legs and Stride picked up the pace. He was still technically walking, but the resulting extra movement caught her unprepared. She squeaked and tightened her hold around Adam's waist, pressing herself against his solid, relatively stationary back.

This time, she definitely felt him laughing.

"We can slow back down..."

"No, no," she said immediately, trying to sound braver than she felt. "Just give me a minute."

He paused. "No rush."

She suddenly realised how close she was against him

and carefully loosened her grip a little. A very little.

~ ~ ~

They rode for another half hour.

Usually Adam allowed Stride to take the familiar route at a much faster speed so the more sedate pace was enabling him to see things he would often miss. As he pointed out his favourite spots and views he felt Amy relax against his back, adding a whole new level of enjoyment to the journey.

She asked question after question about everything she saw; plants, insects, birds, crops, an interestingly shaped rock. He was no expert, but he told her what he could. Having grown up in a big, noisy, dirty, overcrowded city, everything was new and fascinating and her enthusiasm was endearing. Adam couldn't imagine a life not surrounded by the beauty of God's creation and the wide open spaces of the area where he'd lived for his entire life. He was enjoying the ride so much he didn't want it to end, although he was equally as excited to get to their destination.

He'd been waiting to do this for a long time, ever since they'd started corresponding and he knew he wanted her to be his wife. And although nothing turned out as he thought it would, the more he got to know Amy, the more he knew he still wanted to share this with her. The more he knew he wanted to share everything in his life with her.

When they reached a wooded area, Adam brought Stride to a halt and twisted to look back at Amy. "Close your eyes."

He expected her to ask why, but she simply closed her eyes without question. In a moment of clarity, he realised it was because she trusted him. This scared, vulnerable, brave, strong woman trusted him. It almost made him feel lightheaded. He'd thought he was prepared for the responsibility of being a husband, but this feeling, this knowledge that she was relying on him to keep her safe and trusted him to not harm her, was both terrifying and elating at once. He prayed with all his heart that he could live up to her belief in him.

As he started Stride walking again she tightened her arms around his waist and leaned her forehead against his back. The experience was far from unpleasant, but he knew it was because she was still nervous about being up on Stride so he didn't prolong it, much as he wanted to.

After less than half a minute, he brought Stride to a halt. "You can open your eyes now," he said, looking back at her.

She opened her eyes and looked straight into his and for a moment his heart stopped beating. Pulling himself together with effort, he nodded to their right. She moved her gaze and gasped, her face lighting up in amazement like he knew it would.

They stood in a grassy clearing dotted with wildflowers and surrounded by trees that dappled the sunlight over the ground. One side of the clearing was open and what lay there held Amy's delighted attention.

A wide, tranquil lake stretched into the distance, reflecting the peaks of the mountains beyond. The deep blue water undulated gently, lapping against the rocks dotted along the shoreline. Trees lined the shores to either side, creating a patchwork of green, yellow and bronze. The buzz of insects, the gently moving water, and the birdsong of the forest were the only sounds. And the tearing of grass as Stride bent his head to the fragrant growth beneath his feet.

"Oh, Adam," Amy murmured, "it's so beautiful."

He'd known she would love it as much as he did. Even though they'd only met two days ago, he'd somehow known.

"This is my favourite place in the world," he said. "I come here to pray or when I'm feeling like I need some peace or just to sit. When I'm here, I feel like everything is OK."

She moved her eyes back to his. "Thank you for bringing me here. It's the most beautiful thing I've ever seen."

They were so close, almost touching. If he leaned forward just a tiny bit, he could...

Forcing himself to look away, he swung his leg over Stride's neck and dropped to the ground then turned and held his arms up to Amy.

She looked down at Stride's back. "Um..."

"Hold onto my shoulders and do what I did. I won't let you fall, I promise."

She swallowed and nodded, reaching out to place her hands onto his shoulders. He took hold of her waist, lifting her towards him as she pulled her left leg across Stride's back. It was all going so well, until her foot caught on the edge of the saddle.

She fell forward with a yelp, throwing Adam off balance. He stumbled backwards with a cry of surprise and fell into the thick grass, Amy landing on top of him.

For a few seconds he lay still, catching the breath that had been knocked from his body. Amy was sprawled across him, her head face down on his chest and her hands still clutching his shoulders.

"Are you all right?" he gasped, trying to see her face which was covered with a tangle of blonde.

She nodded against his chest and lifted her head. Raising one hand, she pushed her hair out of her eyes. "Are you?"

He did a quick mental check of his body. It seemed to be in one piece. "Yep."

A shaky smile stole across her face. "That actually went better than I thought it would."

They stared at each other for a few moments and then erupted into laughter.

Amy lowered her head to his chest, her whole body

shaking as she laughed into his shirt. Adam dropped his head back onto the grass, closing his eyes and laughing at the sky until he ran out of breath. Something nudged at the side of his face and he opened his eyes to see Stride staring down at him as if he'd gone mad. He moved one hand from Amy's back and patted the horse's muzzle.

"It's OK, boy. We're OK."

Reassured, Stride walked away to the edge of the clearing and started work on a patch of greenery.

Amy rolled from on top of Adam and sat up, raising her hands to her head. "I'm sorry. I don't think I'm a natural when it comes to horses."

He sat up, his gaze inexorably drawn to her fingers combing through her hair. "Don't worry, it just takes a bit of practice. We'll work on getting on and off first."

The sound of her laughter buzzed blissfully through his chest. He could have listened to her laugh all day. Reaching out, she plucked a leaf from his hair, her fingers brushing his skin as she did so. It was the lightest of touches but Adam froze, his face tingling from the contact. Amy looked down with a shy smile.

She's not staying, he told himself. *She doesn't want to be with you. You will only ever be friends, that's all. Don't get attached. One broken heart is enough for a lifetime, don't risk another.* Even as he thought them, he knew the words were empty. He was already attached. He had been from the moment he first saw her.

He brushed at his hair, dislodging a few pieces of grass, and climbed to his feet.

Amy took the hand he offered her and stood. "I could spend the rest of my life looking at this," she said, gazing out at the lake.

Watching her face, he said, "So could I." He quickly moved his eyes to the lake when she glanced at him. "Well, now we're on solid ground and still in one piece, I'm hungry."

He laid out the blanket he'd brought on the grass close to the shoreline then removed Stride's saddle and bridle while Amy unpacked the food.

"He won't wander off?" she said when Adam joined her on the blanket, leaving Stride to his tasty undergrowth.

"No, he always stays close to me. And we come here a lot so he knows the area. I could have left the saddle on, but he always seems happier without it."

"You care about him a lot, don't you?"

Adam glanced at the horse who, he had to admit, was probably his best friend. "We've been together a long time."

She finished arranging their lunch and held out her hands, smiling.

Adam took them in his and tried to concentrate on being thankful for the food rather than for the opportunity to hold Amy's hands again. "Would you like to say the blessing?"

She looked uncertain for a moment then nodded and closed her eyes. "Father, thank You for this wonderful place and for the beauty of Your creation. Thank You for Your mercy in bringing me here where I'm safe." She paused for a moment. "And thank You for Adam and his kindness to me. Please bless him. Oh, and thank You for this food and all you give us. In the Name of the Lord Jesus, Amen."

She darted glances at him as she unwrapped her sandwich. "Why are you smiling?"

He shrugged and tried to wipe the grin from his face. He was only partially successful. "It was a nice blessing."

She was thankful for *him*.

He would probably be smiling for the rest of the day.

They ate slowly, savouring the view, talking, enjoying each other's company. It was comfortable and wonderful and ignited in Adam a feeling of warmth and peace he wasn't used to lately. By the time they reached the dessert of apples and grapes, he would have been happy for their time at the lake to never end.

At the appearance of the apples Stride wandered over and Adam cut a slice and handed it to him. When he'd finished it he looked at Amy hopefully.

"Stop begging," Adam said, reaching up to pat Stride's shoulder and then gently pushing him away. "It's unbecoming."

Stride shook his head and wandered to the lake for a drink.

"How long have you had him?" Amy said, watching him lap at the water.

"Eight years, since he was a foal." He remembered the ungainly young horse his father had entrusted to his care, a bundle of nervous excitement with legs that looked too long for his body. He'd bonded with the animal straight away. Just two or three years before that, he had been much the same. "My father gave him to me as a kind of peace offering."

Amy didn't say anything, but she gazed at him silently, obviously waiting for him to elaborate.

"I grew up here, in Green Hill Creek," he said, looking towards the distant mountains. "My family lived in town and my pa worked at the smithy with Jesse's father. But when I was seventeen my grandpa died and my pa moved us to live with my grandma and take over the farm. I didn't want to go. I had my friends here, and there was a girl..." He glanced at her. "Well, my whole life was here. I could have stayed, but my pa needed help with the farm and my younger brothers were still in school. But I wasn't at all gracious about it, to put it mildly. Me and my pa never did see eye to eye; he said I always had my head in a book and I thought he didn't understand me. Anyway, not long after we moved to the farm, one of the horses gave birth to a foal and my pa gave him to me."

"Did it help?" she said. "Between you and your father, I mean."

He drew one leg in and hugged his knee. "Not much. I was still angry. And when I finally stopped being angry, we just didn't speak hardly. I know he wanted me to take over the farm eventually, but I was never going to be a farmer. When my uncle, my ma's brother, got sick and nominated me to take over as Postmaster two years ago, I jumped at the chance to leave. He always did understand me better than my pa did. My brothers were out of school so they didn't need me anymore." He lapsed into silence, staring, unfocused, at one of the napkins on the blanket.

"But?" Amy said softly.

He drew in a deep breath and let it out slowly. "But my pa was furious. We had a screaming fight before I left. I've been home a handful of times since, but we barely speak. My ma comes to visit sometimes, but he doesn't ever come with her. He's stubborn." He smiled slightly. "I guess I am too."

Lost in thought as he was, he didn't notice Stride walk up to him until the side of his face was nuzzled by a large black nose. He rubbed one hand over Stride's muzzle and looked at Amy. He hadn't meant to tell her his whole life story. Something about her made him want to be open and honest. He wasn't used to the feeling.

"So Stride is just about my best friend," he said.

She looked up at the horse and smiled. "I'd say you're just about his too." She paused. "So what happened with Daisy?"

His mouth opened in surprise. "How'd you know the girl I left behind was Daisy?"

She shrugged, the ghost of a smile on her lips. "The way you spoke to each other, familiar, like you were old friends. Like maybe you were more than friends."

94

He never could get over how women seemed to know what was in his mind. Was he that transparent? "It was too far to keep seeing each other, especially with all the work I had on the farm. At the time I was devastated. I was in love, or as in love as I could be at that age. But I think that if we'd been meant to be together I would have done more to make it happen."

"And now? You never thought, after her husband died, that maybe one day you two could...?"

He shook his head. "It was a long time ago. Everything's changed. I've changed. We're just friends now, that's all." He patted Stride's neck and pushed to his feet. While he did want to be honest with Amy, he didn't really want to discuss his relationship with the girl he'd come close to marrying. Given how he was feeling about Amy, it felt inappropriate. And very, very awkward. "How about we do some work on that getting on and off a horse?"

Amy took the hand he held out to her. "If you're willing the risk to life and limb, I'm game."

Stride showed endless patience over the ensuing couple of hours as Amy learned to mount and dismount. There was defeat and triumph, catching and falling, a few bruises, and most of all, laughter. Adam couldn't remember the last time he'd laughed so much. By the time they finished, Amy could get into the saddle by herself, get back down mostly without falling, and even stay on when Stride walked slowly around the clearing.

Eventually they collapsed, exhausted, onto the blanket. Adam stretched out on his back, only wincing a little when he leaned on the hip he'd landed on more than once.

"Does it hurt a lot?" Amy said, her lower lip caught between her teeth.

He smiled and shook his head. "No, it's fine." Any pain was worth it, just to see the look of joy on her face as she rode by herself.

She leaned forward and kissed his cheek. "Thank you for your patience. I must be the worst horse rider ever."

The touch of her lips sent his heart thudding against his ribs. "Probably not *ever*." He wondered what else he could do to make her kiss him again.

Climbing to her feet as she laughed, she wandered to sit on a large, flat rock at the water's edge. Adam narrowed his eyes to slits, hoping she wouldn't notice him watching her. She slipped her shoes off, laying them beside her on the rock, and glanced back at him. He immediately closed his eyes. When he opened them ten seconds later she was rolling one stocking off her foot. He snapped his eyes shut again, his heart pounding even faster.

When the rustle of clothing had stopped, and after he'd given it another half a minute just to make sure, he slowly opened his eyes a sliver. Amy was leaning back on her hands on the rock, her feet dangling off the edge into the cool water of the lake and her face tilted towards the warmth of the sun, her eyes closed. Her face glowed in the sunlight, its rays shining in her rich golden hair.

Adam felt his heart ache. He didn't think he'd ever seen anything more beautiful. The mountains, the lake, the trees, the sky, everything paled in comparison. He said a silent prayer of gratitude to God for bringing her into his life. Even if sometime in the future she did leave, having her here now made Adam happier than he'd been in a long time. After just a few short hours of being with her, the loneliness he sometimes thought he'd carry with him for the rest of his life was gone, vanished in the sound of her laughter and the brightness of her smile. Even if he only had a short time with her, every moment would be worth it.

Somewhere nearby a bird began to sing, its melody mingling with the gentle rustle of leaves in the light breeze.

Amy took a deep breath and smiled, her face a picture of perfect serenity.

Adam raised his head and tucked one hand behind it so he could see her better. "What are you thinking?"

She started, her eyes springing open.

"Sorry, I didn't mean to startle you."

"I thought you were asleep," she said, smiling. "Why do you want to know what I was thinking?"

He moved one shoulder in half a shrug. "You were smiling. You seemed happy."

She looked back over the lake and swept one hand round to take it all in. "Just... all this." Drawing her bare feet up from the water, she flattened them on the rock and wrapped her arms around her knees. "Before the journey here I'd never been out of New York. I couldn't even have imagined so much beauty was out here. I'd seen pictures, but they didn't come close to this. I *am* happy. I think coming here is the best thing I've ever done." She gasped, her hand going to her mouth. "I'm sorry, I didn't mean that lying to you and using you was the best thing I've ever done."

Adam sat up and echoed her stance, pulling his knees to his chest and leaning his elbows on the top, his hands clasped loosely in front of him. He stared out over the lake for a few seconds, measuring his words before speaking.

"Friday, waiting at the station for you to arrive, I was more afraid than I've ever been in my life." He smiled at her look of disbelief. "I'm not exaggerating. I got chased by a pack of coyotes once, when I was thirteen. Had to climb a tree to get away from them. But I wasn't nearly as scared up that tree as I was waiting for you. Finding a woman willing to travel across the country to marry me seemed so romantic and exciting until it actually became a reality and all I could think was, what if you didn't like me or what if I didn't like you or what if we didn't get along at all and the whole thing

97

was a huge mistake or what if... you get the idea. I can't even tell you how relieved I was Friday night, having got to know you a little and finding how much I liked you."

Amy's face sank. "And then I ruined it all yesterday morning."

"But that's the thing, you didn't. I admit that I was shocked at first and angry and hurt, but when I think of all the ways this could have gone wrong, this isn't so bad." He gazed out at the lake. "I've been thinking about today for weeks, when I would bring you here, share the things that are important to me with you, and this is exactly how I hoped it would be. So I didn't get a wife." He shrugged and looked at the ground. Cornflowers dotted a patch of buttercups nearby and he plucked one from amongst the grass. "But I think I found a friend. I'm not wrong, am I?"

Amy was staring at him. He wished he knew what she was thinking.

"No, you're not wrong," she said, her voice soft.

He pushed to his feet, walked over to her and sat beside her on the rock. Hesitating for just a moment, he tucked the cornflower into the hair above her ear, resisting the urge to touch her face as he drew his hand back. The blue of the flower echoed the shade of her eyes.

"So I think, all things considered, this whole situation could have been a whole lot worse, but only a little bit better."

She smiled slightly and nodded, looking out across the lake as her fingers touched the flower in her hair.

Adam dragged his eyes from her face and followed her gaze. He'd made a decision. He was going to do everything he could to convince her that she could be happy here. He would show her how good life could be if she stayed.

Because despite the very real possibility that he might fail and one day lose her, he knew he had fallen head over heels in love with Amy Watts.

Chapter 10

Adam strolled along the street towards the bank, a smile on his face.

He was aware he probably looked like he'd misplaced a few of his marbles, but he didn't seem to be able to make it go away. Ever since the picnic the previous day he'd found his face stretching into a grin whenever he wasn't concentrating. Had he ever been this happy before? He didn't think so, even with Daisy. Amy and he were meant for each other, he knew it. All he had to do was convince her of that, in as subtle a way as possible.

After a while he became aware he was humming. He briefly considered trying to stop, then decided to just go with it. It was easier that way.

He reached the bank ten minutes before opening time. As usual, Jesse was already at his desk in the back room.

"You look cheerful," Adam said.

Jesse leaned back in his chair and twirled a pencil through his fingers, his eyes dancing with amusement. "I'm not the only one. What was all that yesterday about Miss Watts needing a friend and not a husband?"

"We *are* friends."

Jesse pointed the pencil at him. "That is not the face of a man who has just found a new *friend*."

"I didn't say I don't want to be more," he said, smiling. "So how's it going with Louisa?"

It was Jesse's turn to smile as he lowered the pencil onto

the open ledger in front of him. "She's agreed to give me two weeks. That's more than any other girl has. And she's amazing. She's smart and funny and kind and she doesn't speak to me like I'm different. I have a good feeling about this." He closed his eyes and sighed. "You've seen her. Isn't she the most beautiful woman you've ever laid eyes on?"

"Don't you start," Adam said. "First Dan claims Sara is prettier than Amy, and now you're saying it about Louisa. Yes, Louisa and Sara are both pretty, but no one comes close to Amy. The two of you are obviously in need of spectacles."

Jesse burst into laughter. "I think we were all matched right. Oh, by the way, Vernon wants to see you before you open up."

Adam left Jesse still chuckling and made his way to his boss' office. Rotherford Ransom, Mr Vernon's middle-aged secretary who Adam was convinced hadn't laughed since 1850, looked up from his desk in the small area outside the door to the office as he approached.

He drew a silver watch from his jacket pocket and flipped open the lid. "Opening time is in precisely four minutes and thirty-eight seconds, Mr Emerson."

Adam resisted the urge to roll his eyes. "Mr Vernon wants to see me."

Ransom sighed and stood, knocking on Vernon's door and then opening it. "Mr Emerson is here to see you." He withdrew. "You may enter."

Mr Vernon was seated behind his huge oak desk when Adam walked in, his eyes on a pile of papers in front of him. He waved for Adam to take a chair opposite and leaned forward, steepling his fingers over the papers. "I know you have to open up soon so I'll make this brief, Mr Emerson. This situation with Miss Watts is deeply troubling to me."

Adam frowned. This wasn't what he was expecting. "Sir?"

101

"The public expect the employees of any bank to be honest, of sound character and beyond reproach. We are, after all, dealing with their hard-earned money. Nothing can be seen to besmirch the good standing of anyone who works here, so I'm sure you can understand why the living arrangement you currently enjoy with Miss Watts is disturbing in the extreme."

"Sir, you were in the service yesterday when I told everyone what is happening. I assure you, I treat Amy, Miss Watts, with the utmost respect. Nothing improper is going on. She is simply staying in my house. I promise you, that is all."

Vernon sat back, heaving a sigh. "Be that as it may, it is not necessarily the truth that people see, but what they believe to be true. You are a man and a woman living under the same roof unwed and unchaperoned, and that is something I cannot tolerate from one of my employees."

Adam began to panic. "But, Sir, I..."

Mr Vernon raised a hand to cut him off. "I'm sorry, but I have no choice but to give one week for Miss Watts to find alternative accommodation. If she is still residing with you at the end of that week, your employment with the Green Hill Creek bank will be terminated."

Adam's jaw dropped. "But... you can't... I need this job. I can't live on the stipend from the post office alone. And Amy has nowhere else to go."

"Those are my terms, Mr Emerson. It is your choice whether to follow them or not. Now, I believe the doors are due to be opened in less than a minute. I would rather they were not late."

"But, Sir..."

"You are dismissed, Mr Emerson."

Adam stared at him, too stunned to say anything more. Vernon had lowered his eyes back to the papers on his desk.

Feeling numb, he stood and left the office. He didn't even look at Ransom as he walked past his desk and back along the corridor to the room where Jesse was working.

"Adam? What's wrong?"

He stopped in the middle of the room, not sure what he was doing. "I..." He squeezed his eyes shut for a moment. "Vernon just told me that if Amy doesn't move out within a week, I'll lose my job."

Jesse gaped at him in astonishment. "*What*? He can't do that!"

"It's his bank, he can do anything he wants. And he has." He rubbed at his eyes. "Please don't tell anyone, not even Louisa. I don't want Amy to find out."

Jesse slammed his pencil down and started to push back from the desk. "I'm going to talk to Vernon."

"No, don't," Adam said. "I don't want you risking your job too."

"I'd like to see Vernon find another qualified accountant within fifty miles of this place."

"He could bring someone in. It's not worth the risk. He's not going to change his mind anyway. I can find another job much easier than you can, you know that."

Jesse shook his head, frowning. "It's wrong. He shouldn't be allowed to get away with it. It's not easy for *anyone* to find work around here nowadays."

Adam managed to dredge up a small smile. "But you need your job, especially now, what with you about to be a married man and all."

Jesse snorted. "I know I'm charming, but even I need a little more time than seventy-two hours. But what are you going to do?"

Adam headed towards the front room to open the bank.

"I have no idea."

Chapter 11

Amy stared up at the painted wooden sign above the barn doors.

PARSON'S LIVERY & SALES STABLE

The letters were black on a cream coloured background and arched over a silhouette of a galloping horse. They had an almost jaunty feel. Bring your horse here, they said, we will look after him as if he were our own.

They made Amy nervous.

"Are you sure you want to do this?" Adam had said to her before he left for the bank this morning. "You don't have to work at the livery. You could wait until there's an opening somewhere else. I don't mind at all."

He'd seemed more nervous about her working here than she was, until this moment.

You can do this, she said to herself.

Determination lifting her head, she strode to the door.

"Thought you were going to spend all day out there, girl," George said from his seat at the desk as she walked inside.

Amy deflated. "I... um..."

"Never mind, you're here now. That your lunch?" He nodded at the canvas bag Adam had lent her in which she'd packed a canteen of water, a cheese sandwich and two apples.

"Yes."

"All right, follow me."

He led her to the far end of the building, past the rows of empty stalls, to where a set of large double doors tall enough to allow a man on a horse through without ducking opened onto a dusty paddock and a large field beyond. Around fifteen horses grazed peacefully in the lush grass. Amy spotted Stride with a beautiful white horse whose coat reflected the light, making it appear as if it was glowing.

"You can leave your bag and anything else you bring with you here," George said, pointing into a large alcove to the left of the open doors where a stool sat beneath a hook on the wall.

She hung her bag on the hook and placed her hat and jacket over it.

George looked her up and down, nodding. "Much better than the dress. I hope you have more like it because you're going to get dirty in here. No way to avoid it."

He turned away and she trailed after him, wondering if Mr Lamb's store sold trousers and sturdy boots in her size and if the two dollars Adam had given her would cover it all. Maybe when she had some more money she could get Isaiah to make her some boots. He was the best cobbler in town, after all.

"Tools are here," George said, indicating another alcove on the other side of the doors packed with shovels, rakes, brooms, buckets, a wheelbarrow, and all sorts of other horse-related paraphernalia. "Always wash them up at the pump out back before you put them in here. There's a brush to scrub them with next to the pump."

Amy followed him through the doors to the outside.

"All the straw and horse manure goes on that pile over there." He pointed across the paddock to a heap of straw buzzing with flies.

105

"What happens to it?" she said, wondering that it wasn't bigger.

"Farmers come and buy it from me. It's good for the soil. Makes the crops grow bigger."

Amy wrinkled her nose. "We eat things that grow in horse manure?"

"Never been on a farm before, have you?" George said with a snort. "Best not to think about it. And always wash your vegetables good and clean."

She followed him back inside. "I will, believe me."

"Your first job is to clean out all the stalls that have been used. The shovel, rake, broom and wheelbarrow is what you'll need. Put all the old bedding on the dung pile. When you've finished that, wash out each stall. I want them scrubbed clean, walls, floor, doors. They haven't had a good clean for a while so it'll likely take you some time and be hard work, but I don't want any half measures. Take however long you need, but do it right."

"Yes, Sir."

"If anyone comes in wanting to buy anything or stable their horse here, call me. I'll be outside. Got some fence posts need replacing. Anyone who keeps their horse here will know to come out the back. Any questions?"

Amy looked around her at the twenty-four stalls lining the walls. It seemed like an awful lot. "No, Sir, I think I've got it."

"I'm not one to stand on ceremony, girl. Things will go much better between us if you just call me George. None of this 'Sir' nonsense. I know my place and it ain't in the realms of 'Sir'."

"Yes, Sir... I mean George."

He narrowed his eyes at her. "Are you sure you're up to this? Ain't too late to back out. This is tough work, even for a man. I don't need you saying you can do it then deciding you can't when it gets too hard."

"You don't know the meaning of the word tough until you've spent hours on your knees scrubbing out a range in a baking hot kitchen in the middle of summer," she said. "I can do this. I won't let you down." She wasn't sure who she was trying to persuade, him or herself, but she tried to make it look good with an added smile.

George didn't look like he was convinced. "If you say so. Oh, there are leather gloves with the tools. They'll be too big for you, but use them. Your hands will blister if you don't. I ain't spending money on a smaller pair only to have you up and leave after your first day. I'll come and tell you when it's time for lunch."

He walked back out the doors, leaving her in the middle of what looked like an insurmountable number of dirty stalls.

"I can do this," she muttered. "I can. Lord, please give me the strength to do this."

~ ~ ~

When her lunch break came around four hours later, Amy had cleared all the stalls of straw and manure and scrubbed three until they were gleaming.

"How you holding up, girl?" George said as he walked inside, removing his hat and wiping his arm across his forehead.

"I'm fine," Amy lied. She felt like her arms were about to fall off.

"Well, have a rest and eat something. You'll need your strength for the afternoon."

Amy stood, wincing a little as her back protested, and wiped her hair away from her forehead with the inside of her elbow. Although even that was filthy. She trudged outside to the pump to wash up, flinching as she flexed her hands in the cool water. The gloves had been far too big and kept slipping off. In the end she'd just given up and left them off, but it wasn't doing anything for the skin on her palms. She hoped it would toughen up soon.

She fetched her bag and took it out into the fresh air, finding a barrel just outside the paddock fence to sit on. Taking out her sandwich, she watched the horses as she ate. She'd hoped to be able to spend more time with them, but maybe George would let her do something else when the stalls were scrubbed of their build up of grime. It had been quite some time since they'd enjoyed anything more than a cursory clean, judging by how much dirt she was removing.

When she'd finished the sandwich and one apple and emptied the canteen, she got up from the barrel, her muscles protesting. Attempting to stretch the aches away, she wandered up to the fence and leaned her arms on the top, cutting her second apple into chunks with her penknife. Seeing her, Stride trotted over, nuzzling his face against her arm in greeting.

"Good afternoon, Stride," she said, rubbing his forehead. "You're looking handsome today."

She held out a chunk of apple in her palm and he delicately removed it with his lips, munching the morsel as she stroked the sleek, black mane between his ears. Behind him the white mare she'd noticed earlier had followed Stride, but stood back as if afraid to approach.

"Who's your friend?" she said, cutting another chunk of apple and holding it out to her. "She's a real beauty."

The white horse looked at the apple, then at Amy. She swished her tail, but didn't come any closer.

"It's all right, I won't hurt you." Amy held out the apple further. "It's really tasty."

The horse took a step back, shook her head and snorted, and trotted back out into the paddock. Amy offered the apple to Stride who was eyeing it pointedly.

"You won't get that one to come near you." George said, walking up beside her and resting his elbows on the fence. He patted Stride's shoulder.

Amy watched the white horse bend her head to tug up a dandelion leaf. "Why not?"

"I've had her for six months now. She was left abandoned, tied up beside the road. Someone brought her to me. Terrible shame it was. Beaten and almost starved, I didn't even think she'd live. Didn't give her a name for two weeks, until she started to gain some weight back. She healed eventually, but she won't let anyone near her. Didn't even like being near the other horses much until Stride took a fancy to her and followed her around until he won her over. She'll follow him anywhere now which makes it a lot easier to get her in at night. But people, no. Not even me, and she knows me better'n anyone."

Realising no more apple was forthcoming, Stride walked away to rejoin the white mare. The two looked striking together, the stallion's midnight black coat contrasting with her porcelain colouring.

"What's her name?" Amy said.

"Clementine." He shrugged when she looked at him. "I knew a girl once with that name, prettiest thing I ever saw. Just seemed to fit."

"So what happened with Clementine?"

George continued to watch the horses. "I married her."

Something about his somewhat scruffy appearance, as if grooming was something he did reluctantly and only when absolutely necessary, had made her think he was on his own. "I didn't know you were married."

His expression didn't change. "She died a year and a half later, giving birth to our son."

A pang of sadness swept over her. She knew the pain of

losing a loved one. "I'm so sorry."

He shrugged. "It was a long time ago."

"What happened to your son?"

"He grew into a fine young man. Lives here in town. Works in the hotel." He glanced at her out of the corner of his eye. "Told me about a certain young lady that came in Saturday asking for work. He was a mite taken with her."

Amy gasped in realisation. "You're Zach's father! I had no idea. You look nothing alike."

"He takes after his ma. She had the most beautiful red hair." He stepped back from the fence and took a watch from his pocket. "You got ten minutes more for your break. You should..." His eyes landed on her hands and he reached out to take hold of one, turning it over to reveal the sore, red skin on her palm. "Have you been wearing those gloves?"

"They're too big. They kept coming off. It was going to take me forever to finish if I wore them."

He huffed out a breath, frowning. "Come with me."

Amy followed him back to the livery and hung her bag back onto her hook. Then she joined George where he was sitting at the desk beside the front doors.

"Sit," he ordered, indicating a chair in front of him.

A blue glass jar stood on the desk next to the leather gloves. He removed the lid and scooped out a small amount of brown, greasy salve onto one finger.

"Give me your hand."

Amy held out her right hand and he gently worked the salve into her damaged skin. It was soothing, but she still hissed in a breath when he hit a particularly painful spot.

"You should have told me you couldn't wear the gloves," he said, frowning.

"I didn't want to bother you."

"Ain't no bother when one of my workers is hurting, girl." He took some more of the salve and started on her other

110

hand. "Didn't they look after you at that kitchen you worked in?"

"Not really. If we got hurt, we had to fix ourselves. And then we had to work extra for the time it took us. The housekeeper wasn't exactly the compassionate sort."

George pushed the lid back onto the jar. "Well, when I leave this earth and stand before the Lord, I won't have Him telling me I treated folks badly. When you're here, you're my responsibility."

He picked up one of the gloves and slid it onto her hand then opened a drawer and pulled out a tangle of string. Holding the glove firmly in place, he wrapped the string around her wrist, palms and fingers until it was secure.

"Make a fist," he said when he'd finished.

She flexed her hand. The glove stayed in place. Nodding in satisfaction, he started on the other hand.

As she watched him work, a thought came to Amy. Was this what it felt like to have a father? Was this what she'd been missing her whole life, someone to look out for her and take care of her when she was hurt? Despite the short time she'd known him, she felt a rush of affection for George. She'd thought working at the livery was a last resort, but maybe it was the best thing that could have happened to her.

"Thank you," she said when her second hand was securely wrapped in glove and string.

"That should do for today," he said, returning the jar and the remainder of the string to the drawer and standing. "If it gets loose, come and find me."

He walked back towards the paddock doors, stopping at one of the stalls she'd scrubbed. For a few seconds he stood, staring at it. Amy held her breath. Finally he turned and carried on outside.

Amy went to study the stall, searching for anything she'd done wrong, but she didn't find anything. With a shrug, she went to refill her bucket.

Chapter 12

Adam lounged on the settee, reading his Bible. At least, trying to read his Bible. He wasn't concentrating too well.

His job. He could lose his job.

He'd spoken to Mr Vernon again before he left the bank to try to convince him to reconsider, but he wouldn't be swayed. He'd got the idea into his head that Amy living with Adam was in some way compromising the bank's reputation and he wasn't going to let it go, no matter how much logic was thrown at him. Adam had no idea what to do.

He'd been working part time at the bank since he moved back to Green Hill Creek. It fit in perfectly with his duties at the post office and for the most part he enjoyed it. It had been a godsend for the extra income he needed too. Where would he find something else? If he didn't have the bank, he might be forced to find full time work and give up the post office. He desperately didn't want to have to do that. Being the postmaster was the best job he'd ever had.

But how could he ask Amy to leave? Where would she go?

What would he do without her?

But she was planning to leave anyway, once she paid him back. It would be foolish to give up his job for someone who would be gone eventually.

But this wasn't just anyone; this was Amy, the woman he'd known for three days but was already longing to spend the rest of his life with.

Pushing one hand into his pocket, his touched the house key he'd had made for her this afternoon. He'd told her this was her home. He *wanted* it to be her home.

Closing the Bible, he dropped his head onto the back of the settee with a groan.

"What do I do, Lord?"

A few minutes later, with no answer forthcoming, he lifted his head again to see Amy through the window, walking into the back yard. He drew in a breath and let it out slowly and, as the door opened, plastered on what he hoped was a convincing smile.

She returned his smile when she saw him, making his own transform into the real thing.

Her hair was escaping from her braid, rogue strands frizzing around her face, and her clothing was rumpled and covered with muck. But even exhausted, dishevelled and dirty she was the most beautiful thing he'd ever seen.

"Are you all right?" he said, rising from the settee.

She pushed the door closed behind her and slumped against it. "Apart from feeling like my arms are about to melt away to nothing and wishing that my back would go with them, I'm fine."

His smile disappeared. "You shouldn't be working there, it's not suitable work for a woman. George should never have hired you."

He knew immediately it was the wrong thing to say.

"Really?" She planted her fists on her hips, defiant and utterly adorable.

He raised both hands in surrender, fighting a smile. "I didn't mean that how it sounded. You can do anything you want. It's just... you look so tired. He shouldn't be working you so hard."

"It was just harder today because the stalls needed a good scrub. It will be easier in the future because I'll keep up

114

with it all. I just need time to adjust." She shuffled to the sink, using the pump to splash water on her face. "George is really very sweet, and at least he didn't tell me I couldn't come back. I was worried he would."

"Sweet?" he said, taken aback. "George Parsons? Are you sure we're talking about the same man? Owns the livery? Gives the word grumpy a bad name?"

She laughed, turning to face him. "Underneath, he's lovely. You just have to look deeper." She wrinkled her nose. "What's that smell?"

"Um..." He'd noticed the odour as soon as she walked in, but he didn't want to tell her what it was.

She grimaced, looking down at herself. "It's me, isn't it?"

He pushed his hands into his pockets and concentrated on not laughing. "Mm hmm."

"I'm going to need to wash..." she waved her hands at herself "...everything. Maybe I should just go and jump in the creek."

"I'll tell you what, we'll draw the curtains to give you some privacy and I'll take your clothes and shoes outside and wash them while you get yourself clean at the sink in here. Then I'll start supper while you get dressed and rest. How does that sound?"

She gave him a dreamy smile. "Like you're the most wonderful man in the world."

Adam's heart thumped in his chest. If she hadn't smelled so strongly of horse manure the urge to wrap his arms around her would have been irresistible.

He turned away to pull the curtains closed across the window and compose himself. When he turned back Amy was pushing off her shoes with her toes. She pulled her socks off and held them out to him, her nose wrinkling.

"Sorry."

He smiled and took them. "I don't mind."

He bent to pick up her shoes and caught sight of her bare feet. *They're only feet,* he told himself. *Perfectly shaped, delicate, amazingly lovely bare feet.* He grabbed her shoes quickly and straightened.

"Throw the rest out when you're ready," he said, filling a large bucket with water and carrying it to the door. "I'll get started with these."

When he returned for soap, Amy took his hand, pushed up onto her toes and kissed his cheek. "Thank you. You have no idea how grateful I am. You really are wonderful."

Adam's lungs appeared to have stopped working. "I... uh... I'm g-glad to help."

He smiled and turned away. It wasn't until he reached the door that he realised he'd forgotten the soap. Feeling his cheeks heating up, he went back to the sink for the soap, gave her an embarrassed laugh, and fled to the door again, pulling it closed behind him and taking deep breaths of air.

Ten seconds later the door opened and Amy's trousers and shirt came flying out, accompanied by a "thank you" before the door closed again. Adam picked up the clothes and dropped them into the bucket, shaking his head and smiling.

He couldn't give this up, this incredible feeling of warmth and joy. How could he risk losing her?

There had to be a way to make it all work, to keep his job *and* convince Amy to stay.

He would do whatever it took, but there had to be a way.

Chapter 13

"You're late. And what are you wearing?"

"I know, sorry," Amy called as she ran past George to the back of the livery and into the alcove where her hook was. "I had to wait for Mr Lamb to open the store so I could buy some clothes. The ones from yesterday were still damp. Don't come back here, I'm changing."

She unbuttoned her dress and pulled it off, hanging it carefully on the hook, then put on the brand new shirt and trousers she'd bought. The shirt fit well since it was made for a woman, but she'd had to buy boy's size trousers and to get them the correct length they were too large on the waist. She buttoned them up and let go. The waistband settled impractically low on her hips where the hems would be tripping her up if she tried to walk.

Pulling them up again, she held them around her waist and went to the edge of the alcove. Peering around the corner, she saw George standing in the middle of the livery, looking like he wasn't quite sure what to do.

"Do you have something I could use as a belt?" she said. "I had to get boy's trousers. I can alter them to fit tonight, but right now they'll probably fall down if I don't have something to keep them up."

He looked around uncertainly. "Uh, yes. Um..." He rubbed the back of his neck and then patted the red checked neckerchief he wore. Pulling it off, he held it out to her, edging to within arm's length then backing up as soon as she took it.

"Thank you," she said, withdrawing out of sight again. "I'll stay longer tonight to make up for the time I'm late." She threaded the neckerchief through the belt loops of the dark brown trousers and tied it at the front then walked out from behind the wall and twirled. "What do you think?"

George nodded his approval. "Very hardwearing. Practical."

It wasn't what she'd meant, but his answer made her smile. "I'll muck out the stalls first," she said as she headed for the tools alcove. "Could you help me with the gloves..."

She stopped abruptly. A pair of leather gloves was draped over the edge of the bucket. Picking them up, she rubbed the supple tan-coloured leather between her fingers. They felt brand new. When she pulled one on, it was a perfect fit.

She turned to look back at George.

"They fit?" he said.

She nodded silently, blinking rapidly when her eyes started to burn.

He cleared his throat, stared out the doors and said, "Well, get to work then," before striding back towards the front of the building.

Amy looked at the gloves on her hands. He must have bought them especially for her. It wasn't that no one had ever been kind to her in her life, but it was rare enough that when it did happen her emotions tended to get the better of her. And since she'd arrived in Green Hill Creek she'd been bombarded with kindness, first from Adam and now George.

She wiped at her eyes and smiled. Maybe she'd have to try to get used to people being kind to her while she was here. That didn't seem like such a chore.

~ ~ ~

118

Adam looked up at the wooden cross on the Emmanuel Church building and tried to take comfort from it. His Saviour was with him.

If God is for us, who can be against us?

He believed it, he truly did, but it felt just about impossible to not be afraid of an uncertain future.

"Lord, I do believe," he whispered, using the words from the gospel of Mark. "Help Thou mine unbelief."

"Adam?"

He lowered his gaze to see the pastor's wife framed by the open church door, a dusting cloth in her hands. "Good afternoon, Mrs Jones. Is the pastor inside?"

"I'm sorry, he's out visiting a couple of sick members of the church. Can I help you with anything?"

"No. I don't know. I need..." His shoulders slumped. "I don't even know what I need."

She smiled and moved back from the door. "Maybe you'd better come inside."

He followed her to the front of the church where she sat in a chair and patted the one next to her. "What's bothering you?"

He picked up one of the church Bibles from the seat and dropped into the chair. "If I tell you something, you won't tell anyone else, will you?"

"Of course not. Not even my husband, if you don't want me to."

"Well, you can tell him I guess, since I came here to see him anyway." He sighed and rested his elbows on his knees, staring at the wooden floor. "Yesterday Mr Vernon told me that having Amy staying with me without us being wed is tarnishing the reputation of the bank and if she doesn't move out within a week I'll lose my job."

"He *what?*"

Adam looked up, startled by the vehemence of Mrs

Jones' response.

"I'm sorry," she said, her voice lowering in volume, "I know as the pastor's wife I shouldn't speak ill of anyone, but that man can be such a self-righteous, arrogant busybody." She shook her head. "Sorry, go on. Don't tell anyone I said that."

At least someone felt the same way about Vernon as he did. "Believe me, I've thought worse of him the last couple of days. I just don't know what to do. I need that job, I can't live on the wages of a postmaster alone." He flicked through the pages of the Bible he was still holding without looking at it. "But I can't ask Amy to leave. She needs me."

"Would you like me to ask Simon to speak with him, try to make him see sense?"

"I don't think it would do any good. I've tried talking to him, but he's made up his mind even though he was there when Pastor Jones said he supported my decision. At this point it may even make things worse, if that's possible." He leaned back, laid the Bible on his lap, and rubbed both hands down his face. Talking about it made the whole situation seem even more hopeless.

"Miss Watts could come and stay with Simon and me," Mrs Jones said. "Louisa is staying with us, but we can easily find an extra bed. I'm sure they wouldn't mind sharing a room, with them being friends."

"It's very kind of you to offer, but..." He let out a long breath. "This is going to sound irrational, but since I found out about Amy I've had this feeling that she's my responsibility, like I'm supposed to keep her safe, protect her. She said she thinks God brought her to me and I think she's right. I need her close to me. I can't explain it, but I know it."

Mrs Jones placed a hand on his arm. "I'm not saying you're wrong, but are you sure you're not thinking with your heart instead of your head?"

He snapped his eyes to hers, startled. "I don't... I mean, I'm not... we're not..."

She laughed and patted his shoulder. "Adam, stop panicking. It isn't a sin to like a girl."

If she could tell, maybe Amy could. Maybe *everyone* could. No wonder they didn't believe his relationship with Amy was innocent if all they could see was a lovelorn man yearning after her.

"Is it that obvious?"

"Probably only to a woman who's known you since before you could walk."

Only slightly reassured, Adam returned his attention to tracing the knots and patterns of the wood beneath his feet. "I admit it, I like Amy, but this..." he searched for the right word, "...*compulsion* I feel to keep her safe, it's more than just that I want her around. Something happened to her in New York that forced her to run across the country. If you'd seen her the morning after she arrived it would have broken your heart. She was so afraid. I don't want her to ever be afraid like that again. I have to know that if she needs me, I'm right there for her. Does that make me sound insane?"

"No. It makes you sound like a man in love."

He raised his gaze to her knowing smile. He'd grown up with that smile. There was no hiding from someone who knew him like his mother's closest friend did, so he simply nodded.

"If you feel that God has brought this girl to you to look after, then that's what you must do, meddlesome busybodies with nothing better to do be dashed. The Lord will guide and provide. He always does."

"Thanks, Mrs J," he said, sitting back. Telling someone had made him feel a little better, if no less worried.

Mrs Jones reached her arms around his shoulders, giving him a warm hug that made him smile. "You can always talk

121

to me about anything, you know that."

"I do."

He moved to stand, forgetting the Bible was still on his lap. It dropped to the floor where it flopped open. A verse caught his eye as he bent to pick it up.

Trust in the LORD with all thine heart; and lean not unto thine own understanding. In all thy ways acknowledge Him, and He shall direct thy paths.

Adam couldn't help chuckling.

"What is it?" Mrs Jones said.

"Nothing. Just, I think God has a sense of humour."

Chapter 14

There was a washtub filled with warm, soapy water in the back yard when Amy got home from her second day at the livery, the washboard leaning ready against the side.

When she walked into the parlour Adam looked up from the stove where a pot of water was steaming. "How was your day?"

She flexed her arms, just because she could. "Less of me's aching than yesterday."

"That's good." He wrapped a cloth around the handle of the pan and carried it to the sink, adding it to the water already there and then checking the temperature with his finger. "I figured you'd enjoy hot water for your wash today."

She took in the towel folded on the drainer with a bar of soap lying on top, her washcloth next to it, and the aroma of cooking food emanating from the oven. For some inexplicable reason the whole tableau made her want to burst into tears.

Adam rushed over to her, his smile disappearing. "Oh, hey, what's wrong?"

She shook her head, pressing her lips together and blinking back tears. "Nothing. Just... all this." She waved a hand around the kitchen. "You did all this for me." Her voice rose to a squeak on the final word and she cleared her throat, embarrassed.

His smile returned. "Well, if I'd known it was going to make you cry I would have warned you first."

A laugh bubbled up in her chest and she wiped the backs of her hands across her eyes. "I'm sorry, I don't know what's wrong with me. I'm just not used to being looked after."

"I like looking after you," he said, tapping his wet fingertip lightly on her nose. "I've only had myself to take care of since I moved back here. I was getting lazy."

One tiny touch and her heart was racing. She hoped he couldn't hear it. "Well, thank you."

He bent forward in an elegant bow. "It is my pleasure, my lady."

She kicked her shoes off, removed her socks and handed them to him. "Even the socks?"

He grinned. "Especially the socks."

~ ~ ~

Amy finished buttoning up her dress and checked her reflection in the mirror hanging above the washbasin to tidy her hair.

Thankfully, she wasn't nearly as sore as she'd been the previous evening when she got home from the livery, even though she'd been scrubbing stalls for most of the day again. At least she'd done all of them now. From now on all they'd need would be a light clean every day to keep them sparkling, which would give her more time to do other things to improve the building. She'd told George she could increase his profits and she'd meant it. She already had plans.

The sound of splashing water drifted up from the yard below her window as Adam washed her clothing. A smile crept onto her face as she thought about how he'd had everything ready for her return. She couldn't begin to understand why he was doing all this for her. Allowing her to stay in his home was one thing, but all the rest? It was as if he truly cared for her, although why he should she had no idea. He had no reason to that she could see. Even so, she couldn't help feeling a warm glow at his eagerness to help her.

A warm glow. She rolled her eyes at herself in the mirror. She was beginning to feel like one of the ladies in Katherine's beloved romance novels, with Adam as her handsome, dashing hero. The thought brought a soft laugh and a shake of her head. This wasn't a romance, she wasn't a heroine, and there would be no happily ever after, at least not the kind in the stories. Adam would make a convincing hero though, she knew that much. It would be a very lucky woman who finally won his heart.

Her eyes drifted to the top drawer of her dresser, as they did every time she was near. She shouldn't read them. They would make her feel even more guilt than she already did. In addition, there was a good chance it would only make her like him more and she didn't want to like him more. She was struggling to keep her feelings under control as it was.

But would they make it any more difficult than being here with him every day already did? She talked with him all the time, surely reading his words wouldn't be any different.

Letting out a huff of frustration with herself, she opened the drawer and took out the small pile of envelopes. She carried them to the bed, sat down and spread them out on the cover in front of her.

The mystery of Adam's letters had taunted her ever since she'd received the first one after answering his advertisement in the special insert in the paper from the Western Sunset Marriage Service. She had steadfastly avoided reading any of them, knowing that if she did, if she got any sense of the man she was planning to lie to and cheat into helping her get across the country, that her nerve might fail her. Instead, Katherine had read each one, telling Amy if he asked any questions, but never reading her his actual words. Amy had answered the letters without knowing exactly what it was she was responding to.

She'd wanted it like that, no contact at all. Nothing to endear her to him.

In truth she wasn't at all certain why she'd brought them with her in the first place, but now her curiosity burned within her. What was in them? What had he said? How had he felt before meeting her?

Maybe she'd just read the first one for now, that was all.

She checked all the dates on the postmarks and arranged them into order, from the first one he had written to the last. Taking the top one from the pile, she studied the name and address on the envelope in Adam's neat handwriting, touching it with her fingertips as if she could feel the strokes of his pen. Then she carefully slid the paper from inside.

Swallowing a flash of nerves, she began to read.

Dear Miss Watts,

Thank you for allowing me to correspond with you with a view to the possibility of matrimony. It was such a pleasure to receive your letter.

First, let me introduce myself. My name is Adam Emerson and I am 25 years old and live in a town called Green Hill Creek in northern California. I doubt you'll have heard of it as it is small, but growing steadily.

I run the post office and have done for the past two years since my uncle nominated me to take over from him as postmaster when he became ill. It still seems new to me, but I am enjoying the work very much and have a good relationship with the people of the town. I also work mornings as a clerk at the bank. Between the two jobs, I am fully able to support a wife and, eventually, a family.

I am in good health, a little over six feet tall and have dark brown hair and blue eyes. My mother tells me I'm handsome, although I think mothers always say that of their sons! But I do not think I am unpleasant to look at.

I find I cannot describe what I wish for in a wife as far as appearance is concerned, because I think all women are beautiful in different ways. But what I do know is that I would like someone who first and foremost loves God. I accepted the Lord Jesus into my life when I was a child and I feel that only a woman who understands what that means could understand me. Other than that, I would like someone who laughs a lot. Someone who likes to have long conversations, but who also takes joy in simply having fun. Someone who likes to be outdoors and enjoys the beauty of nature. I think what I want most is a companion who will stand with me through all of life's challenges, so that we can support and take care of each other. And most of all, someone who I will love and who will love me in return.

I am very much looking forward to hearing from you and anything you would like to share about yourself.

Yours sincerely,

Adam Emerson

Amy pulled her handkerchief from her pocket and dabbed at the tears running down her cheeks. He sounded so full of anticipation, so hopeful. Not for the first time since she'd arrived, she wished things were different. Wished *she* was different.

Pushing aside the thought, she read the letter again. She couldn't help smiling at how formal he sounded. Almost nervous. It wasn't like him at all, and yet it was. She imagined him sitting down at the kitchen table with a pen and paper, planning what to say, writing it down, maybe discarding it and starting again, working on it until he was happy.

I do not think I am unpleasant to look at.

That part made her shake her head. Not unpleasant to look at was such an understatement when it came to Adam.

She thought of his beautiful blue eyes and his handsome face, his dazzling smile and his tall, strong frame. As far as Amy was concerned, he was as far from unpleasant to look at as it was possible to be. He was perfect.

Sighing, she replaced the paper in the envelope and put the letters back into the drawer. Maybe she'd read the rest another day, when she was more emotionally stable than she apparently was tonight. Getting through them without crying would be a good start.

For now, she had to get downstairs and start dishing out the supper. The splashing had stopped and there was no way she would allow Adam to do anything else this evening. If he tried, he was going to have a fight on his hands.

Smiling at the thought, she wiped away the rest of her tears and headed for the stairs.

Chapter 15

"Enjoy your hay." Amy patted Stride's shoulder and left him eating in his stall, the picture of contentment.

After three days at the livery bringing the horses in from the paddock was becoming her favourite part of the day, the only time she really got to interact with them. She also liked working alongside George. During the day he was usually either outside, doing repairs and maintenance or working with the horses.

In the stall next to Stride's Clementine stopped eating and eyed Amy warily as she leaned her arms on top of the door. The nervous horse pressed herself into the farthest corner and pawed at the floor.

"It's all right, girl," Amy said, keeping her voice low. "I'm not going to hurt you."

The white horse stopped kicking up straw, but still looked like she wanted to bolt. Amy watched her for a few more seconds then backed away and walked to where George sat at his desk by the front doors. The front entrance was closed and a kerosene lamp on the desk cast a soft glow.

George's lined face wore the worried frown working on the ledger always seemed to produce. Amy didn't know what was in the leather-bound black book, but there was little doubt it wasn't what he wanted it to be. She longed to help in some way.

There was a wide area beyond the desk in which barrels,

sacks of feed and sundry other items were heaped haphazardly around each other. Movement caught her eye as a plump brown rat burst from behind a wooden box and dashed towards the open back doors.

Amy yelped, putting a hand to her racing heart. She was getting tired of being startled by the livery's copious resident rodents.

"You need a cat in here."

"Cats need feeding," George said, not looking up from his ledger.

"They'd be eating rats and mice. Besides, I'm sure you'd save enough in what they're stealing now to feed a cat or three. I swear I've never seen rats so fat. I'm surprised they can still run."

A grunt was his only reply.

Amy studied the mess around him. "I think this area is wasted."

George raised his head. "What's that supposed to mean?"

Amy walked forward amongst the miscellaneous boxes and sacks. "Just, it's kind of a mess and it's the first thing people see when they come in."

He looked around him. "I have to put it all somewhere."

She picked up a rusting metal feeder that obviously hadn't been used for some time.

"Maybe not that," he said.

"But does it have to go here?" she said, putting the basket down and spreading her hands to encompass the whole area.

"It's always been there."

"But does it *have* to be?"

He scrunched up his face like agreeing with her was painful. "Maybe not. But if it wasn't, where would I put the lot of it? And why would I want to move it anyway?"

130

Ideas were sparking to life. "You sell saddles and bridles and all the other horse stuff, but it's all in that room where no one can see it." She pointed towards the small room which adjoined the main building and housed a collection of horse related paraphernalia, some of which had been covered in thick dust before Amy cleaned it.

"If a person comes in wanting anything, I take them in there."

"I know, but they have to *ask*. If you moved all this in there and moved all that out here and displayed it all nicely, someone who hasn't necessarily come in here for that may see something and decide to buy it. But you need to have it where they can see it. This area is perfect." She held her arms out to either side of her and faced him, smiling. "You could put hooks on the walls to hang bridles and halters and have a rack for saddles and shelves for the smaller items."

He looked unconvinced. "You sound like Zach. He always has all these big ideas. But it sounds like a whole lot of work for nothing to me."

"I've seen how shops do it in New York, the way they get people into the stores so they'll buy things. It will work, I know it will."

"This ain't the big city, girl." Frowning, he turned back to his ledger.

Amy picked her way to his side and sank to her knees, taking his hand in both of hers. He seemed startled at the contact, his eyes widening.

"Please, George, I know something's wrong."

A flash of anger crossed his face.

"I haven't seen what's in the ledger," she said quickly, "but I see how worried you get when you work on it. I want to help. It won't take much work and no money. I'll even do it in my own time, if you like. I might need help moving some of it, but I can do the rest myself. Please let me do this.

131

Please?"

She stared up at him, silently pleading with him to agree.

His expression softened, just a little. "I can't decide if you're the best worker I ever had, or the worst."

She grinned. "Does that mean I can do it?"

He heaved a sigh. "I'll probably regret this, but we can start on it tomorrow."

She squeaked in excitement. "Thank you! It'll be great, you'll see."

"Hmm."

Chapter 16

"There you go, boy. Enjoy your hay."

Amy patted Eagle's shoulder and left the sturdy bay horse chewing contentedly on his food, closing the stall door behind her. She moved along the row, smiling at the sight of all the horses happy and safe in their stalls. A few of them had their heads hanging over the doors to watch her and she took the time to greet each one with a stroke of their silky hair or a pat on their neck.

Some might have found the work she did at the livery unpleasant, with all the muck and cleaning involved, but knowing each of the horses, having them trust her and be happy to see her, made it worthwhile. She sent up a silent thank You to God for bringing her there. There was no doubt in her mind that it was His guidance that had got her the job with George she loved so much.

Reaching the alcove where she kept her belongings, she took an apple and her knife from her bag then picked up the stool and carried it across to Clementine's stall. The white horse stopped eating and watched her warily.

"It's all right, Clem," she said in a soft and hopefully soothing voice, "you're safe with me."

She opened the door to the stall and Clem turned to face her, pressing into the farthest corner of the space. Amy placed the stool down onto the straw-strewn floor inside the stall, cut a slice of apple and placed it onto the seat. Then she backed out, closed the door again, and waited.

And waited.

After ten minutes or so, Clementine took a few tentative steps forward and sniffed at the apple on the stool. Stretching out her lips, she plucked it from the wooden surface and retreated to the corner to eat.

Amy wanted to laugh. Instead, she cut another slice, opened the door, and left it on the stool again. This time it took the skittish horse only five minutes to retrieve the treat. The following time, only one. When Amy placed a fourth chunk of apple on the stool, she left the door open a little, standing in the gap where Clementine could see her.

Five minutes passed.

Ten.

Amy began to wonder if she was rushing things, but when she was just about to close the stall door, Clementine took a couple of steps towards the stool. Amy held her breath. Another two steps brought the horse within reach of the apple. Suddenly, she darted her head forward, grabbed the apple which sat only three feet from Amy, and sprang back into her corner.

Amy instantly cut another piece and placed it on the stool. To her surprise, Clementine almost immediately walked forward and picked it up, this time watching Amy for a couple of seconds before returning to the corner.

Amy removed the stool, closed the door, and leaned her elbows on the top.

"I know you're afraid," she said softly, "but I also know you're very brave. I know someone hurt you, but that doesn't mean all people are bad. It's all right to trust, as long as you trust the right people."

As long as you trust the right people. It was good advice, and not just for horses. There had been few people Amy had trusted in the course of her life, even fewer who'd been worthy of it. Like Clementine, she *wanted* to trust, but fear still held her back. An image of Adam's face came into her mind. Amy longed to be like normal people who could follow their hearts without their brains stepping in and constantly whispering to them all the things that could go wrong. In her whole life, she'd never wished for that more than she did now.

A nose nudged at her arm, making her smile. Stride was stretching his neck around the wall separating his and Clementine's stalls, his nostrils flaring at the slice of apple left in Amy's hand.

"Here you go," she said, giving him the apple and rubbing his forehead as he ate. "I'm sure you don't mind the rest went to your girl. I'll have more apples on Monday. For both of you."

"Amy?" George's voice came from the front of the building.

"I'm here."

She left Stride and Clem and walked to the front door where he sat at his desk. She couldn't help admiring what they'd done so far with the area behind him. George had attached hooks to the walls for the bridles and halters and moved a long rack into place beneath them for the saddles. Amy had polished every saddle and bridle before displaying them. It was already working. Three sets of tack had already been sold and a few other bits and pieces had gone too. She still had work to do, but it was a good start.

George looked up as she approached. "You heading home now?"

"Yes, unless there's anything else you need me to do."

"No, you can go." He handed her a brown envelope. "Your first week's pay."

It was the first time Amy had ever been paid for her work. She took the envelope almost reverently and carefully tore open the top. Inside, she found a five dollar bill and three

135

singles.

"But this is twice what..."

George had returned his gaze to the ledger on his desk. "I've paid you what I've paid you. I'm a fair man and you're a good worker. And your idea with the saddles and such has brought in some sales."

Tears burned at Amy's eyes. Being appreciated for what she did was a new and somewhat overwhelming experience. "Thank you."

He nodded his head, still not looking at her. "You earned it. I'll see you Sunday at church."

Clutching the envelope in her hand, she went to fetch her bag, said goodbye to George and walked outside into the long shadows of early evening. After paying back the two dollars Adam had lent her she could give him four more towards what she owed him and still have two left for a few items she needed.

Turning right, she headed in the direction of the general store.

Chapter 17

Dear Miss Watts,

Thank you for your letter. I was so excited to find it as I was sorting the mail that I accidentally knocked all the letters I'd already sorted onto the floor and had to start all over again! Thankfully I hadn't got very far. I didn't read it straight away though. I wanted to savour it, so I waited until my work was finished. That wasn't easy, I can tell you!

I was so happy to hear of your relationship with God. You are right, without Him life would be very hard. The comfort He has given me, the assurance of His presence, has so often been my light in the darkness, and by the way you spoke I suspect you feel the same way. We are so blessed.

Working in the kitchen in such a large, grand house sounds like very hard work. Do you enjoy it? Perhaps that's a silly question, what can there be to enjoy in scrubbing pots and pans and ovens? But maybe there are some not so bad parts. I hope your employer appreciates your dedication.

For my part, I enjoy running the post office very much. I take pride in being responsible for so many letters and packages and making sure they reach their intended recipients. Each one has so much potential. A letter can be life-changing.

I know this is only my second letter to you, and I wouldn't want you to think I'm prone to dashing headlong into situations without thinking them through first, but ever since I received your first letter I've felt an anticipation, like something amazing is about to happen. Does that sound foolish? Maybe I'm getting ahead of *myself, but I wonder if some time in the future I will look back on these letters as changing my life for the better. Now I sound overly romantic. If my brothers knew I was writing these things they would tease me mercilessly!*

Do you have siblings? I have two older sisters, one younger sister and two younger brothers. Even though I don't get to see them often, we are close. They are all married now, apart from my youngest brother who's only eighteen. And me, of course. I admit that part of the reason I'm doing this is because I miss my family and long to have one of my own. Not that I expect to have children straight away, but just to have a wife, someone to share life's joys and triumphs and difficulties and failures with, would feel like the greatest blessing I can imagine.

I very much look forward to hearing from you again, Amy. May I call you Amy?

Yours,

Adam.

~ ~ ~

"I'm sorry, I overslept. I never oversleep." Adam stopped halfway across the parlour and winced. "That's not true, I often oversleep, but I just pretend that's when I meant to wake up. I just don't usually oversleep this late."

Turning from the stove where she was dishing up an omelette, Amy had to stifle a giggle. His hair looked like it had only had a glancing relationship with the comb, only half his shirt was tucked in and one shoelace was untied. He looked adorable.

"You're bleeding."

He reached the stove. "I'm what?"

She bit her lip and pointed to his face where small trickles of blood were congealing in two different places.

He closed his eyes and sighed. "Is it bad?"

138

"It's only two nicks. Stay there." She fetched a clean cloth, moistened it and dabbed at his face.

"I may have rushed my shave," he said.

She looked down at the rest of him.

"Among other things," he added, tucking the rest of his shirt into his waistband as she continued to clean the blood from his cheek. "Still, two's not so bad. You should have seen me when I first started shaving. For the first month every morning I looked like I'd been battling herds of porcupines."

Amy smiled at the thought of the young Adam covered in tiny self-inflicted cuts. "How old were you?"

His eyes drifted to the side as he remembered. "I must have been close to eighteen because Daisy and I were courting. She was the reason I started. I'd been thinking of growing a beard because, well, I was getting to the point where I could. You know what boys that age are like. Anyway, Daisy kept dropping not so subtle hints that I was getting too hairy for her liking so I started shaving, but I wasn't very good at it. She didn't stop laughing for a good five minutes when she saw me the first day." He chuckled and his gaze unfocused, wandering back eight years. "And the second and the third. It was quite an event the first time I managed to not cut myself at all. Daisy kissed every inch of my face and told me it was just because she finally could without tasting blood."

Amy wiped the last of the blood away and swallowed the pain blooming in her chest. *I'm not jealous. I am not jealous.* "I think they've stopped bleeding now. Do you have any iodine?"

"Oh, no. I mean yes, I have some, but I'll be fine without it." He took the cloth from her and, to her surprise, leaned down to kiss her cheek. "Thank you for taking care of me."

She smiled and lowered her eyes to hide her blush. Her gaze settled on Adam's feet. "Just one more thing."

Crouching, she laced up his shoe. When she straightened her gaze lingered on his hair.

He swivelled his eyes up. "What?"

"Um... just..."

She reached up with both hands and ran her fingers through his hair, taming the worst of the unruly mess. Lost in the feeling of the soft strands slipping through her touch, it was a few seconds before she realised what she was doing. She lowered her eyes to his and found him watching her, half a smile curling his lips. Feeling her cheeks heat up even more, she rapidly dropped her hands to her sides.

Adam leaned forward again, kissed her cheek a second time, and whispered, "Thank you" in her ear.

A not at all unpleasant shiver sauntered down her spine. "I, um, you're welcome." She spun back to the stove, almost knocking the frying pan onto the floor. "We'd better eat or we'll be late for church."

~ ~ ~

By the time they reached the church the rest of the congregation was already seated and Pastor Jones was just taking his place on the platform at the front.

Sara waved them over and Amy and Adam quickly took two vacant seats next to her.

"I saved them for you," she whispered to Amy as she sat beside her. "I'm glad you're here."

She smiled, but Amy could see the sadness behind it. The seat where Daniel had sat the week before was occupied by a lady Amy didn't know and Sara's husband was nowhere to be seen.

Amy slipped her hand into hers and gave it a sympathetic squeeze.

When the service had drawn to a close, Adam

diplomatically excused himself and went outside to give Amy time alone with her friend.

"I know you aren't staying, but he seems like a wonderful man," Sara said as they watched him leave.

"He is," Amy replied. "How are you holding up?"

She lowered her eyes to her lap. "I'm all right." The slight tremor in her voice said otherwise.

Before Amy had a chance to answer, Lizzy appeared in the row in front of them. Beyond her, Louisa and Jo stood in the aisle.

"I would like to formally invite you two to lunch," Lizzy said. "Just the five of us. Pastor Jones and Mrs Jones are going to be out for a couple of hours and they told Louisa we could use the house. I know it's short notice, but I think we could all use the time to talk." She reached over the back of her chair and took Sara's hand.

"I don't know," Sara said. "I should probably get back..."

"Please?" Lizzy said, drawing the word out. "It wouldn't be the same without you. I for one could really use your sage advice and I think the rest of us could too. Jesse said he'd take you, me and Jo home afterwards."

Lizzy was a marvel. Since the five of them arrived on the train eight days ago, they had all had to deal with the unexpected in their new lives, but Sara perhaps needed this time more than any of them. And yet Lizzy made it sound like she would be doing them a favour by staying.

"Lizzy's right," Amy said. "You're the most stable of all of us."

Lizzy nodded vehemently. "Exactly. The rest of us scatterbrains need you."

Sara laughed softly, shaking her head. "All right, you don't have to lay it on quite that thick. I'll tell Will to let Daniel know I'll be back later."

Lizzy squealed in delight, clapping her hands.

"I'll go and tell Adam he can go without me," Amy said.

She left Sara, Lizzy, Louisa and Josephine chatting together and went outside to find Adam. Most of the congregation was still gathered at the front of the church and Amy wended her way through the crowd in search of him.

She almost stumbled over her feet in her haste to stop when Mrs Vernon abruptly stepped in front of her.

"Miss Watts, how lovely to see you at church."

For some reason she couldn't quite put her finger on, Amy didn't entirely believe her. The fake smile definitely wasn't helping.

"Good morning, Mrs Vernon. How are you?"

"Very well, thank you, if a little surprised."

"Surprised?"

Mrs Vernon looked around them, stepped closer, and lowered her voice. "That you are still residing with Mr Emerson, given the circumstances."

"I'm not sure what you mean."

She stepped back. "Just one day left, Miss Watts. I'm sure you'll do the right thing. Good day."

Amy watched her walk away in bemusement. One day left until what?

She'd just decided to ask Adam if he had any idea what Mrs Vernon was talking about when she spotted him through the crowd and she forgot all about the cryptic exchange. A lump rose to Amy's throat as she watched him chat to Daisy, their closeness apparent in the ease they clearly enjoyed with each other. An image of his ex-almost-fiancée planting kisses all over his young, freshly shaved face rose unbidden into her mind. And then a dark haired little boy, no more than three years old, bounded up to them and raised his small arms towards Adam. Adam smiled and bent to pick him up, settling him on his hip as though it was the most natural thing in the world. Daisy reached out to rub her thumb over a smudge on the boy's face. It was a picture of familial bliss.

A feeling of envy swept through her, so strong that for a moment Amy couldn't breathe. She turned away, praying for God to take the unwelcome emotion from her. It took at least a full minute for her to feel in control enough to walk over to them.

Seeing her approach, Daisy smiled. "Good morning, Amy. It's so nice to see you again."

Did she have to sound so genuinely nice? Jealousy still nipped at Amy and Daisy's friendliness just served to add a healthy dose of shame to the mix.

"Good morning, Daisy." She looked at the little boy. "And who's this?"

"Amy, meet Nicholas," Adam said, turning so that the boy faced her. "Nicky is Daisy's son."

"It's a pleasure to meet you, Nicky," Amy said, holding her hand out to him.

Clearly astonished at being offered such a grown up greeting, Nicholas hesitantly held out his small hand. His eyes lit up when Amy shook it gently.

"You have pretty hair," he said.

Amy placed a hand on her chest with a gasp. "Why, thank you, kind sir."

Nicholas giggled and Adam whispered to him loudly, "I think she has pretty hair too."

Despite all her best intentions, Amy's heart flipped a little. "Uh... I just came to tell you that Sara, Lizzy, Jo, Louisa and I are having a kind of support gathering at the Jones' house so I won't be home for lunch. If that's all right."

She knew she didn't need to ask his permission, but she hadn't been able to resist the desire to slip in a reminder in front of Daisy that they would normally eat together. She suspected she should probably feel ashamed of that too.

"Of course it's all right," he said, smiling. "I promise I

143

won't starve."

"Oh, well, if you're alone why don't you come and join Nicky and me for lunch?" Daisy said brightly.

Amy's stomach sank into her shoes.

Adam's gaze flicked between the two women.

"Come and see my new toys I got for my birthday!" Nicky squealed in excitement.

And he'd seemed like such a nice little boy.

Adam smiled at him. "Well, how can I refuse an offer like that?"

He glanced at Amy and for a moment she thought she saw an apology in his eyes, but it was probably just wishful thinking on her part. She suddenly had an urge to leave as quickly as possible.

"Well, I'll see you later then," she said. "It was nice to see you again, Daisy." It may have been the biggest lie she'd ever told.

"You too, Amy."

She wanted to spend time with her friends, she really did, but as she trudged back to the church entrance Amy couldn't help wishing she'd waited until after Daisy left to tell Adam about it.

144

Chapter 18

Amy folded her arms on the top of the stall door and rested her chin on them. Clementine stared at her.

She stood looking almost relaxed, no longer pressed into the corner. She wasn't entirely comfortable, but three days of apple slices had at least got her away from the wall.

"Well, Clem," Amy said, keeping her voice low and soft, "are you ready for the next step in our friendship?"

Clementine's ears flicked back and forth, signalling her uncertain interest.

"Because we are going to be great friends, you and I."

The horse's expression was impassive.

"So I'd appreciate it if you didn't kick me or anything," Amy said, pushing away from the door.

She opened the stall and placed the stool inside. Clementine took a step forward in anticipation of the apple, but instead of placing a slice onto the stool Amy walked into the stall, closed the door behind her, and sat.

Clementine backed into the corner, her ears flattening. She gave a soft whinny. From the adjoining stall, Stride answered her. Strangely, Amy was put in mind of Adam's voice, always there when she needed reassurance.

She cut a thin slice of apple and bit into it as Clementine watched. Finishing the half a slice, she placed the rest into her mouth and cut a second slice as she ate. Under Clementine's unwavering scrutiny, she ate that one too. And then a third. As she chewed her fourth slice, she cut another and silently held it towards Clementine on her palm, keeping her eyes fixed on her lap.

After a couple of minutes of inaction her arm started to ache. She was about to lower it when Clementine took a step forward. Amy tried to appear relaxed while tensing her arm which was beginning to tremble. Clem took another step towards her and Amy held her breath. Finally, another two steps brought her within range. The horse tentatively stretched her neck forward, paused, then plucked the apple from Amy's hand and backed away. Ignoring the tear trickling down her cheek, Amy cut another slice of apple and held it out again. Clementine immediately came forward and took it, this time staying within reach as she ate.

Slowly, slice by slice, Amy fed her the rest of the apple. By the time it was finished the white horse was standing just two feet away, her ears perked forward as she followed Amy's every movement.

Amy put the knife into her pocket and folded her hands on her lap. To her complete surprise, Clementine lowered her head and nudged her muzzle against her arm. With tears running down her face, Amy almost burst out laughing.

"I don't have any more apple, girl," she whispered.

She raised her left hand. The horse lifted her head, looked at Amy's hand for a moment, then lowered her face towards it. Amy gently touched her fingertips to the silky hair of her neck. When Clem didn't recoil, she moved her hand onto her face. Clem pushed against her palm for a moment then raised her head, looking at the door.

"Well, I'll be." George was standing outside the stall, his eyes wide.

Amy wiped the moisture from her face and stood, slid her hand down the horse's neck, and then picked up the stool and left the stall. Clementine kept her eyes on George, but didn't move.

"I..." He looked as if he'd seen a rock get up by itself and walk. "How in the world did you get her to do that?"

Amy smiled at Clementine who was watching her from the centre of the stall. "She wanted to trust me. She just needed to know that she could."

She took the sack of hay from George's unresisting hands and filled Clementine's feeding rack. Clem immediately walked forward and started to eat, not even flinching when Amy ruffled her mane.

"I never thought that horse would ever let anyone near her again." A smile stretched George's rugged face. "You must have a magic touch, girl."

Amy smiled back. "No, just patience. And lots of apples."

Chapter 19

"Are you sure you don't want me to do it?" George said, for the sixth time.

"Or me," Adam added. "You could take Stride."

"She'll be calmer if it's me," Amy said, tightening the cinch on Clementine's saddle. "I'm not handing her off to someone else after she's trusted me this far, even you two."

George puffed out a frustrated breath. "You're too stubborn for your own good, girl."

She moved forward to where Clem could see her. "I know you're a little nervous, Clem," she said softly, "and to be truthful, so am I. But you know I will never hurt you. We're both going to have fun, you'll see."

Clementine nuzzled against her arm and Amy gave her a pat before moving back to her side.

"Now I'm sure, judging by the way she took to that saddle, that she's been ridden before," George said. "So she'll know what to do. Just take it nice and gentle."

"I only do nice and gentle," Amy said. "Just ask Stride."

At the sound of his name, Adam's horse hooked his head over Clem's back to look at her. Amy laughed and rubbed his nose.

"Come on, Stride," Adam said, tugging him back. "Let's show Clementine how it's done."

Standing Stride where Clem could see them, he used one of the livery's mounting blocks to climb on, then guided him in close to the white horse in an attempt to keep her calm.

"Please be careful," he said to Amy.

"Well, girl, if you're determined to go through with this, now's the time," George said, holding tight onto Clementine's bridle.

Amy stepped up onto her own block, gave Clem a quick rub on her neck, and carefully pulled herself into the saddle, praying all the time.

Clem immediately tensed and took a couple of steps back, jerking her head up and snorting. Stride nickered and looked around for danger.

"Calm down, girl," George said, hanging onto the reins.

Amy wasn't sure if he meant her or Clementine. Her heart thumped as the horse flinched beneath her. She leaned forward and pressed her hand onto the side of Clementine's neck. "It's all right, Clem," she said, trying to keep her voice steady. "It's just me. I'm not going to hurt you. You're safe."

Clementine twisted her neck to look back at her.

"It's all right," she repeated.

A few seconds passed while Clem stared at her, then she lowered her head and Amy felt her relax. Stride nudged the side of her face with his nose.

"Right," George said, breathing out. "Good."

Adam looked pale, but he gave her a tremulous smile. He appeared more shaken by the experience than she was.

Amy let out a long breath and sent up a silent 'thank You'. "Do you think I could ride her around the corral a bit?" she said to George.

He scratched the side of Clementine's jaw and she leaned into his touch. Once she'd realised she could trust Amy, she'd warmed to him too. "I'll lead her first, but she don't seem overly bothered by you being up there."

They walked a couple of laps of the small area before George let go and allowed Amy to ride by herself. Despite all the time Adam had spent teaching her how to ride and the practice she'd had on Stride, Amy still lacked the confidence to take things too fast. But Clem didn't seem to mind. She was remarkably calm as she walked with Stride at her side and after a few minutes George left them to go back inside.

Adam was quiet as they continued to ride at a leisurely pace side by side around the corral, his eyes fixed on the horses.

"Is something wrong?" Amy said after a while.

"No, it just scared me a bit, watching you do that with Clem. If she'd panicked..." He shrugged and blew out a breath. "If you could hold off on doing anything else life-threatening for the next few days, I'd be grateful."

"I'll do my best."

He gave her a small smile and went back to watching Clementine. Amy got the feeling he wouldn't relax until she was back on solid ground. He was worried for her safety. It shouldn't have made her feel good, but it did.

"Can I ask you something?" he said.

"Anything." Where had that come from? She never told anyone *anything*. What if he asked her something she couldn't tell him? Like how she felt about him.

"Why San Francisco?"

She breathed out in relief. That was an easy one to answer. "About three years ago I found a magazine Mrs Courtney had thrown away, on one of the rare times she was home. I never got to read that kind of thing so I took it and read it from cover to cover over and over. There was a feature article inside about San Francisco hotels and they were all so fancy and grand. I dreamed about what it would be like to work in one of them as a maid, maybe work my way up to housekeeper one day. I never really thought I would, but just to be able to see them... I guess it became like a symbol of everything I wanted and didn't have; independence, safety, a future. And then when I read your advertisement and found

150

out you lived so close to there, I just thought maybe this was my chance. It wasn't much of a plan, I admit."

Strangely, as she spoke, the familiar ache, the longing for the wonderful new life of her dreams, didn't come as it previously always had. In fact, as she thought about her whole plan, she couldn't seem to find any appeal at all in the idea of going to San Francisco.

Amy had carried the aspiration for so long that the sudden realisation of its loss shocked her. If she no longer had that desire to drive her, what did she have to aim for?

"It sounds like a fine dream," Adam said, without looking at her.

It did sound like a fine dream, and it had been. So where had it gone? And what would she do now?

She looked at the back of Clem's head as she walked calmly around the corral, ears perked forward, with Stride at her side. Only a week ago she'd been too afraid to let anyone near her. Now she wasn't just allowing Amy to ride her, but she seemed to be enjoying the experience. All because she'd taken a chance and trusted Amy, even though she was afraid.

Amy glanced at Adam beside her. Maybe it was time she started trusting.

And stopped being afraid of opening herself to what she really wanted.

151

Chapter 20

Amy reached up to adjust a saddle on its hook then stepped back to make sure it was straight. Satisfied, she took a couple more steps backwards to take in the full effect.

The display looked good, perhaps even as good as some she'd seen in the city. Gleaming saddles adorned the junction of two walls, their matching bridles hanging neatly from hooks beneath each one. George had brought an old, battered bookcase in from his own home and told Amy she could do whatever she wanted with it. She'd gleefully sanded it down and painted it white with some leftover paint she'd found when they moved everything, and now it displayed all the smaller tack items.

She was toying with the idea of advertising reduced prices on a couple of the saddles that George admitted he'd had for years. She was still working on bringing him around to agreeing with her on that, although she suspected he was being obstinate more out of habit than any real conviction that she was wrong. She didn't mind. She enjoyed their arguments and she almost always got her way in the end. She'd already bought some red paint for the sale signs.

"Hey? Boy?"

At the voice, Amy looked round. A man stood just inside the open front doors. As she turned his eyes widened then travelled slowly down her body. A hand rose to rub at the rough stubble across his chin and one side of his mouth curled into a leer.

"Sorry, Miss."

He stared at her for a moment longer before the hand at his chin moved to pull the hat from his scraggly brown hair.

Amy took an unconscious step backwards. "Can I help you?"

His leer grew. "I imagine you can. I'm lookin' to buy a horse."

She swallowed against her suddenly dry mouth. The way he was ogling her was digging up memories she would rather stayed buried. "I'll go and fetch the proprietor, if you wouldn't mind waiting."

"Whatever you say, darlin'."

His inappropriately familiar speech ignited a flash of anger, but she got the feeling he would only enjoy any chastisement from her so she ignored it and walked as quickly as she could to the back doors, stopping just short of running. She didn't want the man to know he'd scared her.

Bursting into the sunshine, she raised a hand to shield her eyes and looked around for George. It took her a few moments to find him, across the paddock where he was cleaning out one of the feed troughs.

"Are you sure you can't help me?"

Amy almost jumped from her skin, whirling around at the man's voice right behind her. He grasped her arm and she stumbled back away from him, crying out and jerking from his grip. Her hand darted to her pocket before she remembered she no longer carried her knife with her.

The man stepped back, raising his hands and smiling. "Sorry, Miss, didn't mean to frighten you."

"*Amy?*"

Heart still pounding, she looked round to see George running towards her. The man took another step back.

"What's going on here?" George panted as he reached them. Eyes fixed on the man, he stepped between him and

153

Amy. "Amy, are you all right?"

"I..."

"I'm sorry," the man said. "I came looking to buy a horse and I think I startled the lady here. She stumbled, I tried to help her." He held his hands out in a placatory gesture. "I didn't mean no harm. Forgive me if I scared you, Ma'am."

"Is that what happened?" George said, looking at her.

Her eyes flicked between him and the stranger. Was that all it was? Her fear was all too real, but maybe she had just overreacted. It wouldn't have been the first time. "I suppose," she said slowly.

The man lowered his hands and pushed them into his pockets, smiling. He seemed to smile a lot, but she could hardly convict him for being cheerful.

George studied her for a moment before turning back to the man. "So you're looking for a horse?"

"Yes, Sir."

George indicated the paddock. "Well, come and take a look."

The man lifted his hat from his head to Amy then headed towards the paddock, George following. Amy retreated to the door, watched them for a few seconds, then went back inside.

She went to her bag, took her knife out and stared at it. She hadn't carried it on her since her first Saturday in Green Hill Creek and it was only still in her bag for when she needed it to cut up apples. She pushed it back in and closed the flap. She wasn't that person anymore, the girl who was afraid all the time, and she didn't want to go back to being her. She'd merely been startled, like the stranger said. That was all.

Leaving the bag on its hook, she returned to her work.

Ten minutes later, George came in.

"Is he gone already?" she said. "Didn't he want any of

the horses?"

George pursed his lips. "I told him to try elsewhere. Something about him didn't sit right with me. Couldn't bring myself to let him have any of my animals." He ducked his head to look into her eyes. "Are you all right?"

"I'm fine. I just overreacted, like he said." She gave a small laugh that didn't sound at all convincing.

"Well, I'm finished outside," he said, "so how about you explain to me again why I should charge less for those saddles?"

Amy knew he was staying for her benefit and she wanted to hug him for it, but she was certain it would just make him feel awkward. So instead she took him to the display and regaled him with her impeccable logic as to why her ideas would work.

This time, he didn't disagree.

~ ~ ~

"I need to take the money from the sales today to the bank before it closes." George walked up to Amy where she was filling the racks in each stall with hay in readiness for bringing the horses in for the night.

"Should I start bringing them in or wait until you get back?"

"Wait until I get back. And I'm going to close the front up while I'm gone."

"Why? We don't usually close until after they're all in." She walked out of the stall and looked towards the back doors. They were shut. "Is this because of earlier?"

"No. I'd just feel better if everything was secure while I'm gone." The slight frown creasing his already creased forehead said otherwise.

"So it is because of earlier. I told you, I just overreacted.

155

I'm fine."

"I know you're fine. I just want to, that's all." He flicked his hand at her, waving her away. "Stop arguing with me, girl. I'm the one in charge here."

"That's what *you* think," Amy said, smiling.

He shook his head and headed for the front door. "Get all the stalls ready. We'll bring them in as soon as I get back." He looked back when he reached the door. "I won't be long. Bolt this behind me."

"Yes, Sir," she said, putting down the hay she was carrying and jogging to the barn's entrance.

She watched George stride away in the direction of the middle of town for a few seconds before closing and bolting the door and returning to fill the rest of the racks.

She smiled to herself as she worked. Today had been a good day, apart from the episode with the stranger. They'd sold two sets of saddles and matching tack plus a few other items, and all the sales had been to people who liveried their horses there and saw the new display in passing. And this was just the beginning. She had more ideas to tempt people into boarding their horses at Parsons' Livery rather than the larger place on the other side of town. At the moment they were only a little over two thirds full. She knew they could do better.

Outside in the paddock, a horse neighed. Amy stopped what she was doing to listen. After a few seconds, the neigh came again, this time from a different horse. She'd heard them neigh before on occasion, to call to each other, but this sounded different. She leaned the fork she was spreading straw with against the side of the stall and went to the back door. She could hear the horses' hooves thumping against the ground, accompanied by sharp snorts. She was no expert, but she was certain this wasn't normal. Something was wrong.

There were no windows on this side of the building at

ground level and she considered climbing up to the loft to look from there.

A horse screamed in fear. Clementine.

Amy tore at the bolts holding the door closed and ran outside.

Someone grabbed her. One arm locked around her waist, pinning her arms to her sides, while a hand clamped over her mouth. She was yanked backwards into the building.

The door slammed shut.

"You know, I was just going to take the white horse the old man wouldn't let me have earlier," a voice hissed in her ear. "But then that would be a terrible waste with you right here, all alone."

Amy squirmed frantically against the iron hard grip, screaming into the hand over her mouth.

Hot breath skittered like a swarm of ants across her neck. "Ain't no use struggling, darlin'."

Panic pounded against the inside of her head. *Help me, Lord!*

The man lifted her off the ground, carrying her towards one of the stalls. Amy used the only part of her she could move, kicking her feet back hard. One heel connected with a shin. The man shrieked, throwing her away from him, and she stumbled and fell to the straw-covered floor of the stall.

She flipped over to see the stranger from earlier advancing, face twisted into a glare. Amy shuffled backwards on her elbows until she hit the end wall of the stall and screamed louder than she ever had in her life.

"HELLLPPPPP!"

"Ain't no one gonna hear you this far out," he said, bending towards her.

Grabbing a handful of dusty straw, Amy threw it into his face.

He brushed it away, laughing. "That's not gonna help..."

157

Still half on her back, she drew in one foot and drove it into his groin.

The man howled, staggering backwards and clutching at his crotch. "Damn!"

Amy pushed to her feet and lunged for the stall door. If she could get to the shotgun George kept hidden behind his desk...

The man grabbed at her as she passed, latching onto her wrist and spinning her around. His other hand drew the revolver at his belt and swung clumsily, catching her face with a glancing blow.

Pain exploded in her cheek. For a moment, her head spun.

Still clutching her wrist, he swung her back against the stall door. A grunt of pain wrenched from her lips. He pressed the barrel of his revolver to her temple, his face inches from hers.

"Stop fighting or I'll kill you," he rasped.

Close to gagging at his rancid breath, Amy stiffened.

Stop fighting?

Never.

Forcing her body to relax, she nodded. He backed off a little, lowering the gun.

"Good girl. Now..."

Amy brought her knee up between his legs, hard.

The man screamed.

She lunged for the gun, trying to wrestle it from his grasp. A deafening bang sent her heart into her throat.

"*Amy?!*" It was George's voice. The front door shook as something pounded on it.

"George! Help!"

The man grabbed her around the waist. She managed to wrest the gun from his grip, but it slipped from her fingers and spun away across the floor. Amy threw herself after it.

The man, clutching onto her shirt, plunged after her. All the breath exploded from her lungs as she crashed onto the floor. The man landed on her legs.

Her outstretched hand brushed against metal. She wrapped her fingers around the revolver and twisted onto her back.

"Don't!" she shouted as the man reached for her, jabbing the gun into his face.

He froze, his bloodshot eyes crossing as he stared at the weapon. One hand held his crotch. His face was red.

Through the fog of terror, Amy barely heard the back door crashing open.

Then a voice roared, "*Get off of her!*"

A shadow loomed up behind the man and he was hoisted into the air. George's fist slammed into his face and he flew backwards, hitting the edge of a stall and dropping to the floor, unmoving.

Amy lay on her back, panting for breath, the gun still extended in front of her. The barrel shook. George moved to the side out of the line of fire and knelt beside her, gently removing the gun from her grasp.

"Amy, are you shot?"

She swivelled her eyes to his face. Shot? The memory of a gun firing surfaced through the pounding in her brain. Was she shot? She shook her head a little.

He nodded and slid one arm around her back, helping her to sit up. A groan from across the way made her start.

"Will you be all right here?" George said. "I have to tie him up."

She nodded mutely.

"I'll be right back."

He stood, took some rope from a hook on the wall and knelt by the man, blocking Amy's view. From the grunts and complaints that followed, George wasn't being gentle.

Amy drew her legs in, wrapping her arms around them. Her whole body was trembling.

George returned and crouched beside her. "Can you stand?"

Her eyes went to the man lying on the floor. He was on his front, hands and ankles hogtied behind him. He turned his face to look at her and she shivered.

"Amy, don't look at him. Look at me."

She shifted her gaze back to George.

"Can you stand up?" he repeated.

She nodded, although she wasn't sure. She couldn't stop shaking. It was so cold.

"Just hold onto me," he said, sliding one arm beneath hers and helping her to her feet.

When her legs buckled beneath her he scooped her up, one arm beneath her knees and the other around her back.

Amy wrapped her arms around his neck, closed her eyes and pressed her face into his shoulder.

"It's all right, girl, I've got you," he murmured. "Ain't no one gonna hurt you now."

Chapter 21

Adam locked the front door to the post office after the last customer and stretched his arms above his head, yawning.

The day after the train delivered the mail was always busy, what with sorting and people coming in to collect their letters and packages, and today had been no exception. But it had also been his final day at the bank and that had been decidedly more difficult. He was trying very hard to accept the loss of his job, but it wasn't easy. The injustice of it all kept sweeping over him. He'd lost count of the times today he'd had to tell the Lord that he forgave Mr Vernon. His forgiveness didn't seem to be sticking.

After coming home from the bank he'd opened his Bible at random, not sure what he was expecting. The page he found himself on was Matthew's account of Jesus' crucifixion and Adam knew God was speaking to him. If anyone knew about unjust persecution, it was Him. At that moment Adam felt the presence of his Saviour. He wasn't alone.

And if God was for him, who could be against him?

He dropped his arms to his sides and walked back behind the counter and through the door to the parlour. Maybe he'd go to the store and get something special for dinner later. Or maybe he could take Amy for a meal at the hotel. The wisdom of spending the money when he'd just lost half his income was questionable, but it would feel good. And when he told Amy about losing his job, it might go a little way towards convincing her that he wasn't worried and she shouldn't be either.

If he told her. He hadn't yet decided if he would. The last thing he wanted was for her to worry that she was causing him problems and move out. She was bound to find out sooner or later, but he still held out hope that it would all work out before that happened. Somehow.

He was about to go upstairs to change out of his work clothes when a pounding on the front door startled him. A second later it came again. He turned and headed back the way he'd come, a frisson of fear skittering up his spine at the thought of what could be so urgent to lead someone to almost break his door down.

"You need to get to the livery," Walter Alvarez said as soon as Adam opened the door, panting between his words as if he'd been running. "Miss Watts was attacked. She's..."

Adam didn't wait to hear any more. Not even pausing to close the door, he pushed past Walter and took off at a sprint in the direction of the livery, his heart pounding in terror. He realised after a few seconds that he should have asked Walter for more details, especially how Amy was, but all he could think was that she needed him and he had to get to her as soon as possible.

But what if she was hurt badly?

What if she was dead?

He cast the thought aside. She wasn't dead. She couldn't be. God had brought her to him, He wouldn't simply take her away again after so short a time. Adam needed to believe that.

Rounding a bend in the road and coming within sight of the looming wooden building of the livery, he almost sobbed with relief when he saw George seated on a chair outside with Amy on his lap, her arms wrapped around his neck and her face pressed into his shoulder. His relief was rapidly replaced by anger. Where had George been when Amy was attacked? How could he have left her alone?

Another man from the town was with them. Adam ignored him and skidded to a stop in front of them.

"What on earth happened, George?" he demanded. "Why weren't you here?"

The distress on George's face as he looked up almost made Adam sorry he'd snapped, but he felt like he needed to blame someone and right now George was in the firing line.

Amy raised her head to look up at Adam and a void swallowed his gut. A cut was oozing blood on the left side of her face, the surrounding flesh swollen and bruised. The right sleeve of her blouse was torn and dirt stains covered her dishevelled clothing.

His anger melting away, he dropped to his knees in front of her and raised one hand to her face, stopping short of touching it. "You're hurt."

She took hold of his hand. She was freezing.

"It wasn't his fault," she said in a soft, tremulous voice that pierced Adam's heart.

He wrapped her hand in his, trying to warm her icy fingers. He'd failed her. *I should have been here to protect you. That's why God brought you to me.*

At the sound of footsteps behind him, Adam looked back to see Marshal Cade approaching, followed by Deputy Fred Filbert and Walter, who must have gone to fetch them after he'd come to the post office.

Amy swivelled round on George's lap to stand and Adam rose to his feet beside her, putting an arm around her waist to support her when she swayed a little. She leaned against his side, resting her head against his shoulder.

"He's inside," George said to the marshal.

Adam's gaze snapped to the open front door of the livery. The man who'd attacked Amy was in there? For a moment he wished he'd known when he arrived, but then he

163

thought it was probably a good thing he hadn't. He'd have found it very difficult not to go straight in there and do something that would have got him thrown in jail, the last place he should be when Amy needed him.

Marshal Cade glanced at his deputy. "Go and fetch him, Fred, and get him locked up."

"Yes, Sir."

Fred Filbert was unfeasibly tall and wide and looked like he could wrestle a buffalo into submission with one arm tied behind his back. Maybe the man would try to escape and Fred would have to get rough. Adam hoped so.

"Miss Watts," Marshal Cade said, "if you'd like to go home, I can come over later and get your statement on what happened after you've had some time to recover. Would you like me to have the doctor come and check on you? That's a nasty looking cut you've got there."

She touched her fingertips to her cheek. "No, thank you. It probably looks worse than it is."

Angry shouts and the sounds of a very brief scuffle emanated from inside the livery. A few seconds later Fred emerged with a greasy looking man Adam didn't recognise in handcuffs. The stranger's gait was awkward and he winced with every step. Fred had the back of the man's collar fisted in one huge hand as he pushed him out the door.

In a flash of rage Adam forgot his need to keep himself on the right side of the law. He loosened his hold on Amy and stepped forward, hands clenching into fists. Beside him, Amy moved back. He looked down to see her eyes fixed on the man, wide with fear.

Releasing the breath he was holding, Adam deliberately relaxed his hands and returned to her side, sliding his arm back around her waist. She turned into him and lifted one hand to clutch onto his shirt.

Her trust in him wrenched at his heart. He should have

164

been here. He should have protected her.

The stranger glanced at her and leered. George stepped towards him with a growl. Suddenly, the man's smile vanished as he was swung around and pushed forward. With his hands cuffed behind his back, he landed on the ground face first with a pained grunt.

"Oops, sorry," Fred said, his expression impassive as he bent to grab the man's collar again. "Lost my grip there."

He hauled the man upright and propelled him away from them, in the direction of the marshal's office.

Amy's grasp on Adam relaxed somewhat. His on her didn't relax at all. The way he was feeling, someone would have to pry him away from her with a crowbar.

"Let's go home," he said.

Amy looked up at George. "Can you check on the horses? He was out there with them, but I don't know if he did anything. He said he was going to take Clem."

George placed his hand on her shoulder. "'Course I will. Don't you worry about a thing. You just go home and rest."

He glanced briefly at Adam before looking away. Adam stifled a sigh. He knew George cared about Amy and wouldn't intentionally have allowed her to be hurt. Later he was going to have to apologise for his outburst.

They left George talking to the marshal and started for home. Amy was silent; her steps slow as she stared at the ground in front of her. Adam kept his arm around her, trying to support her as best he could. He longed to pick her up and carry her, but he wasn't at all sure she'd want him to.

When they reached the busier part of town passersby began to stare after them and Adam steered them onto a back street leading to the rear of the post office where it was quieter.

They stepped inside the parlour and Adam turned away to lock the door. When he turned back Amy was standing in the middle of the room, looking lost. She raised her sad eyes to his.

Then she burst into tears.

Adam rushed to her side, panicked, as she covered her face with her hands and cried in great, heaving sobs. He raised his hands towards her without making contact, afraid he would scare her or somehow make it worse. What was he supposed to do?

When he couldn't bear the sound of her distress any longer, he gently wrapped his arms around her trembling shoulders and she immediately leaned into his chest, gasping as her frenzied crying robbed her of breath. Not knowing what else to do, Adam finally picked her up, carrying her to the settee and settling her over his lap where she collapsed into him. He squeezed his eyes closed against his own tears, silently praying for the wisdom to know how to comfort her.

After a while her desperate sobs eased and he began to pray in a whisper. "Father, Your daughter is suffering. Please, be Amy's comfort. Wrap her in Your loving arms and strengthen her. Take away her fear and replace it with Your peace." He cupped one hand over her cheek without touching it. "Heal this wound, Lord, and thank You for keeping her. In Your Name, Lord Jesus. Amen."

Her sniffles quietened and she murmured, "Thank you."

He rested his cheek against the top of her head. "Is there anything I can do?"

"Just... keep holding me?"

He tightened his arms around her. "For as long as you need."

He would hold her forever, if that was what she needed him to do.

~ ~ ~

Amy sniffed. Then she sniffed again. Her hand moved to her nose.

"You can use my shirt for a handkerchief if you like," Adam said. "I don't mind."

She began to shake and at first he was afraid she'd started crying again. Then he heard her soft laughter.

She sat up and winced, her hand fluttering near the cut on her cheek. "It hurts to laugh."

"I'm sorry, I'll try to curb my wit."

She laughed again and pushed his arm. "Stop it."

He reached out to push a few strands of hair from her face, sliding them from the congealing blood. "We should clean that up before the blood dries too much."

"Does it look bad?"

"No, just a touch messy. It'll be better when it's cleaned."

If he could have, he would have taken the wound from her onto himself.

He ran upstairs to fetch some clean handkerchiefs from his bedroom, finding it difficult to leave Amy alone even for that short amount of time. When he got back to the parlour he took a bottle of iodine and a bowl of water and sat back down with Amy on the settee.

He handed her one of the handkerchiefs, which she used to wipe her eyes and blow her nose, then set to work cleaning the blood from around the cut. Despite doing everything humanly possible to not cause her more pain, she still flinched a few times. It made him feel like a monster.

After he'd apologised for the fourth time, she touched her hand to his face and said, "Please stop being sorry. I couldn't want for anything more than having you take care of me."

Adam froze, staring into her eyes. When she lowered her hand and looked down with a small smile on her lips, he breathed again.

When he'd finished with the iodine, he sat back to study his handiwork. He'd done what he could. It wasn't a large wound and the bruising made it look worse than it was. Maybe he'd call the doctor, just to be sure.

"Um, did he... are you hurt anywhere else?" He very much didn't want to ask, but he had to know.

"No." She looked at her lap. "He tried, but I fought back as hard as I could."

He reached out to take her hand. "I am so proud of you. You're the bravest person I know."

She raised her eyes and smiled and suddenly he couldn't look away. He longed so much to take away everything bad that had ever happened in her life and replace it with all the love in his heart.

How could this depth of feeling have taken hold of him in such a short time? But perhaps it had started long before they met. He'd felt an undeniable connection to Amy from the very first letter she'd written to him, so much so that by the time she arrived he was ready to fall in love. It was as if she'd been made just for him. And, he hoped, he for her.

A knock at the front door made him start and Amy dropped her gaze and let go of his hand. Whoever it was instantly became Adam's least favourite person in the world.

"I, um... I'd better answer that," he said, rising. Why was he so flustered?

Marshal Cade and George stood on the covered porch outside the front door.

"Is Miss Watts up to answering some questions?" the marshal said.

"She's doing better." Adam stepped aside to let them in. George didn't meet his gaze as he entered. Might as well get this over with. "Look, George, I'm sorry I got angry at you. I know you wouldn't do anything to hurt Amy."

Expelling a deep sigh, George finally looked up. "No, you were right, I should have been there. I knew there was something off about that varmint, but I still left her alone. It's my fault."

Adam saw his own guilt echoed in the older man's eyes. "I think we're both feeling at fault here."

"And it isn't neither of your faults," Marshal Cade said. "So stop beating yourselves up over it. It won't do either of you any good, believe me. I've seen enough guilt in my time to know when it's deserved and the only person guilty here is that rascal I've got in my jail."

"Aren't you supposed to be unbiased?" Adam said, smiling.

"Only when I don't know if the perpetrator is guilty," he said. "No doubt of that in this case."

"Right," George growled.

Adam led them through to the parlour where Amy was still on the settee.

"Ma'am," Marshal Cade said, removing his hat. "How are you feeling? Are you up to telling me what happened?"

She nodded, although Adam could see the slight tremble of her lips. She looked at George. "Are the horses all right?"

"They're fine. He just scared them, was all. Got them all inside now, safe and sound."

Some of the tension released from her shoulders. "That's a relief."

He walked over to sit in the armchair close to her. "How are you?"

She patted his hand. "I'll be all right."

Adam pulled up a chair from the table for the marshal then went to sit beside her. She slipped her hand into his.

"OK," the marshal said, pulling a small paper pad and pencil from his shirt pocket. "George has told me everything he knows, but how about you start at the beginning so I can fill in the blanks."

Amy began with the first time the man had arrived at the livery and related the full story, how he'd made her uncomfortable, then not being sure about him, and how he'd returned, lured her from the livery, and attacked her. Her description of their fight had Adam's mouth hanging open. He knew she was as strong and determined a woman as he'd ever met, but he didn't know of any female, and not many males, who would have been able to handle themselves against a much stronger attacker the way she had. When she told of how she'd kneed him in the crotch the second time Adam almost cheered. He wanted to go down to the marshal's office and take a shot himself.

By the time she finished Marshal Cade was shaking his head as he finished scribbling his notes. "Miss Watts, maybe I should deputise you. You are one tough lady, if you don't mind me saying so."

A smile crept onto her face.

"And I think it may give you some satisfaction to know that he's still in a lot of pain," he said, grinning.

To Adam's surprise, she laughed. "I don't know how Christian it is of me to be pleased to hear that, but I truly am."

At her laughter, some of Adam's anger melted away, and even George cracked a tiny smile.

Marshal Cade pushed the pad and pencil back into his pocket and stood. "I've already found one wanted notice that's probably him and I'm going to send telegraphs to some of the other marshals around to see if they've heard of him. Believe me, he's going to jail and he won't be getting out for a good long while."

"Thank you, Marshal," Amy said. "That makes me feel much better."

"He should be relieved too," he said with a smirk. "I don't think he'd survive another round with you."

Adam escorted him back through the post office to the front door. "He truly won't get out?" he said as the marshal stepped outside, out of earshot of the parlour.

He replaced his hat. "As I said, this isn't his only crime and I'm guessing a bit of digging will produce more. The only place he's going is to prison and the only thing you need fret about is taking care of that brave lady of yours."

Adam opened his mouth to say she wasn't *his* brave lady, but then thought better of it and simply said, "Thanks, Marshal, I will." If anyone wanted to think of Amy as his, he wasn't going to object.

When he got back to the parlour Amy was on her feet, one hand on her hip and the other pointing at George. "So you will not even *think* of not letting me come back to work. Is that clear?"

George spotted him at the door. "Adam, please tell this girl that it's far too dangerous for her to work in the livery. I won't be the cause of her being hurt again."

Adam's gaze flicked to Amy. She turned her ire-filled eyes on him. "I... uh..."

After the events of the past hour he wanted nothing more than for her to stay with him at all times where he could ensure nothing bad ever happened to her again. But he had to be realistic. "George, I understand how you feel, believe me. But I know Amy well enough to know that's never going to happen. Better you just let this warrior woman carry on working for you. I think it's safer for both of us that way."

She gasped, her apparent outrage tempered by the sparkle in her eyes, and grabbed a cushion, throwing it at him.

Laughing, he caught it out of the air. "See? Even I'm not safe."

George rolled his eyes. "I ain't gonna win this argument, am I?"

171

"Nope," Amy said. She took his hand. "Stop worrying and stop blaming yourself. You're one of my favourite people in the world and I don't want you to be sad. So stop it."

He harrumphed, but Adam could see the wisp of a smile before it was stamped out. Not even George was immune to Amy's infectious charm.

He placed a hand on Amy's shoulder. "Get some rest, girl. And take care of that face." Then he turned and strode from the room.

Adam followed him to the front door.

"Take care of her," George said as he stepped out.

"You know I will."

George looked past him to the open parlour door and lowered his voice to a whisper. "When you gonna tell her how you feel about her?"

Adam's eyes widened. "How...?"

"Honestly, boy, if I've seen a more lovesick man than you in all my days, I can't recall it."

Was there anyone in Green Hill Creek who didn't know how he felt about Amy? "I'm working on it."

"Well work harder."

When Adam returned to the parlour Amy had started work on the potatoes for their evening meal. She was facing away from him, standing at the sink, but she wasn't moving.

He walked up to her and touched her arm. "Amy? Are you all right?"

It took her a few seconds to respond and when she did her voice trembled. "I'm still scared. Why am I still scared?"

He stepped in close behind her, encircled her in his arms and said softly, "Tell me what I can do."

A tear caught a shaft of sunlight shining in through the window as it fell into the sink. "I don't know."

Adam squeezed his eyes shut and leaned his forehead against her hair, willing her fear away with every piece of his breaking heart. "How about I hold you until you're not scared anymore?"

She nodded and he led her to the settee where they sat and he held her tight, praying silently, until she stopped trembling and fell asleep in his arms.

Chapter 22

Dear Amy,

First of all, thank you for allowing me to be so familiar. I'm beginning to feel as though we know each other, even in the few letters we've exchanged. Am I wrong? I hope not. I await each of your letters with such anticipation. Thank goodness Green Hill Creek has the railroad now or the amount of time I'd have to wait for them would be torture!

I can't imagine what being an only child would be like. My brothers and sisters and I are all so close in age that growing up there were always other children around me. My mother is a truly strong woman! There were times when I longed for the peace of it just being me (particularly when my brothers were pestering me), but I think I would have been lonely. I hope you didn't feel that way at all. I should think your parents showered you with love and attention as their precious only daughter.

I was so pleased to hear you like horses. My own horse is named Stride and he and I spend a lot of time together. Perhaps if you come here you would like your own horse? I would love to take you riding and show you the country around here. The beauty of the mountains will take your breath away. I've lived in this area all my life and I still enjoy just sitting and looking at them. In fact, at this moment I'm upstairs where there is a wonderful view I know you would love. I may be getting a little ahead of myself, but I am looking forward so much to introducing you to the north Californian countryside. Forgive me if it's too soon to be thinking like that, but I can't seem to help myself.

I'll be honest with you, Amy, I like you very much. I've been praying a lot about our future and I am hoping you have too. I'm trying to trust God to lead me in all I do and I'm hoping very much that He leads us to be together. I hope that doesn't scare you, but I want to be honest about how I feel. I hope you know that you can be honest with me too.

Kindest regards,
Adam.

~ ~ ~

When Amy woke the next morning the sun was already high in the sky.

Horrified, she leapt out of bed, washed her face and struggled into her clothes, practically all at once. She ran down the stairs and found Adam seated at the table in the parlour. He smiled as she burst into the room.

"What's the time? I'm late!"

She rushed to the cupboard to find something for her lunch. The quickest thing was a couple of apples. They would have to do. When she turned to get her bag, Adam was standing right behind her. She jumped, startled. In her haste, she hadn't heard him leave the table.

He took her hands in his. "George isn't expecting you. I went down there while you were still asleep to say you wouldn't be coming in, but he hadn't thought you would anyway."

Although she knew Adam's motives were kind, she was a little irritated at him for making the decision that she wouldn't be going to work without asking her first. "But he needs me."

He smiled, which irked her even more because it made her insides wobble. It was very difficult to be annoyed with him when her insides were wobbling. Plus, he was still holding her hands. That wasn't helping at all.

"George was running the livery for a long time before he hired you," he said. "He can cope on his own for today."

"But my face doesn't even hurt anymore." It didn't, so long as she didn't touch it. "I'm ready to go to work."

"But I'm not ready for you to go." He sighed and looked down at their entwined hands. "I wasn't there when you needed me. I should have been there to protect you, but I wasn't."

He felt guilty? How could he possibly feel guilt for what another man did?

"You're not responsible in any way for what happened. You can't be with me every second of the day."

"I know, and it isn't logical to feel like this, but I can't help it. At least for today I need to be with you. So either you take the day off from the livery or I come with you."

"What about the bank?" She suddenly realised he was as late as she was. "Wait, shouldn't you have left already?"

"I don't have to go into the bank today." He smiled again. "So here's my idea. I was planning on doing deliveries today, so we could make a picnic, you could come with me on my rounds, then we could go to the lake and spend the afternoon. What do you say?"

Amy's objections faded. She couldn't deny it sounded like an extremely good idea. "I think that's an inspired way to spend a day playing hooky."

~ ~ ~

After they'd had breakfast, Adam went to fetch Stride while Amy prepared the food.

They would be travelling by buggy so Amy packed sandwiches along with two slices of vegetable pie she and

176

Adam had prepared the evening before when she'd woken up, feeling much better for having slept. And for having spent quite some time wrapped in Adam's arms. They'd also made apple pie so she wrapped two slices of that along with a pear each, some grapes, and an apple for Stride.

Adam's voice called through the post office as she was finishing. "I'll load everything up. You can come out whenever you're ready."

"Almost finished," she called back, tucking a cloth over the food she'd packed into a basket.

Stride bent his head towards her when she got outside and she rubbed his neck, moving the basket back out of his reach when he surreptitiously stretched his nose towards it.

"It's for later," she said. "And you can't fool me. I know you've already had breakfast because it's often me who gives it to you."

Adam jumped down from the buggy and took the basket from her, tucking it in behind the seat, next to the mail bag. "If he got to eat everything he wanted he wouldn't be able to fit into his stall."

"Doesn't he mind being harnessed to the buggy?" Stride always seemed to Amy like he wanted to be running free.

Adam smiled and patted his side. "He has good reason to look forward to delivery day. You'll understand why once we get going." His eyes drifted down to her feet and then back to her face. "You changed. That's the one you've been working on, isn't it?"

Amy looked down at the sage green dress she'd put on after he left. She'd bought the material out of her first week's pay and finished it two nights ago. It was meant to be for church, but for reasons she suspected had very much to do with Adam, she'd wanted to wear it today.

Shrugging one shoulder, she attempted nonchalance. "It is. I thought, since we'd be meeting your customers I should look presentable."

A small smile quirked one corner of his mouth, tiny wrinkles warming his eyes. "You always look presentable, but that colour suits you. You look stunning."

Amy gasped in a small breath as her insides somersaulted several times before landing in a panting heap in the vicinity of her navel. Adam held her gaze until she felt like she would drown in his blue eyes, not caring in the slightest that she'd never take another breath.

The spell was broken when Stride nudged Adam's arm with such insistence that he stumbled to one side.

"Well," he said, his voice sounding slightly breathless as he glanced at his horse and gave a small laugh, "looks like Stride is eager to be off. Are you ready?"

Ready for what?

Amy struggled to corral a coherent thought. "*Oh*, to go. Um..." Was she ready? Where were they going again? "Uh, I need to fetch my shawl. I'll only be a moment."

She fled back into the house, gasping in a few deep breaths as she retrieved the brown shawl from where she'd left it on the settee.

Pull yourself together. All he did was say you look stunning and then gaze into your eyes as if you were the only woman in the world. At least, that was how it had felt. She was probably over-romanticising it.

But his eyes gazing into hers...

Don't make me slap myself, Amy.

Squaring her shoulders, she marched back outside, determined to maintain some semblance of dignity. And this time she managed to keep herself more or less together, even when Adam flashed her a smile that made her stomach feel like it had become a thousand tiny butterflies. Things got a little hairy when he put his hands on her waist to help her into the buggy, but once she was seated it only took a few

178

seconds to regain most of her faculties, even though the skin beneath the dress where he'd touched her was still tingling.

What was wrong with her today? Was it possible that the time she'd spent the previous evening wrapped in the comfort of his embrace had had more effect on her than simply calming her fears?

"Looking fine today, Miss Amy," Isaiah called from his rocker as they rode past.

"Thank you, kind sir," Amy called back, smiling and waving to him.

"Hmm," Adam said as they turned onto a side street.

"What?"

"Seems maybe I should be watching out for Isaiah. I may have some competition."

"For what?" And then realisation struck; he meant her. At least, she thought he meant her. Did he mean her?

Adam merely smiled mysteriously and returned his attention to the road ahead.

~ ~ ~

It took half an hour, more or less, to reach the first delivery, a small farmhouse nestled in the foothills surrounded by fields of assorted crops, most of which Amy didn't recognise as they weren't near harvest time yet. She was ridiculously proud of herself when she correctly identified a small plot of carrots.

Stride apparently needed no guidance as he came to a halt in the open area in front of the wraparound porch. A huge barn off to the left dwarfed the tiny house. It also dwarfed the tiny, wizened woman who hobbled out of the door of the barn and made her way towards them, leaning heavily on a gnarled walking stick.

Stride nickered at her approach.

179

"Good morning, Mrs Byrne," Adam said, jumping from the buggy.

Her wrinkled face broke into a grin. "Good morning to ye, Postmaster Emerson." She moved her gaze to Amy. "And who's your pretty young lady?"

Amy found herself wanting to grin at being called Adam's young lady, especially when he didn't correct the assumption.

"This is Miss Watts," Adam said as he reached into the mail bag. "Amy, meet Mrs Byrne. She runs this farm."

"It's a pleasure to meet you, Mrs Byrne," she said, wondering how on earth this small, ancient woman ran all of this. "You have a beautiful farm."

"Well, thank ye, Miss Watts. I do have a bit o' help with it from me strappin' sons and grandsons," she replied, as if she could read Amy's mind. She walked up to Stride and rubbed his nose. He bobbed his head and nickered again. "Oh, I know what you want."

She reached into a deep pocket at the front of her apron, withdrew a handful of strawberries, and fed them to the eager horse one by one.

Adam looked up at Amy and winked. She smiled in understanding. So that was why Stride looked forward to delivery day.

"Here's your mail," he said, handing Mrs Byrne a bundle of envelopes and a small package.

She brushed her hands on the front of her apron then took the letters and slipped them into the pocket from where she'd produced the strawberries. Stride took the opportunity to peer inside, just in case she'd missed any.

"He does get fed, I promise you," Adam said.

Mrs Byrne laughed and scratched behind Stride's ear which he seemed to enjoy almost as much as the strawberries. "My boys are exactly the same." She glanced up at Amy,

180

leaned forward as if she was about to tell Adam a secret, then said in a very loud whisper that Amy had no trouble hearing, "Hold onto her. She's a beauty."

Adam darted his eyes to Amy, replying in an equally theatrical whisper, "I'll do my best, Ma'am."

Amy put one hand to her mouth to cover her smile, although she couldn't do anything to hide the blush heating her cheeks.

"Mrs Byrne is very forthright," Adam said as they rode away.

"I noticed that."

"Nice lady though. Stride loves her."

"I noticed that too. So her treats are why he likes going on deliveries so much?"

Adam chuckled. "Oh, it's not just her."

They spent the rest of the morning travelling, taking mail to those for whom getting into town was difficult. Most of those they visited were older and Amy discovered that Adam didn't just deliver the mail. He would always ask after their wellbeing and if there was anything he could do for them. During the course of the morning Amy helped fix a broken fence, found a missing pair of spectacles, held Adam's jacket while he unblocked a sink, and retrieved a cherished necklace only she could reach from beneath a huge chest of drawers so heavy it hadn't been moved for fifty years.

And every single person they visited had something delicious for Stride. The horse was in his element.

Amy's respect for Adam grew even further, if that were possible. He wasn't just the postmaster, he was a lifeline for the isolated people around Green Hill Creek.

"It's wonderful what you do for these people," she said as the buggy ambled in the direction of the lake after leaving the last homestead on Adam's route. "What would they do without your visits?"

181

She felt Adam's arm raise and lower against hers in a shrug.

"The church has people who visit the ones who can't come into town when they can, but I think they like the regularity of me going. My uncle did the same thing when he was postmaster. When he nominated me to replace him after he got sick, he told me one of the reasons he wanted me to take over was because he knew I'd continue to come out here every couple of weeks. Not that I mind you thinking it's completely altruistic on my part, but I admit I enjoy doing it. And Stride would never forgive me if I stopped."

Amy watched the horse's head bobbing ahead of them, his sleek mane ruffling gently in the breeze. "He certainly seems to enjoy the attention. And the treats."

Adam glanced at her then back at the dirt track they were following. "I really liked having you along. Maybe we could work something out that you could come with me every time. If you'd like to."

Smiling, she kept her eyes ahead. "I'd like that very much."

Ten minutes later they arrived at the spot where they'd had their first picnic, the Sunday afternoon after Amy arrived in Green Hill Creek. It was just as beautiful as she remembered and while Adam unhitched Stride from the buggy she stood staring out over the lake, breathing in the warm spring air and absorbing the peace surrounding her.

I want to stay here, she thought. *I want to stay in this beautiful place with this wonderful man for the rest of my life. I don't want to be anywhere else.*

It wasn't the first time she'd considered what it would be like to stay, but it was the first time she'd truly admitted to herself that it was what she wanted more than anything.

She didn't know when it had happened, but sometime in the past two weeks her fear of the uncertainty of relying on other people had faded, and what happened to her yesterday had been the final proof she needed. Not only had she had the strength to fight off her attacker, but Adam and George had steadfastly been there for her. She knew now that being alone was no longer what she wanted. Staying here, with Adam, was.

But would he want her in return?

Stride sauntered past her and bent his head to the lake's clear water. She turned from the tranquil scene and wandered over to help Adam with the picnic.

"Do you think that maybe next time we come here we could bring Clem?" she said as they worked. "I'd like her to see the world outside the livery and paddock and I'm sure she'd love it here."

"I think that's a great idea," he said, taking the last of the food packages from the basket and setting it aside. "And I'm sure Stride would love to have his girl along. He might not even mind sharing the food."

After they'd finished eating, Adam stretched out on his side, his head propped up on one elbow as he gazed out at the lake. Amy pulled her legs up beneath her skirt and wrapped her arms around them, studying him surreptitiously. He seemed relaxed, but not sleepy. If she was going to do this, now was as good a time as she was likely to find.

She drew in a deep breath and let it out slowly. "My father died when I was less than a year old. It was an accident in the factory where he worked. My mother told me he was a good man and loved us very much, but I never knew him."

She kept her eyes on the lake, but out of the corner of her eye she saw Adam slowly sit up, his gaze fixed on her.

"My mother got ill when I was six and she died too," she continued, before she lost her nerve. "Since I was all alone and had no relatives, I was sent to an orphanage. It was a place no child should ever have to go. We were made to work, had no schooling, got sold out to people who only wanted free labour. I've heard there are good orphanages, but the Mayfield Home for Destitute Children wasn't one of them. When I was ten, a couple took me to cook and clean for them. I hated it. After I'd run away three times they sent me back to the orphanage so I ran away from there too and spent a few years on the streets. It was dangerous and hard and sometimes I was so cold and hungry I thought I would die, but I learned how to survive. You'd be surprised how many children there are on the streets of New York with no one to look after them but each other. A lot of the time I was happier out there than I ever was in the orphanage."

She sighed, dropping her eyes to the grass at her feet and wondering what happened to the friends she'd made back then, children like her with only each other.

"But I was caught and sent back when I was twelve. Then when I was fourteen I was taken in by a rich couple, the Courtneys. They lived in a big, grand mansion and I thought I'd struck gold. It was hard work, but I had a warm bed and regular meals and Mr Courtney told me I was getting paid, that it was all being put into a bank for me and when I was twenty-one I could do what I wanted with it. I was stupid enough to believe him." She shook her head at her naivety, even at that young age. "Then when I was sixteen, he started taking an interest in me."

She heard Adam draw in a sharp breath but she didn't look away from the grass.

"I learned to stay away from him, make sure I was around other people all the time, and I slept in a room with four other girls so I was safe then. I was just biding my time until I could get my money and leave. I had my dream of going to San Francisco, I just had to wait until I was twenty-one and would have the money to get there."

184

She paused, trying to find strength she couldn't feel. Adam stayed silent. She wanted to look at him, see what he was thinking, but her gaze remained locked on the grass in front of her. Her hands fisted around the material of her skirt.

"On my twenty-first birthday I went to see Mr Courtney, to ask him for my money. He said with all my bed and board none of my wages were left, but that I could have something if I..." She wiped one hand across her suddenly burning eyes and swallowed. "If I went to his bed every day for two years. When I told him I wouldn't, he tried to force himself on me. I'd been stupid, going to him alone, but I was so eager to get my money and start my plans. Mr Rand, the butler, came at that moment and I escaped, but from then on the way Mr Courtney looked at me scared me even more. I knew he was just waiting for his opportunity. I had to get far away from him, but I had no way to get out of the city and no way to get employment anywhere else.

"Then I found the special insert in the newspaper that had your advertisement in it."

She stopped and drew in a shuddering breath. She hadn't told anyone her whole story before, not even Katherine. It wasn't that she was ashamed of her past, but growing up in an orphanage and on the streets didn't exactly make her a lady. And Mr Courtney's inappropriate attentions had made her feel tainted, even though she'd done nothing to encourage him. Could Adam want someone like her now he knew the truth?

He shuffled forward until he was sitting at her side. She continued to stare at the ground in front of her, unable to look at him.

"Amy," he whispered, touching her arm.

She slowly raised her eyes to his and in that moment she knew all the dreams she'd had of San Francisco no longer meant anything, and she didn't mourn them at all. The only future she dreamed of now was with Adam, the man she'd fallen in love with.

He took her hands, wrapping them in his own. "You are safe with me," he said, an intensity to his voice. "I will never let anyone hurt you again. And you will always have a home with me, for as long as you want it."

They stared at each other, their faces only inches apart. Adam's gaze flicked to her lips and back up again. Her eyes went to his mouth and saw his neck move as he swallowed. His head tilted towards her.

Then he stopped, his eyes closed, and he let out a long breath. Leaning forward, he pressed a soft kiss to her forehead.

"Thank you for telling me," he murmured, his breath brushing across her skin. "Your trust means a lot."

To her disappointment he sat back and let go of her hands. For a moment she'd thought he was going to kiss her, and not just on the forehead.

"I haven't been completely honest with you," he said.

Her heart rate picked up at his serious expression, and not in the good way it had when his lips made contact with her skin.

"I was hoping I'd never have to tell you this, that Vernon would change his mind, but you've been honest with me and I feel like I owe you the same." He breathed out a long sigh. "I didn't take today off from the bank. Yesterday was my last day working there. I lost my job."

Amy gasped, her eyes widening. "No! Why?" And then realisation drew an icy finger down her spine. "Was it because of me? Did he fire you because of me?"

He took her hands again, holding them tight. "No, he fired me because all he cares about is money and wouldn't know compassion if it bit him on the backside. The Monday after you arrived he called me into his office and told me if

186

you didn't move out I would no longer have a job there. But it's all right."

How could he be so calm about this? She pulled her hands from his grasp so she could wave them about to emphasize her words. "But, but, I could have moved out. I could have gone to the boarding house. I can still go to the boarding house. I can go to Mr Vernon and explain and tell him I'm moving out and get him to give you your job back and why are you smiling?"

He looked as though he was trying not to laugh. "Because I've never been surer that I did the right thing than I am right now. Vernon can keep his job. The last thing I want is for you to move out. Besides, God brought you to me, remember? If it's a choice between obeying my Creator and Saviour and obeying my boss, God gets my vote every time."

"But..." She'd cost him his job. How could that not bother him? And then a memory came back to her. "I never used to get to see the newspaper."

He frowned, confused. "You... what?"

"I never ever got to see the newspaper, but that day the housekeeper, who usually delivered it to Mrs Courtney, had to deal with an emergency in one of the bedrooms when a bird got inside, and she gave it to me to take. That insert fell out and when I saw what it was I kept it." At the time she'd thought of it as luck, but could it all have been the Lord's doing to bring her here?

Adam was grinning from ear to ear. "Sounds like a miracle to me. That proves it. I'm not worried and you shouldn't be either."

A smile tugged at the corners of her mouth. "Maybe you need to drop your Bible for confirmation."

"Well, funny you should say that, but the day after Mr Vernon gave me his ultimatum, I was in the church..."

Chapter 23

Adam lay in his bed, staring up at the ceiling. He couldn't see the ceiling in the dark, but he stared anyway.

Today had been one of the best days of his life, although he'd had at least three of those since Amy arrived. But today... today had been incredible. Spending the whole day in her company, going on his rounds, which were so much more fun to do with her along. The way she'd opened up to him and told him her story. It had been hard to hear how much she'd been through, but that she trusted him enough to share her life with him gave him hope that she would stay if he asked her.

And that was why he was staring at the ceiling. He hadn't asked her.

All during their time at the lake, for the hours they'd talked and relaxed and gone for a stroll, and when Amy nodded off on the blanket and Adam gazed at her face for the entire half hour she slept, he'd thought about asking her. Then as they rode home with the sun sinking in the sky, painting the clouds purple and red and lighting up Amy's beautiful face, he'd thought about asking her. As they made supper, naturally falling into the comfortable rhythm they'd found together after two weeks of living under the same roof, he'd thought about asking her. And as they relaxed on the settee after the meal, reading, he'd barely got through two pages in an hour because he couldn't stop thinking about asking her.

But in all that time, he didn't *once* actually ask her to stay. He didn't even hint at it, apart from mentioning her coming with him on his postal rounds in the future. And he suspected that may have been too subtle for her to get his entire meaning, which had been, *Please, please, please stay with me for the rest of my life and I love you and marry me and have my children and grow old with me and never, ever leave.*

He wanted to bang his head against a wall.

The problem was, in addition to thinking about asking her to stay he had also been obsessively considering all the ways it could go wrong. Chief amongst those was she didn't feel the same way about him as he felt about her and that declaring his undying love would scare her away.

But then again, if he didn't ask her she'd leave eventually anyway.

He scrubbed his hands over his face in an attempt to erase his nervous indecision. Why was being in love so hard? He lowered his eyes to the wall that separated his bedroom from hers. Maybe he should just get up, march in there, and tell her he loved her with all his heart.

It was possibly the worst idea he'd ever had, but that was where he was right now. Instead of making that mistake, he rolled over and groaned into his pillow, pounding his fist into it for extra emphasis. This was ridiculous. He should just ask her and deal with the consequences afterwards.

But tomorrow. He'd ask her tomorrow.

Not tomorrow morning though, because Amy was insisting on returning to work and he didn't want any discussion that would ensue to feel rushed. Or, if he was very lucky, any kissing that would ensue.

But most definitely tomorrow afternoon, after she got home. That's when he'd ask her to stay.

Undoubtedly then.

189

Chapter 24

Amy moved the brush down Clementine's flank in one final long stroke and lowered her arm. "Beautiful," she said, admiring the horse that she couldn't help thinking of as hers, even though she wasn't. Yet.

Clementine turned her head to nudge Amy's shoulder and Amy laughed. "I can't keep brushing you forever," she said, rubbing her forehead. "You'll lose all your hair."

The horse nudged her again.

"Oh, all right, just a little longer."

"Are you spoiling that nag again?" George's voice called from the other end of the livery.

"She's not a nag," Amy called back as she resumed brushing. "She's the most beautiful horse in the world."

Clementine bobbed her head.

"And she completely agrees with me." She smiled, imagining George rolling his eyes.

"Just don't neglect your other duties. I'm not paying you for nothing, girl."

"This place is spotless and all the horses are fed. I earn my pay and you know it."

A grunt was the only response, making Amy smile again. "Don't listen to him, Clem, he loves you really," she said, loud enough for George to hear.

Boots clomped outside the livery. It was late, close to six, and they didn't usually get customers at this time. Anxiety pinched at Amy's gut.

George is here, she reminded herself.

Being her first day back at work after the attack, he hadn't left her on her own all day, other than to use the outhouse. And even then he'd made her come outside so she was within shouting distance.

I'm safe here.

She put Clementine's brush down onto the stool and rubbed her hands off on the front of her shirt.

"Marshal?" George said. "What's going on?"

"Amy Watts, where is she?"

Amy's heart slammed into her throat at the all too familiar voice. It couldn't be him. It couldn't.

She shrank back into Clementine's stall, pressing herself against the back wall, her heart pounding. Sensing her fear, Clem laid her ears back, eyes wide and feet shifting nervously.

"Who are *you?*" George demanded.

"George, is Miss Watts here?" Amy recognised Marshal Cade's voice.

She forced herself away from the wall and crept forward, peering around the edge of the stall. From where she stood in the shadows she could see George facing the livery's front door, arms folded across his chest and feet planted wide. The other men were out of sight, beyond the door.

"I am Franklin Courtney of New York City and you are harbouring a thief and fugitive from justice," the man's voice boomed.

It was the voice of Amy's nightmares, a voice she thought she'd escaped by coming almost all the way across the country. A voice she couldn't hear without remembering that day in his study, her anger turning to fear as he'd grabbed her, his breath hot on her neck, his hands grabbing at her skirts.

191

She stepped back, looking around her. They had a view of both front and back doors, but maybe she could escape through a window.

"Mr Courtney," Marshal Cade said, "I think it best if you allow me to handle this..."

"Step aside, man," Courtney said in the imperious tone he always used with those he felt beneath him. Which was just about everyone.

"I don't know who you are," George said, his voice dripping with warning, "but this is my property and you would do best to stay out of it."

"George," the marshal said, "an arrest warrant has been issued for Miss Watts. Please don't make this harder than it needs to be. If you stand in my way I'll have to take you in too, and I really don't want to do that."

In the process of carrying the stool to the window at her end of the building, Amy froze at the words 'arrest warrant'.

"What could you possibly want to arrest Amy for?" George snapped. "That girl ain't never done harm to anyone."

"She's a thief," Courtney said.

Thief? Anger flared in Amy's chest, momentarily eclipsing her fear. He was accusing *her* of theft? She almost marched to the door to tell Courtney what she thought of him.

"I don't believe it," George said.

"What you believe, *Sir*, is of no relevance..."

"George," Marshal Cade cut in, "is Miss Watts here? The warrant means I can search the property."

Amy hurried to the window and placed the stool beneath it. She didn't want to get George in trouble. She had to get away before they found her, although where to she didn't know. At the thought of leaving Adam her heart wrenched so hard it caused her physical pain, but what

192

choice did she have now?

She pushed the window open, wincing when its rusty hinges gave a harsh squeak.

The argument at the door stopped.

"She's in there!" Courtney roared.

Amy glanced back to see him push George aside and lumber towards her. Rational thought fled. She pushed off the stool and scrambled through the window, feeling a hand grab at her shoe as she slid through the gap. Outside, she landed on the grass and leapt to her feet.

"Miss Watts!" Marshal Cade shouted.

He was running from the livery doors towards her. Without any thought as to where she would go, Amy launched herself in the opposite direction.

"Miss Watts! Stop!"

She barely heard the marshal over the blood pumping in her ears. Glancing back to see him sprinting after her, she hit something solid, rebounded backwards, and landed in the dirt of the road.

Deputy Filbert towered above her, his tall, wide form blocking out the sun and barring her way like a brick wall. She scrambled backwards on her elbows and pushed to her feet, turning to run. Marshal Cade stood in her way. He grabbed her arms. Amy pulled away, but his grip clamped tight.

"*No!*" she screamed, fighting to break free. "Let me go!"

"Miss Watts, stop!"

"I won't," she sobbed, pounding against his chest. "I won't let him take me."

Two arms wrapped around her from behind. "Amy, be still."

At the sound of George's voice, she stopped struggling.

"It's all right, Lee, I've got her."

The marshal looked at George, nodded and released his

hold on Amy. She twisted round in George's arms and sobbed against his chest, her words punctuated with tearful gasps. "Don't... let them... take... me."

"It's all right, girl," he said, his voice gentle. "I won't let anyone hurt you."

"Marshal Cade, I demand you take Amy into custody at once."

She stiffened at the sound of Courtney's voice and peered around George. Her former employer was jogging towards them, his face red as he gasped for breath from the exertion of trotting the fifty yards or so up the street.

He leered at her in between pants. "Otherwise, I'll have to take her back to New York myself."

George turned to face him, holding Amy at his back. "If you want her," he growled, "you'll have to go through me."

Courtney paled, taking a step backward. He swallowed and looked at Marshal Cade. "Marshal..."

"Mr Courtney," Cade said, an edge to his voice, "we are capable of dealing with matters of the law here. Justice will be served."

Courtney's eyes darted between him and George. "Yes, well, just see that it is."

The marshal turned to Amy. "Miss Watts, I'm sorry but I'm going to have to take you into custody. I have no choice." To his credit, his expression said it wasn't what he wanted to do.

She shook her head, tears rising to her eyes. "No, please, I don't want to be locked up."

"It's all right, Amy," George said. "We'll sort this out. I promise."

Her eyes darted around the street. A small crowd had stopped to see what was going on and more were approaching. There was no way out.

She took a deep breath and let it out slowly. Then she

squared her shoulders, wiped at her eyes with her sleeve, and looked up at George. "Will you tell Adam?"

"No, girl, I won't, because I'm staying with you." He narrowed his eyes at the deputy marshal. "But Deputy Filbert will, won't you Fred?"

Fred Filbert looked between him and Cade. "Um..."

"Go ahead, Fred," the marshal said.

Clearly relieved to not have to disobey either of them, the huge deputy jogged off in the direction of the post office.

Marshall Cade swept a hand in the direction of his office along the street. "Miss Watts, if you please?"

"'If you please?'" Courtney mimicked. He stepped towards Amy, reaching for her. "I'll take her myself..."

Amy yelped, jerking her arm from his fingers.

"Get your hands off her!" George stepped between them, raising his fist.

Courtney stumbled backwards. "Marshal, stop him!"

George advanced on Courtney, Marshal Cade not making any move to stop him.

"It's your duty!" Courtney almost screamed, raising his hands in front of his face.

"George," Cade said with a sigh, "leave him be. Think about Miss Watts."

George stopped and his head lowered, his shoulders rising and falling as his fist slowly unclenched. Then he turned, walked back to Amy and put his arm around her shoulders, guiding her in the direction of the marshal's office.

It was a long walk along most of the town's main street from the livery to the marshal's office and it felt to Amy like every resident of Green Hill Creek was out as they stopped to watch the little group pass. Any of the town's population who didn't already think she was a hussy would now think she was a criminal. So much for her hopes of making a home here.

George kept his arm around her protectively, darting frequent threatening glances at Courtney. Amy didn't look at her former employer at all. Just his voice made her sick to her stomach; his face would give her lasting nightmares.

It felt like it took forever to reach the single storey brick building that housed the Marshal's office and local jail and, despite the reason for her being there, Amy was relieved to get inside and away from the curious stares of the townspeople. The room they entered contained two desks, a few chairs and a table against the wall, a cupboard, and a general feeling of mild clutter.

Marshal Cade pulled two chairs away from the wall and set them in front of one of the desks. "Have a seat, Miss Watts."

Amy sat on the edge of one of the chairs, twisting her hands together in her lap.

"George?" The marshal said, nodding towards the second chair.

"I'll stand," George said, taking a place behind Amy and placing his hands onto her shoulders. He turned and fixed Courtney with a warning glare.

Courtney loitered by the door, obviously afraid to come any closer. At least Amy could take a small amount of satisfaction from that.

"There's no necessity for you to be here, Mr Courtney," Marshal Cade said.

"This is a public building," Courtney replied, "so I'm entitled to stay."

The marshal huffed an irritated sigh. "Suit yourself." He turned his attention to Amy. "Miss Watts, the warrant for your arrest states you are being charged with the theft of seventy-five dollars from your employer, Mr Franklin Courtney of New York City. I am required to detain you until the circuit judge arrives, when he may set bail if the trial is going to last longer than a day."

Amy swallowed against her dry mouth. "When is the judge arriving?"

"Monday is when he's due."

Three days. She could survive three days in jail. She'd done it before, in far worse places than this.

"I have to make sure you have no weapons on you," Marshal Cade said, "which would normally involve me patting you down, but in your case I'm happy to take your word for it. Do you have any weapons? Knives, guns or the like?"

She shook her head.

Courtney snorted. "What kind of backwoods operation..."

"Mr Courtney," the marshal snapped, "I am a hair's breadth from throwing you out of here. Don't push me." He stood and opened a door behind him. Beyond, Amy could see bars. "The federal marshal came yesterday to take the prisoner, so you have the whole place to yourself. If you have anything you'd like brought from your home, I can send someone for it. Meals are good, at least."

He held out a hand towards her. Amy rose from the chair and allowed him to usher her through the door. In the room beyond were three barred cells, each containing two low, uncomfortable looking cots. Marshal Cade unlocked the door of the closest and stepped aside to let her past.

She walked to the door and stopped, her heart pounding. If she went in there she'd be trapped. She looked back at George behind her and he immediately stepped forward and wrapped his arms around her.

"I'm not gonna let anything happen to you, girl," he said quietly. "We'll sort this whole thing out, you have my word on that."

Nodding against his chest, she forced herself to let go,

197

trying to produce a smile but not quite succeeding. Turning away, she walked into the cell.

With a clanging finality that made her stomach jolt, the marshal closed and locked the door behind her.

Chapter 25

For the second time in three days, Adam sprinted along the road to find Amy.

Behind him Deputy Filbert followed at a slower pace, but Adam couldn't wait. Reaching the small crowd of gawkers surrounding the entrance to the marshal's office, he pushed his way through and burst into the building. He collided with a rotund older man wearing a thin moustache and expensive looking clothes, standing just inside the door.

The man stumbled, grabbed the edge of a desk, and whirled around to glare down his nose at Adam. No small feat with Adam at least six inches taller.

"How dare you! Are there no manners in this God-forsaken backwater of a town?"

In that instant, Adam knew who this man was. Courtney, the man who had terrorised Amy for years. Anger flared so strong that Adam took a step towards him, his fist clenching. It took every ounce of willpower he had to stop himself from throwing himself at the man and pummelling him into the floor.

Very deliberately, he turned away and walked to the door leading to the cells.

Marshal Cade was standing next to George in front of the closest, where Amy stood on the other side of the bars, looking more forlorn than Adam had ever seen her.

He went to the cell and gripped the bars, wishing he could yank them apart and pull her out. "Are you all right?"

Amy placed her hands over his and nodded, gazing up at him through a film of moisture. "I'm sorry."

"You don't have one thing to be sorry about." He looked back at Marshal Cade. "Let me in there."

Cade sighed. "You know I can't do that, Mr Emerson."

Adam told himself the marshal was just doing his job and forced himself to be civil. "You locked her up, you can lock me up too."

"So you're the poor sap who paid for her to run away," Courtney sneered from the doorway. "I'll bet it was a disappointment when you found out she's frigid."

Adam closed his eyes and gritted his teeth, trying not to give in to his anger.

Then he had an idea.

"Quite frankly," Courtney went on, "I'd leave her to you if she hadn't stolen from me."

Adam ignored his taunts and looked down at Amy through the bars. "Do you trust me?"

She nodded immediately. "Yes."

He smiled, squeezed her fingers, and walked back out into the main room.

Courtney opened his mouth to speak. Before he could, Adam drew his arm back and slammed his fist into his face. Courtney spun round and would have fallen if he hadn't hit the wall. He clamped one hand over his nose and whimpered.

In the cell room, George let out a bark of laughter.

Marshal Cade rushed into the room. "Mr Emerson, what on earth do you think you're doing?"

"Arrest him!" Courtney sputtered, pointing a bloody hand at Adam. "You saw it, he assaulted me! I demand you arrest him!"

Cade ran one hand over his hair. "Emerson, what...?"

"Do it, Marshal," Adam said calmly. "Arrest me. Throw

me in a cell."

Marshal Cade stared at him as realisation dawned. He shook his head slowly, half a smile curling his mouth. "All right then."

He took the keys to the cells from his pocket and walked over to Amy's cell.

"Wait, hold on," Courtney said.

"You wanted me to arrest him," Cade said, pushing the key into the lock and turning it. "I'm arresting him."

"But... but... you can't put him in with her. What about the other cells?"

The marshal held open the door for Adam to enter. "I'm expecting a run on cells tonight. Gotta keep those ones clear."

Amy rushed into Adam's arms, clutching onto him in a way that made his heart leap.

"Now, Mr Courtney," Cade said, "I suggest you go back to the hotel. Judge will be round Monday. We'll work this whole thing out then."

Courtney sputtered for a few seconds then turned and stomped to the door.

"Oh, and by the way," the marshal called as he left, "doc's down the road to your left. You might want to get that nose seen to. It's not looking so good."

"I think I'll make sure he gets back to the hotel," George said, heading for the door.

"George..." Cade began.

"Don't worry, I'm not going to hurt him," he said as he walked out. "I'm just going to scare him a little."

"Are you OK?" Adam said, stroking one hand over Amy's silky hair.

She raised her face to look up at him and nodded. Inappropriate as it was under the circumstances, he wanted to kiss her so badly it made his head spin.

Thankfully, Marshal Cade interrupted his train of

thought before he could embarrass himself.

"Maybe you should tell me what's going on here."

Amy sighed and lowered to one of the cots in the cell. Adam took a place next to her, resting his hands on his thighs. He'd much rather have rested them around Amy again.

She gasped. "You're hurt!"

He looked down at his right hand which was beginning to develop a bruise across the knuckles. Hugging Amy had effectively dampened the pain, but now he realised it was hurting.

"For a man with all that padding, he has a hard face."

"You need me to get the doc down here?" Cade said.

Adam flexed his fingers a few times. "No, I don't think it's broken. I'll be fine."

"You didn't *have* to punch him," Amy said, taking his hand gently.

"I know, but with what he was saying making me so angry, it seemed like a very good way to kill two birds with one stone. I don't think I'm very good at turning the other cheek when it's yours."

He brushed the pad of his left thumb against the side of her face and she smiled.

Cade cleared his throat. "I'm still here."

Amy let go of his hand and looked at her lap, her cheeks colouring. Adam wanted to hug her again.

"So?" the marshal said. "What's the story with this Courtney?"

Amy let out a long breath. "I worked for him back in New York, right from out of the orphanage at fourteen. He told me my wages were being kept for when I turned twenty-one, but it was a lie. When I confronted him, he told me the wages only covered my bed and board. And he said..." She faltered, her eyes on the floor. Adam wrapped his good hand around hers. "He said the only way I would leave with anything was if I went to his bed. When I refused, he tried to force himself on me. That's when I knew I had to get away." She raised her eyes to Cade. "I swear I only took what was owed me, and not even a fraction of that."

The marshal puffed out a breath, shaking his head. "That no good, slimy... You didn't report him to the law?"

"It would have been my word against his and he has lots of important friends. I was just a maid. No one would have believed me."

He planted his hands on his hips and looked up at the ceiling as if searching for answers there. "So that's how he got the arrest warrant signed by the district judge. Probably had one of his bigwig friends telegraph him. I think I'll go and have a talk with him. Fred will be in the office, so just give a holler if you need anything. Dinner will be round later." He sighed. "I wish I didn't have to keep you in here, but with that warrant, my hands are tied."

"I get it, Marshal," Adam said, trying very hard to get it. "Just do everything you can to get Amy out of this."

"That I will." He smiled at Amy, nodded to Adam, and walked out, leaving them alone.

Next to Adam, Amy's gaze was focused on her hands twisted in her lap. The way she'd run into his arms when he walked into the cell had taken his breath away and he wanted to hold her again, but he wasn't certain if he should. He moved his arm towards her then stopped. What if she didn't want him to touch her? The last thing he wanted was for her to feel uncomfortable. She was, after all, trapped in here with him. Should he ask first?

"Amy, may I..."

She sniffed. A tear dropped onto her hands.

His heart breaking, he lifted his arm and placed it around her shoulders. She immediately turned to him, her

203

hands clutching at his shirt and face burying in his shoulder. He wrapped both arms around her trembling body.

He felt like such a failure. All he wanted to do was protect her from everything bad in the world and he couldn't even do that. How was he supposed to save her from people like Courtney when the sum total of his power was deciding when people got their mail?

My grace is sufficient for thee: for My strength is made perfect in weakness.

The Bible verse simply popped into his mind, to his astonishment. He knew he shouldn't be surprised that God would answer him, and yet he still was. He offered up silent thanks for the reminder that it was God's power that mattered, not his own. He also apologised for being surprised.

"God is with us," he whispered into Amy's hair. "He won't let you down. And for what it's worth, neither will I."

She wiped at her eyes. "Why do you care so much? Everything you've done for me, losing your job, and now you're in jail because of me."

"We talked about this yesterday, remember?"

"I know, but you haven't just done this because God told you to help me. I think you care about me. Don't you?"

He swallowed, his mouth suddenly dry. "Yes, I do."

"Why?"

It was the perfect chance to tell her he loved her. Well, maybe jail wasn't the best place, but she'd given him the opportunity. All he had to do was say the words. *I love you. I've loved you almost since the day I met you. Stay and become my wife and I will spend the rest of my life doing everything in my power to make you happy.*

"Because..." *Tell her!* "Because..." *Just say it!* "Because we're friends, and friends care about each other." *Coward.*

She seemed to consider his words, then lay her head

204

back against him and whispered, "You're the best thing that's ever happened to me."

He tightened his arms around her and felt her relax against him. He hoped she couldn't hear his heart thudding in his chest.

He couldn't tell her, not now, not in a jail cell with the threat of a trial hanging over her head and the man who'd made her life unbearable in the hotel just down the street. They'd get through this first, then he'd tell her.

Definitely then.

Chapter 26

Word travelled fast in Green Hill Creek and within an hour Amy and Adam were receiving visitors.

George had already brought them some items from home that they'd need; books, paper and pencils, clothing, towels, soap.

Amy almost giggled at the hint of colour on his cheeks and the awkward way he'd said, "It's all in there," and then cleared his throat when he handed Amy the bag of clothing, including undergarments, she'd asked him to fetch for her.

Adam rigged up a sheet across the corner of the cell to give her privacy to wash and change and it felt good to get out of the clothes she'd been working in all day. By the time Pastor and Mrs Jones arrived Amy felt almost normal, other than being locked up in a jail cell. Without Adam with her, she knew she would have been terrified.

"We have the whole church praying for you," Pastor Jones said. "The Lord is with you, I know that for a fact."

Mrs Jones nodded vehemently.

The support was unexpected and a complete surprise to Amy. "But you don't even know if I'm guilty."

"We know you're a good person," Mrs Jones said. "Whatever happened, we're not here to judge, just to show God's love in a difficult world."

During her life Amy had met a number of pastors back in the big city. Some of them had been good, some of them hadn't, and she knew well there were people who claimed to speak for God and yet didn't. Jaded as she'd become over the years, however, it was still painful when someone who should have been a refuge turned out to be as selfish and cruel as everyone else. The Jones' unwavering support and concern was like a balm to her soul.

At around six Amy heard voices coming from the main office. One of them was Marshal Cade. The other sounded very familiar. "Is that Mrs Goodwin?"

Adam looked up from his book. "Sounds like it."

A minute later the door to the cells opened and the marshal walked in carrying a wooden tray covered in a cloth. The smell preceded him.

Amy and Adam looked at each other and grinned, saying together, "Mrs Goodwin."

"I see you have also had the immense pleasure of Mrs Goodwin's cooking," Marshal Cade said as he balanced the tray on one hand and unlocked their cell with the other.

Adam stood and took the tray from him. "I didn't know Mrs G provided meals for the jail."

The marshal leaned against the open doorway, hooking his thumbs into his belt loops. "I don't have the budget for the hotel and there is no way I'm giving any business to the saloon. So it was either hire her or I'd have to do it. Although come to think of it, my cooking might be more of a deterrent to criminal behaviour than the threat of being locked up. But Mrs Goodwin also brings me and Fred a meal, so my motives aren't real pure." He smiled. "Enjoy your food."

As the marshal left, Adam held out his hands for Amy's and closed his eyes. "Lord, You know how Amy and I are feeling and You know it isn't easy being here and not knowing what's going to happen, but I know that You're here with us. Help me to let go of my fears and trust You, and thank You for letting me be in here with Amy and for bringing her into my life. And thank You for Mrs Goodwin and her wonderful cooking. In Jesus' Name, Amen."

Amy whispered a shaky, "Amen." When she opened her eyes, Adam was watching her.

He let go of her hand and brushed a tear from her cheek. "Please don't cry."

"How can you be grateful for me when I've landed you in jail? If it wasn't for me none of this would be happening and you'd be in your own home."

"I'd much rather be in jail with you than at home on my own." A smile lit his face. "Besides, Mrs G's cooking is well worth being locked up for."

She laughed softly and wiped at her eyes. "Better not tell anyone or Marshal Cade will have people clamouring to get in here."

~ ~ ~

Two hours after the delicious supper, the marshal walked into the cell room.

"I'm off for the night," he said, unlocking the door and handing Adam the kerosene lamp that had been lit earlier against the falling light. "I'm really not supposed to give this to you, but I figure I can trust the two of you to not try to burn the place down. Deputy Fielding's on duty tonight so just give a yell if you need anything."

Adam didn't know Eric Fielding well. He'd come to town a little after Marshal Cade, having served under him during the war, and had married a local girl. But Adam knew that if Lee Cade trusted the man, he could too.

"Thanks, Marshal."

Cade sighed and shook his head. "I hate keeping the two of you in here. There's just no cause for it, but if I violate the terms of the warrant at all it might affect the trial."

Amy came to stand beside Adam at the door. "I'll be all

right, Marshal, it's only for a couple of days. But does Adam really have to stay too?"

"Yes, he does," Adam said firmly.

"But..."

"I'm not leaving you alone here and that's final." He looked at the marshal. "If you need an excuse to keep me here, I'm willing to go and punch Courtney again. Just say the word."

Cade snorted a laugh. "It's tempting, but I think I can just keep you here on the threat."

Adam heaved a sigh. "Pity."

Amy threw him a stern look. "You're incorrigible." Then she slipped her hand into his and smiled. "Thankfully."

He was *this* close to just giving in to his feelings and kissing her, not caring that the marshal was right there.

"Well," Marshal Cade said loudly, "I'll say goodnight then. Sleep well." Shooting Adam a knowing smile, he locked their cell and walked back into the front office, closing the door behind him.

Adam set the lamp on a small table Deputy Filbert had brought in earlier and joined Amy where she was staring down at one of the cots.

"I don't know if I'll be able to sleep," she said. "I've spent the night in jail a couple of times, when I was living on the streets, and I didn't sleep at all either time. It should have felt safer than sleeping on the street, but it didn't. I guess I felt trapped if anyone tried to get to me." She hugged her arms around herself. "You could have gone home, you know. You could have slept in your own bed."

"You think I could sleep knowing you were in here?" He studied the two cots, an idea forming. "I think we can do something with this."

He dragged one of the cots against the back wall of the cell, opposite the door. It spanned almost the entire width of

209

the tiny area. "Sit," he said, indicating the cot, "and if you could put your feet up too?"

She looked confused, but nevertheless obeyed, pulling her shoes off and setting them beneath the cot then folding her legs next to her.

Adam pulled the other cot in front of hers, pushing them together. He turned off the lamp, leaving the room lit only by the moonlight filtering in through the small window, then he sat, pushed off his shoes and shuffled under the blanket. He stretched out on his side, propping his head up on one elbow and smiling up at her. She followed his lead, lying facing him and pulling the blanket up to her chest.

He took her hands and enveloped them in his, laying his head on the flat pillow and staring into her eyes. "Now anyone who tries to get to you will have to go through me first, and that won't happen. You don't have to be afraid. I'll keep you safe."

A smile crept onto her face. "I believe you."

She did, he could see it in her eyes, even in the dark. She trusted him. He prayed that he would never let her down.

"Goodnight, Adam," she whispered, closing her eyes and snuggling his hands beneath her chin.

"Goodnight, Amy," he replied, his racing heart making him feel anything but tired.

Despite her statement that she wouldn't sleep well, her breathing settled into the deep, slow rhythm of slumber within minutes. Adam lay awake for a long time, watching her.

What would he do if she was convicted at the trial? There was no way he could let her go to the state prison. Worse, what if Courtney somehow wrangled it so she would have to serve any sentence back in New York? Adam's need to keep her safe was like a burning flame inside him. He wouldn't be able to protect her there.

Could he run away with her? Take her to Mexico or Canada where they would be safe? Could he leave his family and live as a fugitive? Would Amy want that?

With a deep sigh, he closed his eyes.

Father, I don't know what to do. I feel like I'm about to burst. Please, don't let this happen. Give the judge compassion and mercy and wisdom. And help me to let go and trust in You.

As he prayed, a feeling of peace washed over him and he felt some of the tension melt away. He opened his eyes to see Amy's beautiful, slumbering face. Being careful not to disturb her, he leaned forward and brushed a light kiss across her forehead.

Then he closed his eyes again and surrendered to sleep.

Chapter 27

The following two days and nights passed remarkably quickly, given that Amy was locked up with Adam in a seven foot square cell and surrounded by bars. Or maybe it was *because* she was locked up with Adam that the time seemed to fly by.

They both had books to read and George brought them his chess set. Amy had always wanted to learn to play and after a while spent teaching her Adam pronounced her a natural, although she was fairly sure he was just saying it to make her feel better. They also had more visitors, but much of their time was spent just the two of them, talking, and Amy loved every second of it.

She had thought she knew a lot about Adam, but it turned out there was so much more to discover. He described his childhood growing up in Green Hill Creek, his parents and five siblings, their move to his grandparents' farm and then his return to the town five years later. His tales of his family made her wish she'd had one of her own.

He even told her briefly about his romance with Daisy which wasn't her favourite part, even though she wanted to know everything about him. Jealousy wasn't an emotion she was comfortable with, so she gave it to the Lord and just enjoyed that Adam was being so open and honest with her. Then she gave the jealousy to the Lord again because she seemed to be having trouble letting it go.

For her own part, Amy talked about her years of

growing up in the orphanage and on the streets of New York, and then her time with the Courtneys, making sure to tell him the good parts as well as the bad so he didn't think her life had been one long tragedy.

Finally, the night before the trial was due to take place they lay on their cots, facing each other.

"So you know my hopes for the future are pretty much a wife and a family," Adam said, blinking sleepily. "What are yours?"

The moonlight filtering through the small window turned his hair jet black, highlighted the contours of his face and transformed the blue of his eyes into liquid silver. Amy didn't know how to answer him. All her hopes and dreams, so uncertain in the past, now rested solely with him.

"I want... I want to belong somewhere," she said. "And I want to be safe and happy."

He gazed into her eyes for a few long seconds before smiling. "We'd better get some sleep, so we're refreshed for tomorrow."

She returned his smile, feeling her eyelids drooping already. "Goodnight."

Just as she drifted off to sleep, she heard Adam whisper, "You belong here."

Chapter 28

Amy smoothed her hand down the front of her green dress then raised it to feel for any hairs that might have strayed from her bun.

She peered into the mirror on the wall of her bedroom. "Do I look all right? Respectable?"

"You look like a fine, upstanding woman," Adam said from across the room.

She sighed and turned away from her reflection to look out the window. She couldn't help wondering if this would be the last time she saw her beautiful view of the mountains. Would she be taken to the jail today? Would she be allowed to come back for her things?

Wrapping her arms around herself, she realised she was shivering. When had it got so cold? As if she'd said it out loud, her shawl was draped around her and Adam's hands rested on her shoulders.

"Don't be scared."

She wiped at a rogue tear. "Easier said than done."

He gently turned her to face him and took her hands, wrapping them in his own, the heat from his skin warming her freezing fingers.

Closing his eyes, he lowered his head. "Dear Father God, thank You for bringing Amy here. Thank You for her courage and her strength and her kindness and thank You for the happiness and joy she's brought into my life. Lord, You know Amy had no choice in what she did, the desperate situation she was in. Please give the judge wisdom and compassion, that he will do the right thing and let her go. Please bring Your justice to this trial. Please give Amy Your strength, courage and peace now, Lord, and help her to feel Your presence with her today. Father, help us to not be afraid and trust in You. In the Name of Your Son, Jesus Christ, Amen."

Amy opened her eyes and threw her arms around him. "Thank you," she said, her voice muffled in the crook of his neck. "For everything."

He held her tight and for a moment, wrapped in his arms, she felt a joy that rose above her circumstances. For that moment, she was soaring like an eagle.

A knock on the door brought her back to earth.

"Miss Watts, Mr Emerson, you ready?"

Adam pressed a kiss to her forehead and stepped back. Amy let him go reluctantly. If she could have, she would have held onto him forever.

Deputy Filbert took up most of the landing outside the bedroom door.

"Thank you for letting me come home to get ready," Amy said, having to crick her neck to look up at him in the confined space.

He nodded, holding his hat against his ample chest. "Don't worry, Miss Watts, Judge Hamilton's a fair man. I'm sure he'll do what's right."

Amy hoped he was correct, but fear still coiled its cold tendrils around her gut as she followed the deputy marshal down the stairs and through the post office to the street. George was waiting outside, scowling at everyone looking in their direction, and he and Adam took their places either side of her as they walked through the town towards the hotel where the trial would be held.

It felt as if the whole town was scattered along their route and Amy had a deep urge to run away and hide as they walked along the busy street. A sizeable crowd was gathered at the entrance to the hotel.

First she was a harlot, now a thief. She couldn't help wondering how, even if she was acquitted, she would be able to stay here. Adam had already lost his job at the bank because of her, could he also lose his position as postmaster? Lose his home? Would George suffer because she worked for him? The thought of having to leave was more painful even than the thought of going to jail, but she wasn't at all sure she would have a choice. She couldn't hurt Adam and George, not anymore.

Inside the hotel the small ballroom had been crammed with chairs, every one of which was occupied. Amy clutched her hands together as she followed Deputy Filbert to the front.

She saw friendly faces; Sara, Lizzie, Jo and Louisa were together, sitting near Pastor and Mrs Jones, Daisy and other members of the church. She also saw unfriendly faces, first and foremost Mr and Mrs Vernon who sat off to one side making no effort at all to hide their disapproval. The majority of those present seemed in agreement with them, judging by the looks Amy received from the gathered spectators.

Deputy Filbert showed her to a table at the front with a single chair. Adam and George sat behind her in the front row of seating where Marshal Cade had apparently saved them the two chairs beside him.

Mr Courtney was already seated at another table to her right. With him was his lawyer, Mr Williamson, who Amy had seen a few times at the house in New York. One night a few months previously, when Courtney had invited a few of his upper class, boorish friends for drinks, and more drinks, the inebriated lawyer had tried to corner Amy in the hallway. After almost a lifetime of escaping tight situations she'd had no trouble escaping his clumsy advances, and the next time she'd seen him sober he had apologised profusely and with much embarrassment and pleading that she never tell his wife. Nevertheless, being anywhere near the man still made her uncomfortable.

In front of the wall facing her was a long table with several unoccupied chairs tucked in behind. After a few minutes a door in the wall beyond the table opened and two men walked out. The first was dressed in a black suit and long black coat and appeared to be in his early fifties, although it was hard to tell with much of his face hidden behind the biggest, bushiest moustache Amy had ever seen. It dominated his face, stretching from his upper lip to his extensive sideburns, and she couldn't help wondering if he was married how he ever managed to kiss his wife around the astounding facial hair. Surely she would be suffocated in the thing.

The whole effect was somewhat intimidating and Amy had to clutch her hands together in her lap beneath the table to stop them from trembling.

The second, younger man carried a pile of papers which he placed on the table in front of the judge as he pulled out a chair in the centre of the row and sat, placing a gavel next to the papers. The younger man took a chair to the far left of the table. Amy guessed he was the judge's clerk. He was clean-shaven, probably to provide a little balance.

Courtney rose from his seat, strolled up to the judge's table and held out his hand. "Your Honour, I'm Franklin Courtney, the wronged party in this trial. I'd like to thank you for hearing the case so promptly. I believe we have a mutual friend in New York city, Judge Matthew Farley? We're both members of the same gentleman's club. He mentioned you and he went to law school together."

Ignoring the hand hovering in front of him, Judge Hamilton glanced up at Courtney. "Ah yes, Farley. How is

217

the self-serving, spineless bigot?"

"Uh..." Courtney's hand dropped to his side. He gave a nervous laugh. "I, erm, don't really know him that well, to be honest. Just in passing. Haven't seen him in months."

The judge lowered his eyes to the paperwork in front of him. "Please take a seat, Mr Courtney. It's against regulations for me to speak with either the plaintiff or defendant before a trial."

"Of course it is. You wouldn't want any accusations of partiality." Courtney laughed again. Judge Hamilton didn't look up. "So I'll just go and sit down then." He backed away, turned and walked rapidly back to his chair.

A few minutes of silence from the judge followed. The assembled crowd, who had quietened when the judge and his clerk entered, began to murmur. Amy glanced back at Adam and he smiled encouragingly. She tried to feel encouraged.

Finally, the judge looked up, took hold of the gavel on the table before him and pounded it three times onto the wooden surface. There were gasps of surprise from the crowd. Someone yelped. Amy couldn't be sure, but she thought she saw the hint of a smile beneath the huge moustache.

The clerk rose to his feet. "Court is now in session. Judge Ebenezer Hamilton presiding."

For a small, wiry man, he had a voice that cut through the air like the crack of a bullet. The room silenced instantly.

"All right," the judge's voice boomed through the room, "let's get this trial started. For those who've never attended a trial before, what I say here goes. You may address me as Judge Hamilton or Your Honour. All those in the audience, you are here as spectators, not participants, so keep your opinions to yourselves. Keep to those rules and we will all get along fine." He looked down at the papers again. "Mr Franklin Courtney, I see you've brought your lawyer with you." He fixed his gaze on Courtney's lawyer and raised his eyebrows which were almost as impressive as his moustache.

Mr Williamson stood, said, "Arthur Williamson, esquire, Your Honour," and sat again.

Judge Hamilton moved his eyes to Amy. "Miss Watts, do you have legal counsel?"

"Um, no, Sir. I mean, Your Honour." Was she supposed to stand when she spoke to him? He didn't correct her, so she assumed not.

He nodded. "Have you ever been to a trial before?"

"No, Your Honour."

"Well, what will happen is that Mr Williamson will detail the charges against you and call any witnesses or present any evidence he may have. You'll have the opportunity to give your own defence. I'll let you know when it's your turn to do that."

"Thank you, Your Honour." Amy relaxed just a little. Despite his imposing appearance, the judge seemed kind. She hoped he was fair as well.

"Right," he said, leaning back in his chair, "let's hear it, Mr Williamson."

Courtney's lawyer stood and walked from behind the table. "Your Honour, we will show that Miss Amy Watts, when in the employ of my client, Mr Franklin Courtney, stole the sum of seventy-five dollars from him, absconding with the money across the country here to Green Hill Creek."

"Well, go ahead and show me then," Judge Hamilton said.

The lawyer seemed slightly thrown. Maybe they did things differently here than he was used to in New York. "Uh, yes, Your Honour. I'd like to call Mr Franklin Courtney to the witness... um..." He looked around. "...stand?"

Judge Hamilton inclined his head to a chair at the opposite end of the table to where the clerk sat.

Williamson looked at the simple seat as though it had offended him in some way. "Ah, yes." He gestured for Courtney to take the seat. "Sir."

Marshal Cade rose and walked forward with a large, leather bound Bible in his hand and held it out to Courtney. "Place your left hand on..."

"Yes, yes, I know what to do," Courtney snapped, putting one hand on the Bible and raising the other. The marshal was clearly not on his list of favourite people.

"Do you swear to tell the truth, the whole truth and nothing but the truth, so help you God?"

Courtney lifted his chin in an attempt to look down on the taller man. "I do."

Williamson walked forward as Marshal Cade returned to his seat. "Mr Courtney, would you describe to us the details of Miss Watts' employ in your household and the circumstances of the theft?"

Courtney smiled, clearly revelling in the rapt attention of the assembled townsfolk. "I certainly will."

What followed was a litany of lies and half-truths about Amy's time working for the Courtneys. He peppered her years of service with thinly concealed allusions to other thefts and deceits, made it sound like his deep kindness was all that had kept her in his employ, and even accused her of trying to seduce him on more than one occasion. Amy had to clamp her lips together and sit on her hands to stop herself from leaping up and shouting that none of it was true. She kept darting glances at the people behind her. Adam and George and her friends looked angry with Courtney, but most of the rest of the people appeared either shocked or were nodding and whispering to each other as they looked at her, as if to say yes, we knew all along she was no good.

Amy looked down at the table in front of her and tried to shut out the sound of Courtney's lies. What was the purpose for his coming all the way here? Why couldn't he have just let her be? It wasn't like the money she'd taken meant anything to him, he had more than enough to squander for the rest of his life. The train ticket for him to come here alone would have cost double what she'd taken.

Finally, after an entirely fabricated tale of how she'd been seen stealing the money from Courtney's office, Williamson handed a piece of paper to the judge. "Your Honour, this is a signed statement from another of Mr Courtney's staff, Mr James Sutton, that he witnessed the theft."

Amy looked up at that. How did Courtney dare to drag James into this? The man had no hint of morals. Didn't he fear God at all?

Mr Courtney stood and returned to his seat, casting a smug look in her direction. A desperate desire to claw his eyes out swept over her and she quietly asked God to forgive her and help her to forgive Courtney. Eventually.

"Do you have any more witnesses, Mr Williamson?" Judge Hamilton said.

"Yes, Your Honour. I'd like to call Miss Amy Watts to the stand."

She looked up in surprise. Could he do that? Would she get to tell her side now?

The judge indicated the chair Courtney had just vacated. "Miss Watts, would you sit here?"

She rose on shaky legs and looked back at Adam. He gave her a smile and she tried to take courage from it, but her heart was pounding as she walked to the seat, said her oath on the Bible, and sat.

Mr Williamson walked up to her. "Miss Watts, I'm going to ask you one question and I remind you before you answer that you are under oath before God."

Maybe he should have reminded Courtney of that, she

221

thought.

"I understand."

"Did you take the sum of seventy-five dollars from the office of your employer, Mr Franklin Courtney, without his permission?"

Amy took a deep breath in and out. "Yes."

Shocked voices rose around the room. Mr Williamson looked taken aback, his eyebrows reaching for his receding hairline. Clearly it wasn't the answer he had been expecting.

The judge's gavel banged hard three times on the table. "I will have order in my courtroom." When the hubbub only receded a little, he barked, "Either shut up or be thrown out!"

The noise died almost as rapidly as it had started.

"Uh... well..." Williamson looked back at Courtney then at Amy. "Well, in that case the prosecution rests." Raising his shoulders in a slight shrug, he returned to his chair next to Courtney.

"Miss Watts," the judge said, "would you like to say anything in your defence?"

"Yes, Your Honour."

He nodded for her to proceed, the moustache bouncing a little as he did so.

Amy looked out at the people in the room, the people she had hoped would become neighbours and friends. By their expressions, most of them had condemned her already. She moved her gaze to Adam and he smiled again. Even under the circumstances, it warmed her.

Help me, Lord Jesus. Give me the words to say.

She looked at the judge. "First of all, James Sutton couldn't have written that statement. James is a lovely, kind man and a hard worker, but he has a bit of trouble with thinking sometimes and he can't read or write. He also wasn't anywhere near when I took the money. He works in the stables. He's not even allowed in the main house."

222

Judge Hamilton looked at Mr Williamson. "Is this true?"

Williamson leaned sideways to whisper to Courtney. Courtney whispered back.

"Yes, Your Honour, it's true that he didn't write it himself. However, those are his words, as dictated."

The judge looked at the paper on which was written James' alleged statement. "'I observed Miss Watts move with all stealth into the office and abscond with the money secreted on her person.' Quite a statement for a feebleminded man, wouldn't you say? And if Mr Sutton can't write, this is not, in fact, a *signed* witness statement. Is that correct?"

Williamson and Courtney exchanged whispers again. Amy wasn't surprised Courtney would make such an error. She doubted he'd even met James, much less spoken to him. It made her angry that he would use the lovely, innocent man to further his lies, assuming he would go along with anything he was told if it came to it. James was the sweetest person she'd ever met and would be utterly distressed if he found out. She hoped he never did.

"The statement is paraphrased, Your Honour," Williamson said. "And it would appear that no, it is not his actual signature on the document."

"Then unless it was your intention to mislead me you should have said that in the first place," Judge Hamilton said, his stupendous moustache and eyebrows joining together in a deep frown. "This may not be the sophisticated, enlightened city of New York, but we try to dispense justice just the same."

A momentary look of panic crossed Mr Williamson's face, as if he was a child who'd been caught with his hand in the cookie jar. "Yes, Your Honour. I mean no, Your Honour; it wasn't my intention to mislead you. At all."

The judge returned his attention to Amy. "You may continue, Miss Watts."

223

She swallowed and surreptitiously wiped her palms on her skirt as all the moisture seemed to leave her mouth and migrate to her hands. The last thing she'd ever wanted to do was tell anyone about what had happened to her. Even telling Adam had been difficult and she trusted him more than anyone in the world. Now she was faced with the whole town knowing her shame. But she was left with no other options. The truth was the only weapon she had on her side.

"I started work for Mr and Mrs Courtney when I was fourteen, straight out of the orphanage..."

She tried to keep her focus on Judge Hamilton as she spoke, specifically on the moustache as it had become a bizarrely comforting presence, but she couldn't help darting glances towards Adam for support. And as she spoke about her experiences, and especially what had happened when she confronted Mr Courtney in his office, she noticed people starting to cast disapproving looks at her former employer. When she related how he'd attempted to bribe her into going to his bed and then tried to force her when she refused, a murmur of anger rippled through the room.

Finally reaching the end of her sorry tale with her arrest and imprisonment, Amy lapsed into silence, staring at her hands in her lap and feeling as if she'd been drawn through a mangle. If there'd been any thought that telling her story would give her a sense of release, it no longer remained. All she felt was drained.

"Thank you, Miss Watts," Judge Hamilton's moustache-filtered voice broke into her thoughts. "Do you have anything else to say or any witnesses you would like to call?"

"No, Your Honour."

"Very well, you may return to your seat. I will retire to deliberate..."

"Pardon me, but may I say something?"

Amy looked up in surprise at the woman's voice coming

from the back of the room. It couldn't possibly be her, could it?

A woman in her mid-forties rose to her feet from a seat by the door and walked towards the front of the room. Her light brown hair was gathered into an elaborate style on the back of her head and she wore a dark blue travel dress with acres of fabric, most of it behind her.

Mr Courtney's jaw dropped. "*Millicent?*"

"Forgive me, Your Honour, but I would like to testify."

Judge Hamilton raised his eyebrows. "And you are...?"

"Mrs Millicent Courtney, Your Honour. Wife of Franklin Courtney."

Courtney and Williamson were whispering frantically to each other.

"Were you witness to Miss Watts taking the money in question?" the judge said.

"No, Your Honour, I wasn't home at the time, but I believe I can clarify the circumstances."

He shrugged. "Well, if no one has any objections..."

"We object, Your Honour," Williamson said, leaping to his feet.

Amy had no idea what was going on. Why would Courtney object to his wife testifying? Surely she was there to back him up.

"On what grounds, Mr Williamson?" Judge Hamilton said.

Williamson's strained smile made him look like he'd just sat on a pin. "Mrs Courtney stated she wasn't there when the crime occurred. What can she possibly have to add?"

"Oh, shut up, Williamson," Mrs Courtney said. "As usual, you have no idea what you're talking about."

Courtney's lawyer looked like he didn't know whether to be angry or apologetic. "Madam..."

"I'm going to allow her to testify," the judge said. "A

225

young woman's freedom is at stake; I want as much information as I can get before I take it from her. Miss Watts, you may return to your seat."

Amy walked back to her table. Adam shrugged and shook his head. George's gaze was fixed on Mrs Courtney.

She took the oath and sat, crossing her ankles and folding her gloved hands in her lap. "Your Honour, if you attended law school in New York, perhaps you know my father, Judge Leonard Ravensworth?"

The moustache tilted up at the corners. "Sadly I never had the pleasure of meeting Judge Ravensworth, but his reputation and integrity are legendary. How is he?"

"Retired now, but as robust and active as ever."

"That's good to hear. I've always regarded him as a credit to the judiciary. It's an honour to meet you, Mrs Courtney."

She smiled. "Thank you, Judge Hamilton."

At the sound of a loud huff, Amy looked over at Courtney. His arms were crossed over his chest and he was glaring.

"Please, Mrs Courtney," Judge Hamilton said, "in your own time."

"First of all I'd like to apologise for my appearance. I arrived on the train not half an hour ago and I haven't had time to go to my room to freshen up. I'm a mess."

"If that's her in a mess," Amy heard George mutter, "what's she look like gussied up?"

"I can confirm that when we brought Amy from the orphanage, she was indeed promised that her wages would be set aside and given to her when she reached the age of twenty-one. It was the same for other girls we employed from the orphanage. I have been spending a lot of time away from home and I had assumed that this was being done in my absence. I now see that I should have been paying closer attention to affairs my husband said he was overseeing."

Mr Williamson stood abruptly. "Your Honour, may I once again point out that this has no relevance to..."

"Sit *down*, Mr Williamson," Judge Hamilton snapped.

"Yes, Your Honour." Courtney's lawyer sank back into his chair and was immediately accosted by Courtney whispering angrily into his ear.

"Please, Mrs Courtney," the judge said, "continue."

"As I said, I was not at home when the incident with the money occurred so I cannot comment on that. However..." She sighed and looked at Mr Courtney. "I can say that I am not terribly surprised to hear about my husband's behaviour towards Miss Watts."

A shocked murmur rippled around the crowd.

"It causes me no little shame to admit this, but my husband's philandering is not unknown to me. He frequents drinking establishments and houses of ill repute with no regard for propriety."

"I saw him go into the saloon!" someone shouted from the back of the room.

"Me too!"

"Quiet, please," the judge said as more people spoke up.

"I didn't think he would ever go so far as to try to force himself on someone," Mrs Courtney continued, "but I have no reason to doubt Miss Watts' veracity that he did." When she moved her eyes to look at Amy, Amy was surprised to see them shimmering with tears. "I'm so sorry."

Amy drew in a shuddering breath and nodded, feeling a sudden affinity for the woman. It seemed she wasn't Courtney's only victim.

"Thank you, Mrs Courtney, for your testimony," Judge Hamilton said. "You may return to your seat."

There was half a minute of silence as Mrs Courtney returned to the back of the room and Judge Hamilton looked

227

through his papers.

Finally he looked up and said, "I'm going to take a little time to deliberate my verdict. The trial will resume in one hour."

With that he stood and left through the door by which he'd entered, his clerk on his heels. A few seconds later Courtney and Williamson rushed past Amy towards the exit, angry glares and a few choice words from members of the crowd following them. At least some had believed Amy's testimony.

She looked around. What was she supposed to do now?

Marshal Cade ambled up to her. "Well, Miss Watts, Mr Emerson, it's coming up on lunchtime. How about we get ourselves a bite in the restaurant here?"

Amy didn't know whether to laugh or cry. "You're supposed to make sure I don't try to run away, aren't you?"

"And I was trying to be subtle," he said, smiling. "Look on the bright side, because it's work related I will be paying for the food from the marshal's office funds."

Adam stood and offered Amy his arm. "Would you care to join me in a meal courtesy of local law enforcement?" He looked at the marshal. "You are paying for me too, right?"

Marshal Cade grinned. "Why not? George, you want to come along?"

"Hmm?" George was scanning the crowd.

"I think she left already, George," Adam said.

He looked back at them. "Um, what? Who?"

Adam was obviously fighting a smile. "Mrs Courtney, she left already."

"She, um, I wasn't..."

"Come on, George," Amy said, reaching out to him with the arm not entwined with Adam's. "She'll be back for the verdict. Come and eat with me. It might be the last chance I get."

She'd meant it as a joke, but the sad look he gave her set off an ache in her chest.

"Don't say that, girl. No decent judge would send you to jail."

As she slipped her arm into his and the four of them headed for the hotel restaurant, she hoped George was right. And that Judge Hamilton was as decent as he seemed.

Chapter 29

Amy, Adam, George and Marshal Cade returned to the ballroom/makeshift courtroom fifty-five minutes later.

Mr Courtney and Mr Williamson were already at their table. Courtney kept darting nervous glances at the people behind him as if he expected them to leap up and lynch him at any moment. The tide of opinion had undoubtedly turned against him. At least there was that.

Five minutes later Judge Hamilton walked in, the clerk with him as usual. Amy's heartbeat quickened. Was this it? Would this be her last few minutes of freedom before she was sent to jail for who knew how long?

"Please stand, Miss Watts," Judge Hamilton said from his seat at the long table.

Amy pushed her chair back and stood on weak legs, clasping her hands in front of her to hide the tremble. She looked back at Adam and he smiled, but it failed to reach his eyes. Even though she knew it was selfish of her under the circumstances, she couldn't help but wish she'd married him when she had the chance. Of all the mistakes she'd made in her life, that was the one she regretted the most.

"Miss Amy Watts," Judge Hamilton said, "I have spent much time deliberating my course of action in this case. The treatment you received while in the employ of Mr Courtney was undoubtedly appalling and something no person, man or woman, should have to endure. However, whether or not you were owed the money the fact remains that you did take the sum of seventy-five dollars without permission. I therefore have no choice but to find you guilty of theft."

Amy stopped breathing. She grasped the table in front of her as she swayed.

"Justice!" Courtney exclaimed, his face splitting into a wide smile. He grasped his lawyer's hand and shook it.

Around the room, voices rose in protest, George and Adam's among them.

The judge's gavel returned order. "I will have silence for the sentencing!"

"I'm willing to drop the complaint and spare her jail if she returns to my employ," Courtney said magnanimously, with a leering smile he probably thought looked charming.

"Over your dead body," George growled.

"Mr Courtney," Judge Hamilton said, "this is my court and I will do the sentencing."

"Sorry, Your Honour," Courtney said, looking not at all sorry. "Please, carry on."

The moustache glowered at him for a moment before the judge returned his attention to Amy. "Miss Watts, for the crime of theft I hereby sentence you to two days incarceration, to include time already served. As you've already been in jail for more than two days, you are free to go. And I trust you will lead an upright and lawful life from this point on." One side of the moustache hitched up a little.

Amy's eyes widened. Had she heard correctly? She looked back at Adam and George and the grins on their faces told her she had. She closed her eyes and breathed out. *Thank You, Lord. Thank You.*

"What? No!" Courtney was staring at the judge in disbelief, his jaw hanging open. "You can't do that!"

"I can and I just have," Judge Hamilton said. "In addition, I have to ask you, Miss Watts, if you wish to bring charges against Mr Courtney. If you do, I'm quite happy to have him arrested and returned to New York to stand trial." He fixed Courtney with a withering stare. "You're not the only one with friends in the judiciary system on the east coast, Courtney. I don't take kindly to those who think they can use the justice system for their own ends."

Courtney's mouth flapped up and down like a fish trying to breathe on dry land. He looked from the judge to Amy and back again.

Amy stared at the man who had made her afraid for so many years, teeth clamped together so tight her jaw began to ache. She wanted to do it, to have him arrested and tried and thrown into prison. She wanted to make him suffer for what he'd done to her.

Forgive others as I have forgiven you.

The words were there, in the back of her mind, behind the anger and need for revenge. And quiet as they were, she knew she had to obey.

"No, Your Honour," she said. "I think I would just like to move on and forget I ever knew him."

"As you wish. I have to say, you're more forgiving than I would be." He looked at Courtney. "Well, Mr Courtney, it looks like you've got lucky. I suggest you go home and..."

"Just a moment." Mrs Courtney rose from her seat and walked forward. "Miss Watts may be willing to let this go, and I don't blame her one bit for simply wanting a quiet life from now on, but I'm not. I'm sure there are other girls who would like a crack at my husband and after too many years of neglecting my household I intend to help every single one of them."

The corners of the judge's moustache reached for his eyebrows. "In that case, Marshal Cade, would you take Mr Courtney into custody and keep him until he can be escorted back to New York?"

The marshal advanced on Courtney, Deputy Filbert at

232

his side. "With pleasure, Your Honour."

Panic twisted Courtney's face. "But Millicent, darling," he pleaded, smiling at his wife while struggling against the Deputy's steely grip. "I love you. You can't just throw away our marriage like this. Think of all the good times we've had."

She tapped one finger on her lips, staring at the ceiling. "I'm trying, but do you know I can't remember a single one."

George snorted a laugh. Mrs Courtney glanced at him and smiled, her cheeks taking on a slight pink tinge.

Marshal Cade jerked Courtney's hands behind him and pushed his wrists into handcuffs.

Courtney moved his attention to his lawyer who was packing papers into his satchel. "Arthur, do something!"

"Franklin, my advice to you is to close your mouth and don't say anything more. And when you get back to New York, find yourself another lawyer."

Courtney glared at him. "You can't do this to me! I'll get you expelled from the club. I'll... I'll have you blackballed in every society establishment. I'll..."

He continued to shout threats as Marshal Cade and Deputy Filbert dragged him, struggling, from the room.

Amy was still standing at the table, overwhelmed and slightly stunned. She couldn't quite believe it was all over and that she was free, not just of her incarceration, but of Courtney.

She was finally, truly free.

A hand wrapped gently around her arm and even without turning she knew who it was. Looking up into Adam's face, she desperately wanted to sink into his arms, her place of comfort and safety. But there were so many people in the room and she didn't want to besmirch her reputation now it was just beginning to improve. All around them the trial's audience were rising from their seats, the hubbub rising with them as they discussed the events of the morning.

"Miss Watts?" Judge Hamilton emerged from behind his table and walked towards her.

Amy wanted to hug him too, although for entirely different reasons. "Thank you, Your Honour. I can't begin to tell you how grateful I am."

The moustache waggled. "I became a judge for days like these, Miss Watts. I should probably be thanking you. I hope you can build a good life for yourself here."

She resisted the urge to look at Adam. "Thank you, Sir."

"I thought you might like to know that I will be presiding over a trial next week for a Mr Ely whose alleged crimes, among many other things, include attacking a young woman in the livery here in Green Hill Creek a few days ago. I thought you might like to know that, although I will obviously hear all the evidence with impartiality, considering what I've read so far it's likely he will be gracing the state prison with his presence for a very long time." The moustache quivered and creases appeared around his eyes. "I also thought you'd like to know that, according to reports, he still can't walk straight."

Amy clamped her teeth together to stop herself from laughing. Next to her, Adam chuckled and George barked a loud "Ha!" that startled everyone in the vicinity.

"If you'll excuse me, Miss Watts." Judge Hamilton gave her a small bow, waved at his clerk to follow, and disappeared into the crowd.

"Well, praise the Lord," George said. "I don't think..."

He stopped abruptly, his eyes focused beyond Amy. She looked round to see Mrs Courtney walking towards them. George cleared his throat, his hands twisting his hat in front of him.

"Miss Watts," Mrs Courtney said, "I just wanted to say

again how sorry I am. And I would very much like to speak with you in private later, if that's all right? Whenever you're free."

"Of course," Amy said. "After this we'll be going straight home so any time will be fine. It's the post office down the road." She indicated Adam and George. "May I present Mr Adam Emerson and Mr George Parsons."

George gave her a nervous smile. "It's a pleasure to meet you, Ma'am."

"We're very grateful for what you did here today," Adam said.

Mrs Courtney sighed. "It was something I should have done a long time ago."

George cleared his throat for a second time. "May I escort you to wherever you're headed for now, Mrs Courtney, Ma'am?"

She smiled and lowered her gaze demurely. "Well, I was only planning to return to my room, but perhaps you could show me around your lovely town, Mr Parsons? This is my first trip out west and I'm eager to see everything. If you have the time, of course."

George's face lit up. "I would be honoured, ma'am. Do you like horses? We could start at my livery."

Amy couldn't remember George ever looking so buoyant. He offered Mrs Courtney his arm and walked her through the thinning crowd with his head held high. With George's usual plaid flannel shirt and battered denim trousers and Mrs Courtney's blue bustled travel dress and fashionable tiny hat, they made a strange looking pair.

It was some time before Amy and Adam left the hotel. A steady stream of people came to offer their congratulations/commiserations. Amy even experienced her first five woman group hug surrounded by Sara, Lizzy, Louisa and Jo. When they let go she had to wipe tears from her eyes.

She was free, she had friends, people who cared for her, a job she loved.

And then there was Adam.

As the final few stragglers left the room she went to where he was waiting for her on a chair against the wall and sat next to him.

"That was quite a morning," he said.

She leaned against him, resting her head on his shoulder and yawning. "Yes."

He took her hand, entwining their fingers. "Let's go home and you can get some rest."

"I'm fine. It's just the strain catching up with me." The last few words were garbled in another yawn. She suddenly felt very tired.

Adam gave a soft chuckle and squeezed her hand. "Come on, before I have to carry you home."

She ducked her head to hide her blush and smile. Being carried in Adam's strong arms didn't sound so bad. His nearness and the feel of his fingers wrapped around hers was making her blood rush.

He stood, pulling her up with him, and offered her his arm. She slipped her hand into the crook of his elbow and they headed for the door.

Chapter 30

Amy started awake and grimaced, placing a hand to her aching head. She hadn't meant to fall asleep.

She was lying on the settee in the parlour, beneath a blanket she didn't remember fetching. Across from her, Adam was rising from the armchair.

"How long was I asleep?"

"A couple of hours, more or less. The knock must have woken you." He walked towards the door leading to the post office.

"Knock?" Her groggy brain finally roused itself. "Mrs Courtney! I must look a mess." She scrambled to untangle herself from the blanket, sit up, and smooth her hair and clothing all at the same time.

"You look perfectly fine," he said, glancing back. "I'll go let her in. Just relax, she's not your employer any more, remember?"

She folded the blanket quickly, listening to Adam answer the door. Mrs Courtney may not have been her employer, but she still made Amy nervous. Other than when Amy had first arrived from the orphanage she'd never interacted much with Mrs Courtney, with her being away so often. Amy wasn't sure what to expect. The fact that she'd come all this way to help her indicated she was a good woman, but being married to Mr Courtney said otherwise. How anyone could want to marry such a scoundrel, Amy couldn't imagine. Mrs Courtney's actions confused her no end, but it was very likely she had been part of the reason Amy had her freedom now, so she couldn't be all bad.

"Thank you so much for the wonderful afternoon, Mr Parsons," Mrs Courtney said as she walked into the room, George following. "I had so much fun. Perhaps we could do it again?"

His hat clutched in his hands, George was smiling in a very un-George like fashion. "I'd be right pleased if we did, Ma'am."

Mrs Courtney beamed at him and Amy watched, fascinated, as his ears turned a vibrant pink.

He swallowed and moved his attention to Amy. "How you feeling, girl?"

"Much better. I'll be back to work tomorrow."

"There's no rush, whenever you're ready." He nodded to Mrs Courtney, said, "Ma'am," and turned to leave, almost bumping into Adam behind him.

Amy couldn't help smiling at his flustered behaviour. It was so thoroughly out of character.

"Would you like something to drink?" she said to Mrs Courtney as Adam walked George out.

"A glass of water would be wonderful," she said as she removed her hat and fanned herself with it. "It's certainly warm here. But so beautiful. Mr Parsons took me on a buggy ride into the country and the mountains took my breath away."

"I thought the same thing when I arrived," Amy said, gesturing for her to sit.

She went to fetch the water as Adam walked back in.

"I'll give the two of you some privacy," he said, heading for the stairs. "If there's anything you need, Mrs Courtney, just ask."

"Thank you, Mr Emerson."

He smiled at Amy and left the room, closing the door

behind him. Amy brought two glasses of water to the settee, handing one to Mrs Courtney.

"What a lovely young man," she said after taking a drink. A sparkle lit her eyes. "And so handsome."

Amy lowered her gaze, fighting a blush. "Yes."

Mrs Courtney placed her glass onto the small table next to her and folded her hands in her lap. "I want to thank you for agreeing to see me. I wouldn't have blamed you at all if you hadn't wanted to come anywhere near me ever again."

Amy wasn't sure what to say to that, so she kept silent.

"I know that I was lax in my duties to look after you and the other girls who worked in my house and you will never know how sorry I am for that. I should have known what was going on. I should have taken responsibility." She breathed a deep sigh, shaking her head. "I had so many dreams. At the beginning I just wanted to help, to give girls like you an opportunity to work and learn and have a better start in life."

She seemed genuinely distressed. Amy felt a twinge of sympathy.

"If you don't mind me asking, what happened?"

"My marriage happened," she answered, her voice tinged with bitterness. "I married Franklin rather late in life. I was engaged once before, when I was young and very much in love, but he was killed in a carriage accident and I thought I would never love again. Then when I was thirty-eight and had long since resigned myself to a life of spinsterhood, Franklin Courtney came along and swept me off my feet. I had thought I'd grown beyond such things, but it turns out infatuation is no respecter of age. He was charming and exciting and I thought I was in love. But starting a few months after we were married he began to show his true colours. As it turned out, he was more in love with my money than he was with me, if he ever loved me at all. Over the years he indulged in wine and gambling and women and

239

I spent as little time as possible around him, staying with friends or family to avoid the man I'd married in too much haste and was too much of a coward to leave for fear of the scandal and shame." A tear slid down her face. She wiped at it and moved her gaze to Amy. "I wouldn't have even known you were out here and Franklin was coming after you if I hadn't returned when I did. I hadn't planned to go home, but I woke up with an irresistible urge to do so, thank the Lord, and when I found out what had happened I got on the first train I could. I neglected my duty of care to you and for that I am truly sorry. I hope one day you can forgive me, even though I don't deserve it for leaving you with that despicable man."

Amy knew what it was to be blamed for something that wasn't her fault. There was no way she would do it to another. "Of course I forgive you. It seems to me we were both his victims. But what will you do now?"

Mrs Courtney sighed and sat back, wiping at her eyes. "The first thing I'll do is something I should have done a long time ago; get a divorce."

"What about the other girls in the house? Won't he just go back there?"

A smile stole across Mrs Courtney's face. "Oh, Staveley House doesn't belong to him. My father, bless him, never liked him. When he gave us the house when we married he made sure the deeds were put into my name and could never be altered, as well as assuring it would return to him should I pass on. Franklin doesn't have a penny of his own to his name." Her smile grew. "Even if he gets out of jail, he will be utterly destitute when I throw him out. Perhaps one of his friends at his precious gentleman's club will take him in. Of course, he'll have to drop his membership since he won't be able to afford the fees."

She clapped a hand over her mouth, her shoulders

240

quivering, then collapsed back against the settee and burst into laughter. Amy stared at her in surprise, feeling a giggle welling up inside her. It was only a few moments before she was laughing along with Mrs Courtney.

"Oh my," Mrs Courtney gasped, wiping at her eyes, "I haven't laughed like that in so long. I feel so much lighter. Thank you, Amy. This is the best thing that could have happened to me. I think you have truly set me free."

"The praise goes to God, Mrs Courtney," Amy said. "He brought me here. Looks like He was helping you too."

"I believe you are right. And please, call me Millicent."

Amy smiled. "Millicent."

"Oh, goodness, I mustn't forget the reason I came." She dug inside her reticule, pulled out a bulging envelope and handed it to Amy. "It's everything you are owed for all those years of service and I also added a bit more. I know it can't make up for everything you went through, but hopefully it will help you make a new start here, whatever you choose to do."

Amy gaped at the thick mound of banknotes inside the envelope. She'd never seen so much money in her life. "I... I don't know what to say. This is so much."

"Not a penny more than you deserve," Millicent said. "Now, I won't take up any more of your time. I'm going back to the hotel to rest a little, then I hope you and Mr Emerson will join me for dinner in their wonderful restaurant? My treat, of course."

Amy looked up at her from the envelope, her head still spinning. "I... yes, of course. Can I walk you back?"

"Oh no, it's not far, I can make my own way. Um... I was wondering if you'd like to invite Mr Parsons, if you wouldn't mind and if you think he'd like to, do you think that he would possibly care to join us for dinner?"

Amy felt like laughing all over again. "I think there is a

very good possibility he would."

~ ~ ~

Adam sat in the chair by the window in Amy's bedroom, staring through the glass at the distant mountains. A book lay unopened on his lap.

He wasn't certain why, but Mrs Courtney's visit was making him nervous. He was grateful for what she'd done for Amy, but he wasn't certain of her motivations. What if she wanted Amy to go back to New York with her? With Mr Courtney no longer an issue, what if that was what Amy wanted?

He glanced at the door behind him. Staying down there with them would have been intrusive, but he couldn't help wishing he had. He badly wanted to know what was going on.

Turning back to the window, he gazed out at the mountains again. "Father," he whispered, "please work this all out. You know my heart, how much I love Amy and how much I want her to stay. I know You brought her to me and thank You for giving me the opportunity to help her and, once again, thank You for what You did at the trial. If it's Your will that she should be somewhere else, then I guess I need to accept it, but Lord, I don't want to lose her. So while I'm saying Your will be done, I'm also asking You to please make her stay."

"Adam?"

Hearing footsteps and the creak of the stairs, he drew in a slow, deep breath and rose from the chair, pasting on a smile when Amy appeared at the doorway.

"I hope you don't mind." He indicated the window. "I was just enjoying the view."

"Of course I don't mind. This was your room."

Before she arrived. Before colour and joy and light entered his life. "Has Mrs Courtney left?"

Amy nodded. "So you can come out of hiding now."

He followed her back down the stairs to the parlour and immediately noticed the envelope lying on the table. It made his gut twist.

"It turns out she was as trapped by her husband as I was, in a way," Amy said as she cleaned a glass at the sink. "She seems much happier than I've ever seen her. I think she might be developing a bit of an attraction for George too. I know they've only just met, but wouldn't it be wonderful if they ended up together? After what she's been through with that unfaithful cad of a husband, Millicent needs a good man. And George needs someone too."

Adam lowered into one of the chairs at the table, unable to take his eyes from the envelope. It was bulging, as if it contained a lot of... something. "They would certainly make an interesting couple."

"I never got the chance to really know her when I was in New York. Turns out I like her. I think I'd enjoy having her here."

It took a few seconds for her words to sink in. *I'd enjoy having her here.* Did that mean Amy would be staying? Maybe the envelope didn't contain what he thought it did.

He had to know. "What's this?" He tried to keep his voice light. He wasn't sure he succeeded.

She placed the dry glass upside down in its place on the dresser shelf and came to join him at the table. She slid the envelope across to him. "Take a look."

Swallowing against his suddenly dry mouth, he opened the envelope and looked inside. His heart dropped at the sight of all the money.

"Isn't it amazing?" Amy said. "She said it was all the pay I'm owed for the past seven years, plus more. I don't

243

even know how much is in there."

Having worked in the bank for so long, Adam had a reasonable idea of how much there was. Too much. Far too much.

She took the envelope from his hands, withdrew several notes, and handed them to him. "This is for the train ticket and my board for the past three weeks." She took out a few more. "And this is to cover the pay you're losing from your job at the bank and just to say thank you."

He tried to hand the money back to her. "Amy, I don't want this. I didn't do any of it expecting any kind of payment, you have to know that."

She took his hand in both of hers, leaning forward and staring into his face. "I know, but I will never be able to repay you for what you've done for me. You had every right to just send me away after I tricked you into bringing me here, but instead you became my best friend and gave me more support and comfort and happiness than I could ever have wished for." Tears shimmered in her luminous eyes and he watched the slow track of one as it overflowed and rolled down her cheek. "Please take it. I want you to have it."

He reached out his free hand and gently brushed at the tear with his thumb. He hated to see her cry, even if they were tears of joy.

A touch of pink coloured her cheeks and she let go of his hand to wipe at her eyes. "Sorry, it's been a long few days. I feel like I could sleep for a week."

"I know," he said softly. "Believe me, I know."

She pushed her chair back from the table. "Millicent invited us to join her for dinner at the hotel. You don't mind, do you?"

Adam sat back, drawing in a deep breath. "No, I don't mind. Two meals at the hotel in one day. We're living the high life."

She laughed. "Almost as good as Mrs G's cooking at the jail. She asked if I would ask George if he'd like to join us so I'll go and do that now. It was so sweet how she asked, like she wasn't sure if she should but she really wanted to."

"Would you like me to come? I thought I should open the post office for a while as I haven't been able to for the past few days, but I don't have to."

"No, that's all right. I might stick around and do some work if George needs me. I'll see you later."

Adam watched her leave by the back door then placed the money he was still clutching onto the table and lowered his head into his hands. Why did Mrs Courtney have to do that? He wished she'd just left and taken her money with her.

Because now, Amy didn't have any reason to stay.

Chapter 31

The walk home from the livery took far longer than usual the next day.

Several people, some of whom Amy couldn't even remember seeing before, stopped her to say how sorry they were about what had happened and that they hoped she would be happy now Mr Courtney was behind bars.

Everyone in the town seemed to have heard her story. She wasn't sure how she felt about that. On the one hand, even telling Adam had been difficult and what she had previously regarded as a secret humiliation was now public knowledge. But on the other, everyone was very nice about it, offering comfort and support and wholeheartedly denouncing Courtney and his actions. It made her feel not so alone and that maybe she really did have nothing to be ashamed of. And perhaps, for the first time since her mother died, she could make choices based on happiness rather than fear.

Reaching the corner of the road leading to the church, Amy stopped for a moment, then turned from her path and headed in that direction. Mrs Jones smiled and rose from where she was tending the flower pots at the front door.

"Miss Watts, come in! I've been wanting to speak with you."

Amy followed her inside the church. "You have?"

Mrs Jones sat and patted the seat beside her. "I just wanted to make sure you're all right. I can't imagine how much courage it must have taken for you to face that awful Mr Courtney at the trial and to tell everyone what you went through."

"It wasn't easy, but now it's over I'm glad I did it. And folks have been so kind today." Amy smiled and stared at her hands folded in her lap. "I couldn't have done it without Adam. He's made me feel so safe while I've been here." She looked back up at Mrs Jones. "Can I ask your advice?"

Mrs Jones laughed. "That's half the reason I spend so much time in this church, so's people who need to talk know where to find me. And there is very little I love more than giving advice." She winked.

Amy nodded, gathering her courage. "I know I have no right to expect this after what I did to Adam, taking his money and all, and after all the kindness he's shown me, but... do you think there's any chance he might still want me as his bride?"

The corners of Mrs Jones' mouth were twitching like she was fighting a smile. "Are you saying you'd like to stay in Green Hill Creek?"

"I've made some wonderful friends here and I'd like to keep working with Mr Parsons and the horses, but most of all I want to stay with Adam." Amy looked down again, feeling a blush heat her cheeks. "The truth is, I love him, and now I can't imagine spending the rest of my life without him."

Evidently unable to restrain herself any longer, Mrs Jones threw her arms around Amy, hugging her tight before holding her at arm's length and smiling. "Then you must go and tell him."

"Do you think he'll want me? Has he said anything to you?"

"I can't repeat anything said in confidence to me, but my advice to you is to go home and tell him how you feel." Mrs Jones' smile looked like it was about to swallow her entire face.

"Does that mean he *has* said something?"

Mrs Jones didn't reply, but the grin remained in place.

Amy nodded, with a smile of her own. "I should just go home and tell him."

Mrs Jones' cheeks must have been aching. "Good idea."

~ ~ ~

Adam plumped the cushions on the settee for what may have been the fifth time in the space of half an hour. They were plump enough, but he did it anyway.

He turned a slow circle, looking for anything out of place in the parlour, anything that wasn't as perfect as he could make it. Amy may have lived there for three weeks, but tonight he needed his small home to be the most amazing place she'd ever been. Admittedly that was probably hoping for too much, but Adam needed all the hope he could get.

Because tonight he was going to tell Amy he loved her and ask her to marry him.

It had to be tonight. She had no more reason to stay now she'd paid him the money back for the train ticket. He had to give her a reason to stay with him, show her how good life could be if she gave him a chance. Convince her she could love him.

He just wished he had some nicer furniture. And a bigger house.

A knock at the back door almost made him jump out of his skin. It took him a couple of seconds to register that it couldn't be Amy because she had her own key. And the door wasn't locked anyway.

Trying to slow his racing heart, he went to the door and opened it. "Daisy?"

"May I come in?" She looked as nervous as he was, her

normal smile absent.

"Of course."

He stepped back to allow her inside and followed her to the settee where she sat, flattening his cushions. She was dressed in a pale blue blouse and skirt instead of the black of mourning she'd been wearing for the past four months. He was impressed he'd noticed at all, given his preoccupation with his impending proposal to Amy.

Daisy clasped her hands in her lap and gave him a strained smile. "I'm just going to come right out and say this because if I don't I'll lose my nerve."

"All right," he said carefully, not entirely sure what was going on.

"We've known each other a long time."

"Yes."

"And we've always been friends."

"Yes."

"And we loved each other once."

"Yes."

"And you are very important to me."

"You're very important to me too."

She sighed, twisting her hands in her lap. "You never told me you were looking for a wife. You never even hinted that's what you wanted."

Slightly confused about what she was getting at, Adam gave half a shrug. "I didn't really tell anyone. I just didn't want anyone to know until it happened."

"If I'd known, I would have..." She stopped and looked at her hands again.

"Would have what?"

"I would have told you that I thought that maybe, one day, you and I would try again. Pick up where we left off."

Adam let out a long breath. He'd never wanted to have this conversation, even though on occasion he suspected it may have been coming. "When I first contacted the agency, Gareth was still alive. In a way, seeing how happy you two were together made me want that too."

"I don't mean then. I meant, since he died I've had the idea that if I ever got married again, it would be to you. It just seemed to make sense. We know each other so well, we're still good friends, Nicky loves you. But when Amy arrived and then you didn't get married... I just need to know, is there any future for us?"

Memories of their time together came back to Adam. Daisy had been everything to him and he'd loved her as much as his young heart had been able. And yet, thinking of how he now felt about Amy, he realised his feelings back then couldn't compare. He'd been a boy when he loved Daisy. Now he was a man and he knew Amy was the only one for him. Much as he'd adored Daisy, they were never meant to be together.

"Daisy, you'll always be one of the most important people in my life, but things have changed. I've changed. I still love you, but only as a friend."

She nodded, still focused on her hands. "I had a feeling that might be your answer, but I had to try."

He reached out and touched his fingers to her chin, raising her face. "Even if my answer had been different, I don't think you're ready for a new husband. Not so soon after Gareth."

A tear slid down her cheek. "I miss him so much. I feel so alone. I have Nicky and my friends and my family, but not having that one person... it's so hard."

That was a feeling he knew well. "I know. I haven't lost anyone, but I know."

She tilted her head to one side in a gesture he knew well. "That's why you paid for Amy to come all this way, isn't it? You must have been devastated when it didn't work out."

He looked away, suddenly not wanting to meet her searching gaze.

"Ha!" She sat back, her usual smile back in place. "Or maybe it did work out. Are you..." Her hand went to her mouth. "You are, aren't you? You're in love with her."

Was he wearing a sign? Did *everyone* know how he felt about Amy? Was he that transparent? "I'm sorry. It's not that I'm choosing her over you..."

She smacked his arm playfully. "Oh, don't be silly. I wouldn't expect you to want me when you're already in love with a wonderful girl. This way is much better for my ego."

Adam shook his head slowly, smiling. "You are an amazing woman."

"Oh, I know that. Does Amy feel the same way?"

"I don't know. I'm planning on telling her when she gets home and asking her to marry me. I just hope it doesn't send her running."

She took hold of his hand. "Believe me, it won't." She raised one hand to his face and touched his cheek. "You're a wonderful man, Adam. There is no way Amy doesn't want you. And I'd better get going. I don't want to spoil your declaration of undying love." She gazed at him for a few seconds as if trying to work out a puzzle on his face, then suddenly leaned forward and pressed her lips to his in a lingering kiss before sitting back and winking. "For old times' sake."

Adam couldn't help laughing. "You are outrageous."

"I certainly hope so."

Feeling a sudden rush of affection for the woman he once thought he'd marry, he leaned forward to hug her. "You don't need to worry about finding someone. When you're ready, you'll have your pick of every free man around. And I'll make sure whoever you choose is good enough for you."

"You'd better." She rose from the settee and Adam

followed her to the door. "Good luck. Not that you'll need it."

He narrowed his eyes. "Do you know something you're not telling me?"

She patted his cheek. "Only a woman's intuition. I'm going to go home and pick out a dress for the wedding."

After she'd left, Adam stared out the window without really seeing anything. Was Daisy right? Did he have nothing to worry about? In his experience with women they often did seem to know things he had no clue about, as his sisters frequently reminded him. A smile stole across his face as hope grew in his heart. It was going to work. He knew it.

Turning away from the window, he caught sight of the now flattened cushions.

But first he had more plumping to do.

Chapter 32

Amy left the church with a grin almost as big as Mrs Jones' had been.

Outside the sky was overcast and grey, but Amy felt like her very own sun was shining down on her. She had a thought that she must look strange to those she passed as she walked, but she couldn't seem to stop smiling. She couldn't remember ever being so happy and she hadn't even told Adam yet. If he told her he loved her too, she thought there might be a danger she would explode from joy.

A couple of minutes later she reached the marshal's office. She hadn't any intention of stopping and yet she did, her gaze drawn to the red brick building. And she knew why.

"You really want me to do this, Lord?" she whispered.

No deep, commanding voice echoed in her head, but nevertheless she knew the answer was yes.

She sighed. "All right, if You say so."

She waited for a horse and rider to pass then crossed the road to the squat building in which she'd spent two days and nights.

Marshal Cade was sitting at his desk, writing. He looked surprised to see her when she walked in. She didn't blame him; she was surprised to be there.

"What can I do for you, Miss Watts?"

"I'd like to speak to Mr Courtney," she said quickly, before she had a chance to change her mind.

At that his eyebrows reached for his hairline. "Are you

253

sure? I'd have thought you wouldn't ever want to see that no good bas... heel again."

"I don't," she said, looking at the door which led to the cells, "but this is something I have to do."

His chair scraped across the floor as he stood. "Well, if it's what you want." He retrieved the keys from a hook behind him and unlocked the door. "Do you want me to come with you?"

"No, thank you, Marshal. I'll be fine."

He nodded and stepped aside to let her in, pulling the door closed behind her.

Courtney was in the cell farthest from the door. For some strange reason, Amy was glad he wasn't in the one she and Adam had stayed in. That cell was a reminder that even in the midst of tragedy, something good could happen.

Courtney was lying on his back on a cot, his eyes closed. His nose was still purple from where Adam had punched him and he'd also acquired a black eye at some point since she'd last seen him.

He opened his eyes, looked at her, and closed them again. "What do you want?"

She walked forward until she was just a few feet from his cell. "I wasn't sure when I came in here, but now I know. I came here to tell you that I forgive you."

The laugh that escaped past his yellowing teeth held no mirth. "I don't need your forgiveness. I've done nothing wrong." He sat up suddenly and fixed her with a glare. "And once I'm back in civilisation in New York and my good name is cleared, I'll come back here and..."

"No, you won't." She stepped closer to the bars. "You may not think you need my forgiveness, but you certainly need God's, for what you did to me and all the other girls you terrorised, and for who knows what else you've done. You can't escape His justice, so if I were you I'd think long and hard on that. But you won't come back here. Everyone knows who you are now. I know I'm safe here and I'm not afraid of you anymore." As she said the words, the truth of them struck her, making her smile. "I will never be afraid of you again."

He shook his head derisively and lay down, turning his back to her. "I don't care about you one way or the other."

Amy's smile grew. "I'm not here for your sake, I'm here for mine. Goodbye, Mr Courtney."

She left the marshal's office feeling a hundred pounds lighter. No more fear. It was invigorating. She felt as if she could do anything, and the first thing she wanted to do was see Adam and tell him she loved him. Maybe he felt the same about her, maybe he didn't, but she was going to find out today one way or the other. And she wasn't afraid to do it.

She almost skipped into the back yard of their house, still smiling. For the first time in her life, she felt like things were going just right. She had a home, she had George and Clementine, she had friends. And most of all, she had Adam.

Wonderful, handsome, kind, smart, funny, caring Adam, the man she loved with all her heart. And who, she hoped, loved her too. Or would, one day.

As she neared the back door she heard muffled voices from inside. One of them was Adam's, the other was a woman. Not wanting to interrupt a private conversation, Amy went to the window and peered through the glass.

Inside, Adam was sitting on the settee. With him was Daisy. Both her hands were holding his.

It's probably nothing, Amy told herself, even as her heart beat faster. They're friends. Friends visit with each other. It's all perfectly normal.

As they spoke, Daisy raised one hand and touched his face. Then she leaned forward and kissed him on the lips.

A void ripped open in Amy's gut. Her hand went to her

chest. She felt like she couldn't breathe. She wanted to turn away, to run, but she couldn't tear her eyes from the nightmare before her.

As she watched, Daisy said something and Adam shook his head, laughing. Then he embraced her.

Finally, Amy found the strength to back away.

He'd lied to her. He'd said Daisy was nothing more to him than a friend. There was no one Amy trusted more in the world than Adam and he'd lied to her. He didn't owe her anything, certainly not his love, but still she felt betrayed.

She'd been almost sure he felt something for her, if not love then close. How could she have been so wrong?

Heart thudding in her chest, she turned and fled. She ran through the back streets to the paddock behind the livery. George had left already, but she found the spare key hidden beneath the water trough and slipped inside. She opened Clementine's stall door and the horse walked up to her and nuzzled her shoulder. The simple gesture of affection sent tears coursing down Amy's cheeks and she wrapped her arms around Clementine's neck, pressing her face against her hair.

"What am I supposed to do without him, Clem?"

Wiping at her eyes with her knuckles, she stepped away and fetched her bridle and saddle. A few minutes later she was riding out into the countryside, her heart feeling greyer than the sky above.

Chapter 33

Amy didn't know how long she rode for, but by the time she returned Clementine to the livery the sun was setting. She checked her hooves, left her eating from the hay rack in her stall, and trudged home.

When she got back to the house the sky was dark. Adam was sitting at the table when she walked in.

He leaped to his feet and rushed over to her. "Thank goodness. I was so worried. George said you left work at the usual time and Marshal Cade said you'd been in to see Courtney, but that was hours ago. Where have you been?"

She kept her face turned away, hiding her eyes which she knew had to be red from crying. "I took Clementine and went for a ride. I just felt like I needed to be alone, to get some fresh air."

He touched her shoulder. "Amy, are you all right? Did Courtney say anything to upset you?"

She shook her head. "It's just been a long few days. I'm sorry I worried you. I didn't mean to."

He dropped his arm to his side. "I'm just glad you're OK. Would you like something to eat? I could warm up something."

"No, thank you. I'm tired. I'd just like to go to bed." She felt his eyes on her as she walked to the door at the foot of the stairs, but she didn't look back. She knew that if she looked at him, if she looked into those blue eyes, she would start crying again.

"Oh," he said. "All right. If you need anything at all, I'm right here."

Her heart twisted in her chest and she almost gasped at the pain. She had to swallow before speaking. "Thank you. Goodnight."

"Goodnight, Amy."

Her feet felt like lead as she climbed the stairs to her room. Once inside, she closed the door and collapsed onto her bed, her face buried in the pillow.

Just a few hours ago she had been filled with hope and joy. How could everything have changed in so short a time? Surely one's life being ripped apart should take longer?

Clamping one hand over her mouth to muffle the sobs, she started to cry again.

Chapter 34

Adam sat on his bed and stared into the darkness of the room.

He had no idea what he was doing.

He hadn't been completely honest with Amy when she finally came home. He hadn't just been worried, he'd been frantic, gone everywhere he could think of to search for her, and finally come home when all he could do was wait and pray. When she walked through the door he had almost cried with relief.

He'd longed to wrap her in his arms and never let her go, but he could see she'd been crying. He'd wanted to ask her what was wrong, but the words had caught in his throat. Surely if she wanted him to know she'd tell him. Wouldn't she?

Maybe it was just the whole thing with Courtney catching up with her. Adam hoped and prayed that was it and that she would be all right soon. But right now he didn't know what to do.

She had money now. There was nothing keeping her here. Maybe what happened tonight was her preparing to go. He was terrified she was going to leave and he wouldn't be able to stop her.

What if she didn't feel the same about him? What if telling her he loved her wasn't enough? Or if it even drove her away?

He rubbed one hand across the day's growth of stubble

on his jaw. He was desperate. He needed help. And there was only one place he could think of to get it.

Without turning on the lamp he rose from the bed, dressed quietly and slipped from his room. He listened at Amy's door for a few seconds, but could hear nothing.

Downstairs he wrote a quick note to her in case she woke up before he returned, telling her he would be back in the morning and begging her to wait for him, and left it on the table. Half an hour later he was riding Stride north through the countryside.

There were places he wouldn't have dared travel at night like this, but he knew the route well and that it would be safe, and the moon was almost full, lighting up the landscape. The cool air in his lungs as he rode felt good, clearing his mind. After an hour he slowed Stride to a walk as they neared the familiar group of barns surrounding the whitewashed, two-storey house. Adam guided him to the water trough inside the gate, dismounting while he drank, then led him to the stable.

He opened one of the large doors and walked into the dark interior. The strong smell of horses wafted over him, the sound of movement rustling in the gloom. A soft whinny drifted from the darkness and Stride responded.

Adam found the lamp in its usual place and lit it, creating a soft glow that chased the shadows from the large space. Lining the back wall was a row of stalls from which six horses watched him. Stride pulled away and walked up to a sleek black mare at one end. They nuzzled their faces against each other in greeting.

"Hi, Ebony," Adam said, stroking her neck.

He led Stride into a vacant stall next to Ebony's, removed his saddle and bridle, and set about cleaning out his hooves as he munched on a rack full of fresh hay. Adam didn't hurry. Now he'd arrived, his decision to come here

260

didn't seem so foolproof.

He'd just finished the fourth hoof when the barn door burst open.

"Whoever's there, come out with your hands in the air!"

Adam sighed at the sound of the voice. He put the hoof pick down and walked from the stall to face the tall man with greying dark hair and piercing blue eyes staring at him down the length of an old shotgun barrel.

The barrel lowered. "Adam?"

"Hey, Pa."

John Emerson huffed a breath. "What are you doing out here in the middle of the might? Scared your mother half to death when she saw the light in here. We thought it was horse thieves or something."

"Sorry. I was trying to be quiet."

A tall figure burst into the building, rifle raised. "Pa! Are you all right? Ma said..." The dishevelled young man stopped. "Adam?"

"Hi, Pete."

Pete lowered the rifle and ran one hand over his close cropped dark hair. "What are you doing here in the middle of the night?"

Adam grinned at his youngest brother. "Nice to see you too."

"Are you OK?"

"Yes, I'm OK."

"Then I'm going back to bed." He turned around to shuffle back out the door. "A growing boy needs his sleep."

"You're eighteen, you're not going to grow anymore. And your head's practically in the clouds as it is."

Pete waved a hand without looking back. Adam chuckled softly.

"I suppose you'd better come inside," John said, following his youngest son.

261

"I'll be right in, Pa."

Left alone with the horses, Adam stroked Stride's mane. The horse hadn't looked up from his hay during the entire exchange with Adam's father and brother. Standing in the familiar stall next to his mother, he obviously felt secure enough to keep his concentration on the important job of eating.

"Wish me luck, boy," Adam whispered.

He left Stride to his food, patted Ebony's shoulder on the way past, and headed for the house.

He'd taken two steps through the back door into the kitchen when he was engulfed, from the chest down at least, in his mother's arms. He hugged her close, a smile spreading over his face. There was nothing like his mother's embrace to make him feel better.

Florence drew back and looked up at him, placing her hand onto his cheek. "What's wrong?"

His smile faded and he looked down at the stone flagged floor. She took his hands and led him to the large wooden table in the centre of the room.

"Sit," she said, pushing him down onto a chair.

Pete was sitting across from him.

"I thought you were going back to bed," Adam said.

"I was, but then I thought I'd stick around." His gaze flicked to a selection of bread, butter, tomato, and slices of beef laid out on the table where their mother was taking a seat.

"I get the feeling that has more to do with the food than me," Adam said.

Pete smiled. "As I mentioned, I'm a growing boy. "

"Only outwards."

Pete grabbed a spoon and threw it. Reflexes honed from a lifetime with two younger brothers, Adam ducked out of the way. The spoon hit the wall behind him.

262

He came up grinning. "You couldn't hit the side of a barn with a cow."

Pete seized another spoon and Adam tensed to move.

"Were you two wanting a sandwich?" Florence said, her voice deceptively calm as she layered slices of beef and tomato onto the bread.

Pete's arm, in the process of drawing back to throw, froze before slowly lowering back onto the table. "Yes, Ma'am."

"Yes, Ma," Adam said, smirking at his brother.

Pete stuck out his tongue and Adam had to bite back laughter.

Florence slid plates piled high with thick sandwiches in front of each of them. Despite it being somewhere around three in the morning, Adam felt a pang of hunger.

"Take yours up to your bedroom to eat," she said to Pete.

He was clutching his sandwich in both hands, halfway to his mouth. "Why?"

"Because I need to talk to your brother alone. Now get."

He sighed. "Yes, Ma." He placed his sandwich back onto the plate and stood, looking at Adam. "You gonna be here long?"

He shook his head. "I have to get back by morning."

Disappointment passed across Pete's face. "Oh. Well, see you next time then."

Adam suddenly wished he could stay. "I'll come and say goodbye before I leave."

With a nod, Pete disappeared into the hallway. Adam picked up his sandwich, needing both hands to keep it together, and took a bite. He closed his eyes in bliss.

Florence waited for him to finish the mouthful before saying, "So what's wrong?"

Adam glanced through the open door to the parlour

263

where his father was sitting in a rocking chair, his back to them. He couldn't tell if he was listening, or even if he was awake.

"You know those mail order brides?"

He started at the beginning, when he'd placed the advert with the agency. He told her about the replies that came, the way he'd felt the only one he should answer was Amy, the letters he'd received from her that both confused and intrigued him, the letter he'd finally written asking her to be his wife, the anxious wait for the train.

"I'm sorry I didn't tell you, Ma, but I didn't want you to worry." He stared at the sandwich he'd lost interest in eating. "I didn't want you to know how lonely I've been."

At a touch on his hair, he looked into his mother's tear-filled eyes.

"You're my son, Adam. I knew."

Blinking back his own tears, he took her hand and kissed it.

"So what happened with Amy?"

Keeping hold of her hand, he continued his story with Amy's arrival, her deception, his desire to help her, falling in love, the drama with Courtney, his decision to tell her how he felt, then her disappearance and strange, distant behaviour the previous evening.

"I don't know what to do, Ma. I don't know what changed last night. I feel like I don't know anything anymore. I'm so scared I'll do the wrong thing and she'll leave. Please tell me what to do."

His mother opened her mouth to speak, but was interrupted by a loud sigh from the parlour. The rocker creaked and his father got to his feet and walked through into the kitchen where he stood, hands on hips, staring at Adam.

"Well that's always been your trouble, hasn't it?"

Adam stared up at him in confusion. "I... what has?"

264

John shook his head, puffed out a breath, and began pacing back and forth across the kitchen. "You've always been afraid to stand up for what you want. You think about everyone else and what you think you *ought* to do, but you don't consider what you *want* to do. When I brought the family here, you could have stayed in Green Hill Creek. You wanted to stay, but you didn't."

Adam frowned. "You said you needed me here. You did need me here. I came for you and Ma and Grandma."

"Yes, we needed you, but we would have survived without you. You were old enough to make your own decision, but you didn't. You followed mine." He stopped pacing to face Adam. "The day you left to take over Ezra's post office was the proudest I've ever been of you, son."

Adam's jaw dropped. "But... but we had that argument! You said you didn't want me to go!"

"I didn't say I wanted you to go, I said I was proud that you did what you wanted, not what I wanted you to do."

Adam sat back in his chair. "Well you could have told me that at the time."

Florence was chuckling. "Don't you know after all this time that's not how your pa does things?"

John flashed her a look and she grinned at him.

"So what are you saying I should do now?" Adam said.

His father threw his hands into the air, exasperated. "He still doesn't get it. Do what you want to do! You want this girl to stay, tell her! Do everything you can to convince her to stay. And if she can't see what a good man my son is and how lucky she'd be to have you, then she's just not the right woman for you. That's all."

Adam's head was reeling. He opened his mouth, couldn't think of a thing to say, and closed it again. His father stuffed his hands into his pockets and stared at the range for no apparent reason. Adam looked at Florence. She was

265

wiping at her eyes, a big smile on her face.

"Thanks, Pa."

John nodded without looking at him. "You gonna eat that sandwich?"

"I'll make you your own," Florence said, waving him over. "Eat up, Adam. You'll need your strength for the ride back to tell Amy you love her so we can all come down there for your wedding. Doesn't he, John?"

John sat opposite him and Adam could swear he was almost smiling. "If you say so, woman."

Chapter 35

Amy absently smoothed her hand over the blue quilt on her bed as she gazed out the window at the mountains, half hidden by mist in the distance.

The early morning sun was just lighting up the peaks, making them appear as if they were on fire. The sight was breathtaking and even though she knew she should leave, she lingered to watch for a few minutes. She wanted to imprint the scene in her mind so she could remember it after she was gone.

It wasn't like she wouldn't be seeing the mountains again, it was just that this was *her* view, the view Adam had given her because he thought she would enjoy it. She loved it for that reason above all the others.

Wiping at a tear trickling down her cheek, she stood and picked up her bag and the letter she'd written. With one last look around the room she adored with all her heart, she opened the door and slipped out onto the landing.

Adam's door was closed and she pressed her ear to its surface, hoping to hear him breathing, but there was silence. With her heart aching, she turned away and crept down the stairs.

She placed the letter onto the centre of the table where he would see it, weighing it down with a glass, then looked slowly around the parlour. Despite having been there for only three weeks, the small house behind the post office felt more like home than any other place she'd lived in her life. It was clean, cosy and safe. And it was Adam's.

The tightness in her chest flared, a burning pain that made her hunch in on herself. She knew she was being unfair to him, leaving without telling him face to face, without saying goodbye, but it was the only thing she could do. He would beg her to stay, she wouldn't have the strength to say no, and she'd be trapped, forced to watch his happiness with another woman. Even the thought of him with Daisy was more than she could bear and it would only hurt him to see her pain. Leaving was the only choice Amy had.

"Please make him understand, Lord," she whispered, looking at the letter. "And please give him a happy life."

At the door she looked back one last time, then stepped outside into the early dawn.

The air was chilly and Amy pulled her coat around her as she hurried through the back streets towards the livery. No one else was up at this time, for which Amy was grateful. She didn't want to see someone she knew and have to lie about why she was out so early.

It only took her five minutes to reach the livery and she circled to the back door to retrieve the spare key hidden beneath the water trough. Inside, the horses stirred at her arrival, rustling in the straw of their stalls. Amy took a deep breath of the combined scent of horses, straw, leather, hay and manure. She never would have thought it possible when she'd first started working there, but the smell was familiar and comforting. This place had become almost as much her home as the post office had.

She reached into her bag and pulled out another envelope, placing it onto George's desk by the door and moving the heavy brass inkwell to cover one corner. The envelope was thick with banknotes, four hundred dollars' worth. Part of it was payment for the horses, but the rest was for leaving George so suddenly, and she also wanted to thank him for everything he'd done for her. He'd been the father she never knew.

Another tear escaped and she wiped at it in irritation. She'd become soft here, opening her heart and letting down her defences. That would have to change. She had no illusions that San Francisco wouldn't be as tough as New York, but at least she had money this time. She would be all right, physically at least. In all likelihood, she knew her heart would probably never heal.

She made her way along the stalls to Stride's and frowned to find it empty. That was strange; he always spent the night here. Adam hadn't mentioned moving him, although Amy hadn't really given him much time to talk when she got home the night before. She looked around, but saw no sign that there had been a break-in, and even if someone had managed to get inside why would they only take one horse? Stride would have fought anyone he didn't know, yet his stall was tidy and in order.

She shook her head and moved on to Clementine's stall. She wished she could say goodbye to him, but there was no doubt a good explanation for his absence and George would be arriving within an hour anyway. He would know what to do.

Clementine walked to the front of her stall, whinnying a greeting to Amy and rubbing her face against the hand Amy held out to her. She pulled half an apple from her pocket and gave it to the mare, stroking her head and neck as she ate.

"I wish I could take you with me," she said, "but I know you'd never be happy away from Stride. Just because I can't be with the one I love doesn't mean you can't either." She kissed her cheek, this time not even bothering to wipe away the tears that fell. "I love you, girl."

Sniffing back her emotions, she walked to a stall back along the row. Eagle was a fine, solid horse. Amy would have

269

taken the train, but there wasn't one due for another few days. The bay stallion would carry her to San Francisco without any fuss. She led Eagle from the stall and saddled him up.

After one final, tearful goodbye to Clementine, Amy left the livery for the final time and rode out of Green Hill Creek.

Chapter 36

Adam's heart lifted as he crested the hill and looked down on the dusty, colourful, sprawling community of Green Hill Creek. He raised his face to the bright blue of the early morning sky and laughed as his soul praised God.

"Thank you, Jesus."

This was his Saviour's doing, he knew it.

He had been picturing how it would go in his mind the entire ride back. He would get home and Amy would smile the beautiful smile that always took his breath away. Then he would sit her down and pour out his heart to her, the way he'd longed to ever since they met, she would tell him she loved him too, and then they'd kiss.

He'd been dreaming of kissing those incredible lips for three weeks straight.

Stride shifted beneath him, impatient to get home.

"All right, boy," Adam said, laughing and patting his neck, "let's go."

They galloped down the gentle slope of the hill to join the dusty main road into town and headed straight for the post office. Adam didn't want to wait. He would take Stride to the livery after he'd seen Amy. Maybe she'd even come with them.

Leaving Stride in the yard with a bucket of water and some feed, Adam ran inside. The parlour was empty, but Amy probably wasn't up yet. He wanted to rush up the stairs and wake her, but reason told him it would be best to let her

271

come down in her own time. He would just start breakfast while he waited. Impatiently.

He turned towards the kitchen and stopped at the sight of a glass upside down on the table, an envelope pinned beneath it. His own letter, the one he'd left in case Amy woke before he returned home, was nowhere to be seen.

ADAM

He recognised Amy's handwriting on the front of the envelope. Heart pounding, he tore it open and pulled out the piece of paper inside.

Dear Adam,

You will never know how grateful I am for everything you've done for me. I truly believe that God led me to you. You saved my life in more ways that I can say and I have felt happier and safer in the time I've been with you than I ever remember being. You are a wonderful, amazing man and I am blessed to have spent even this short time with you.

I hope you can forgive me for what I'm doing. I didn't want to leave like this, but I know that you will try to stop me if I wait and that if you do, I won't be strong enough to say no. So I'm leaving now, while I can. Please believe me when I say that you have done nothing to drive me away, this is all my choice.

I will leave a note for George and some money so that he can keep Clementine. She and Stride shouldn't be parted.

I will remember the time I've spent in Green Hill Creek for the rest of my life, and mostly I will remember you. Please don't be sad that I've gone. I pray that you will have a blessed and happy life with a loving wife and children and everything you've ever wanted.

You are the best friend I've ever had.

All my love, Amy.

Dropping the letter, Adam raced for the stairs, taking them two at a time and bursting into Amy's bedroom. She was gone, the bed made and drawers empty. He ran back down to the parlour and looked around, panicked.

He'd begged her to stay in his letter. How could she do this? Why didn't she stay?

Then he saw the corner of a piece of paper sticking out from beneath the stove. Pulling it out, he found his letter to Amy. It must have blown off the table when he went out the door. She never saw it. He was so stupid. Why hadn't he thought to weigh it down, as she had?

He ran out the back door and leaped onto Stride who jumped, startled.

"Come on," Adam said, patting his shoulder, "we need to go."

When they reached the livery, in record time, the front doors were open. Adam rode straight in and dropped from Stride's back. He found George by Clementine's stall.

"Is she here?"

George shook his head, lifting his hand in which was clutched a piece of paper. "She left me this letter, said she was leaving, took one of the horses. What happened? What did you do, boy?"

"Nothing! I don't think." Adam ran one hand over his hair, looking around the livery as if it would provide some answers. "I went to visit my family during the night and when I got back she was gone. What do I do, George? I can't live without her."

"San Francisco. That's where she'll be going."

"But how do I find her? I don't even know how long ago she left."

George stared down at the stone flagged floor, frowning in concentration. "The railroad. She'll be following the tracks. It's the only way she'd know which way to go."

Adam turned and ran back to Stride who had found a pile of fresh hay, calling, "Thanks, George" over his shoulder

273

as he went.

He leapt onto Stride's back and the black stallion looked at him over his shoulder as if to say, "Again?"

"Come on," Adam said to him, urging him back outside. "We have to find Amy."

Chapter 37

Amy idly watched Eagle drinking from the stream then looked up at the blue sky through the branches of the tree they stood beneath.

It was turning into a beautiful day, just like that first Sunday when she and Adam went to the lake for the picnic.

She wondered what he was doing now.

A tear escaped to slide down her cheek and she wiped at it in annoyance. She couldn't afford to be sad. There was a long road ahead of her, a whole new life to experience, and Adam wouldn't be part of that life. He'd chosen someone else and she couldn't blame him. All she'd done was make his life difficult.

If she'd only married him when she first arrived...

But it was too late now. She'd ruined any chance she had to be with Adam and he deserved far better anyway. Leaving was the only thing she could do, even if it felt like her heart was being crushed to nothing.

The sound of galloping hoof beats instantly had her on alert. She went to the saddlebag on Eagle's back and reached inside. A few seconds later a horse and rider appeared through the trees and Amy gasped, letting go of her knife.

Stride slowed and trotted up to her, stopping a few feet away and shaking his head. Adam dropped to the ground from the saddle. He began to approach and then stopped.

"Amy?"

She suddenly felt like crying. Seeing him again was too

hard. "Why are you here? Didn't you read the letter I left? I explained everything."

"I know," he said. "I read it. I still don't understand why you're leaving, without even saying goodbye."

Amy looked at the ground. "I'm going to San Francisco like I planned. I'm going to find a new life."

Adam took another step forward. "That's not what I asked."

She sniffed and rubbed her nose with the back of her hand. "It's what I have to do."

"Why? Why can't you stay?"

She didn't answer. How could she tell him the reason she was leaving was that she couldn't bear to watch as he married another woman? Another traitorous tear slid down her cheek.

Adam stepped forward, his hands hovering in front of him as if he wanted to touch her. "Please, Amy." He took another step towards her, bringing him within arm's reach. "Please don't go. I don't want you to leave."

She looked away, fighting to hold back the tears burning her eyes. "This is why I left without telling you I was going. I don't want you to ask me to stay. I explained in the letter. Please, just let me go."

"Why? Help me to understand. Did I do something wrong?" His voice dropped to barely more than a whisper. "Do you not want to stay with me?"

She couldn't take it anymore. "I can't stay, all right? I can't stay and watch you marry Daisy while my heart is breaking. I just can't." She wiped angrily at the moisture pooling in her eyes.

Adam stared at her, his mouth hanging open. "You... what... I don't... *Daisy?*"

"I saw you kissing her in the parlour yesterday." She didn't mean it to sound like an accusation, but somehow it came out that way.

His eyes widened. "Was that why you were out all evening?"

She nodded, sniffing again and digging in her pocket for a handkerchief. "You held her hand and kissed her and hugged her. And you were laughing." She blew her nose, which wasn't very ladylike, but neither was having a runny nose. And she didn't feel like being a lady.

Adam waited for her to replace the handkerchief into her pocket then touched a finger to her chin, raising her face to look at him. "I didn't kiss her, she kissed me. For old time's sake, she said. Daisy just does things like that. There's absolutely nothing more than friendship between me and her, I swear."

All the breath left Amy's body at once. "You don't love her?"

"No. At least, not in that way."

"You're not going to marry her?"

"Of course not." A small smile played across his lips. "Although if things go according to plan, I will be needing Pastor Jones' services in that respect very soon."

Amy frowned, feeling like there was something she wasn't getting. What she did know was that she'd apparently run away for nothing and made a fool of herself.

"According to plan?"

He took a step back and, to her utter astonishment, sank to one knee in the grass. "Amy, will you marry me?"

For a few moments all she could do was stare. Had he really just proposed to her? "I... beg your pardon?"

He gazed up at her and drew in a shaking breath. "I fell in love with you the first day we spent by the lake, and every day since I've loved you more. I love your strength and your independence. I love your kindness and laughter. I love your beauty and your grace. I especially love your hair which I

277

have been dying to run my fingers through ever since I met you. And I love the way my heart flips every time you smile at me. I am completely in love with you and I can't imagine how I've lived the first twenty-five years of my life without you. My heart belongs to you, Amy, only you. Will you marry me? Will you be my wife?"

He stared up at her, looking more scared than the first time she'd seen him, standing on the platform at the station, waiting for his first glimpse of the woman he thought had come to marry him.

And maybe, without knowing it, she had.

Amy's heart was beating so fast she thought it might burst from her chest. "I didn't think... I..." She let out a combined sob and laugh. "Yes. Yes!"

For a moment, Adam froze, staring up at her as if he didn't know what to do. Then he rose and stepped in close. With a small smile, he touched her cheeks, brushing her tears away, then pressed a lingering kiss to her forehead. The feel of his lips on her skin shivered all the way down to her feet.

She placed her hands on his chest and gazed up at him. "I love you too."

His beautiful blue eyes widened. "You do?"

She smiled at his surprise, quietly astounded he hadn't known already how she felt. There were times she'd been sure it was written all over her face. "With all my heart."

His gaze flicked between her eyes and then dropped to her mouth. Gently cupping the sides of her face, he whispered her name as he touched his lips to hers. Amy closed her eyes, wrapped her arms around his neck and pushed up onto her toes. That probably wasn't very ladylike either, but she didn't care.

She felt him smile against her lips.

And then he kissed her.

Amy's heart fluttered and then burst into flight. She

clutched the back of his collar and pressed closer. One of his hands moved to the back of her head, pushing into her hair, while the other rested between her shoulder blades, fingers fisting in the material of her shirt.

It was the kiss of a lifetime, where time stood still and the whole rest of the world melted away.

When they finally parted, after what could have been hours for all Amy knew, she dropped back down onto her heels and lay her head against his chest, wondering vaguely that her legs could still support her. She sighed in bliss as she felt Adam kiss the top of her head and then rested his cheek against her hair.

His chest rose and fell in a deep sigh. "That was even better than I imagined it would be," he murmured. "And I've done a lot of imagining kissing you in the past three weeks."

Amy lifted her face to look up at him. "Did you know? Even right from the beginning?"

He brushed the fingers of one hand down her cheek. "I knew I wanted to marry you right from the beginning. I didn't know you would until you said yes."

"Really? Right from the start?"

"From the moment I first saw you. I couldn't believe how beautiful you were. And your hair..." Smiling, he let go of her with one hand, held it in front of her, and unfurled his fist to reveal the leather band she'd secured her braid with.

"What...?" She felt the back of her head and found her braid unravelled, her hair loose and free. "When did that happen?"

He grinned and touched his forehead to hers. "Told you I've been dying to run my fingers through your hair ever since we met."

She gasped in feigned shock. "Mr and Mrs Vernon would be scandalised."

"Then I propose we do one thing every day that would

scandalise Mr and Mrs Vernon if they found out." He winked.

Amy bit her lower lip. "Only one?"

Adam burst into laughter and drew her in for another kiss. "Let's go home. We can make a list."

Chapter 38

When they got back to the livery George shocked Amy by catching her up in a hug as soon as she slid from Eagle's back. Then he held her out by her shoulders at arm's length. "Don't you ever go running off like that again. You hear me, girl?"

She smiled and nodded. "I hear you. And I won't."

George looked at Adam as he climbed off Stride. "You finally tell her you love her?"

"Yes, although you saying that would have been real awkward if I hadn't."

George waved him away. "You had long enough, kid. If you hadn't done it by now it would serve you right to have me do it for you."

Adam rolled his eyes. "I'm going to give Stride a good brush. He's had a long night." He draped one arm around Amy's shoulders and kissed her temple, then went to lead Stride into his stall.

George walked to his desk and pulled the envelope she'd left him from the drawer. "Here, you'll be wanting this money back."

Amy pushed it back to him as he held it out. "Keep it, for Clem if it's all right. I'd like to buy her. And I'll pay you to keep her here, like everyone else."

For a moment it looked like he would protest, then he shrugged. "Whatever you want to do, girl. I ain't one to refuse a paying customer."

She grinned up at him. "I'm glad I'm staying."

The hint of a smile tugged at his mouth. "I'm glad too, girl. Now get to work. These stalls ain't gonna clean themselves out."

~ ~ ~

By the afternoon, Amy's sleepless night and early morning were catching up with her. When her yawns had reached the rate of roughly one every ten seconds, George sent her home with the order to "get some sleep before you fall over."

She trudged back to the post office and entered through the back door to the sight of Adam stretched out on the settee with an open book balanced on his chest, his eyes closed and breathing soft and regular. Amy tiptoed across the room and lowered to her knees beside him.

She gently moved a wayward strand of dark hair from his forehead, resisting the urge to press her lips to his soft skin. As she gazed at his slumbering face such an intense feeling of love swelled inside her that she almost laughed. She understood now why anyone would risk the pain and devastation of losing a husband or wife. For the chance to feel like this she would risk anything. This was true love, and it made her feel like she could fly.

He shifted a little in his sleep and the book slid from his grasp. Amy caught it before it dropped to the floor and replaced his bookmark.

Adam's eyes opened slowly, his lips widening into a sleepy smile when he saw her. He raised one hand and stroked it down the side of her face, making her heart stutter.

"I'm sorry. I didn't mean to fall asleep for so long. I was going to have supper ready for when you got home."

"It's only two," she said. "I was yawning so much that George sent me home."

Sitting up, he swivelled his feet to the floor and patted

the seat beside him. When she sat next to him he wrapped both arms around her and leaned back so she could rest her head on his chest.

"I'm not clean," she murmured, closing her eyes and relaxing into him with a sigh.

"I have no complaints."

She smiled, snuggling in against him. "Is this another one of those scandalous moments?"

"Oh, absolutely."

"I was thinking that when it gets around that we're courting, people are going to disapprove even more of us living under the same roof." Feeling his chest shaking in a silent chuckle, she raised her head to see him smiling. "What's funny?"

"Just the thought that we weren't courting before. I've been courting you since the day you got off that train; you just didn't know it."

She stretched up and placed a soft kiss on his lips. "Well maybe I was courting you too."

He cradled the back of her head with one hand and drew her close for another kiss, this one lingering until its warmth filled her all the way down to her toes.

"I went to see Pastor Jones today," he said when their lips parted. "He said we can have the wedding whenever we want."

Amy lay her head back down onto his chest. "In that case, I vote for making it as soon as possible."

He kissed the top of her head, relaxing beneath her. "My thoughts exactly."

~ ~ ~

Amy woke with a start at the sound of someone knocking loudly on the front door.

283

She sat upright as Adam groaned and rubbed one hand across his face.

"Whoever that is had better have a *very* good reason for waking us up." He kissed her cheek and pushed himself off the settee. "Waking to your beautiful face I have no objection to at all. With anyone else, I take exception."

He trudged from the room. Ten seconds later, Amy heard Mr Vernon's voice.

She scrambled to her feet and brushed at her clothing, looking down ruefully at her work clothes. She really should have washed and changed before she fell asleep.

Lifting her hands to check her hair, she found it loose. Despite her horror that she was even more dishevelled than she'd thought, she couldn't help smiling at Adam's sneaky unravelling of her braid again. She found the band on the arm of the settee and just managed to tie her hair back before Adam returned with Mr and Mrs Vernon in tow.

The uncertainty in his expression and slight shrug as they passed him told her he had no more idea what they were doing there than she did.

"Uh, good afternoon, Mrs Vernon, Mr Vernon," Amy said. "Please forgive my appearance, I haven't had a chance to change from my work clothes. Can I get you anything to drink?"

"Oh no, dear, thank you," Mrs Vernon said, smiling as if they were close friends. "We won't be long."

Dear?!

"Please, have a seat," Adam said, indicating the settee.

The Vernons sat and Amy took the armchair facing them, Adam pulling up a seat from the table. Suddenly nervous without knowing why, Amy wished she could hold his hand.

"First of all we'd like to say how very sorry we are about everything you went through at the hands of that awful man,

Miss Watts," Mrs Vernon said. "And about how badly you and Adam were treated by people who should have known better than to believe malicious gossip. It was disgraceful the way some people were so quick to jump to conclusions without all the facts."

Amy kept her face carefully straight. Inside, her jaw was on the floor. Adam glanced at her and his utterly neutral expression told her he was thinking the same thing. Mrs Vernon seemed to have conveniently forgotten that she had been the instigator of the 'malicious gossip' that so shocked her now.

Mrs Vernon elbowed Mr Vernon in the ribs.

He jumped. "Erm, yes. And in light of what has happened I would of course like to offer you your job back at the bank, Mr Emerson."

Mrs Vernon elbowed him again as she smiled at Amy and Adam.

"And as you are such a loyal and valued employee," he continued, "I would also like to offer you a rise of one dollar per..."

Mrs Vernon smacked his thigh with the back of her hand.

"...one dollar fifty per week."

"Well that's, um, thank you, Mr Vernon," Adam said. "I accept." He reached out to take Amy's hand. "The extra money will be very welcome, now that Amy and I plan on being married as soon as possible."

He glanced at Amy and she struggled to contain a sudden urge to giggle. It was as good a way as any to let the town know of their impending wedding.

Mrs Vernon's squeal was so loud and high, Amy almost expected to hear dogs start barking.

She clutched her husband's arm. "Oh, that's wonderful news, isn't it dear?"

285

"Wonderful," Mr Vernon said, giving them a relieved smile. "Congratulations."

"And of course you shall have a few days paid leave for your honeymoon," Mrs Vernon said.

The smile disappeared from Mr Vernon's face. "He will?"

She turned to him and raised her eyebrows. His shoulders slumped.

"Naturally, you can have a couple of days..."

She squeezed his arm.

"...three days..."

She gave him another poke with her elbow, this one so hard it made him yelp.

"...four days *and that's as far as I'm going, woman.*"

She smiled at him and patted his arm. "Thank you, dear."

"Thank you," Adam said, looking stunned. "That's very generous of you."

"Yes, it is," he grumbled, glancing at his wife.

"Well," Mrs Vernon said, standing, "we've taken up enough of your time. I'm so thrilled you will be staying in our little community, Miss Watts. I'm sure we will be great friends. Come along, Emmett."

Adam walked them to the front door, casting an astonished glance back at Amy as they left the room. She walked over to get supper started and when he returned he strode up to her, picked her up and spun her around, laughing.

"I have no idea what just happened," she said as he lowered her to the floor, "but I do know we serve an amazing God."

"Could you believe what they were saying though? As if they weren't the worst ones in the entire thing?"

She touched her fingertips to his face. "We're together,

you have your job back, and we're going to be married. I'm going to try very hard to let the rest go."

Covering her hand with his, he kissed her palm and then dipped his face towards her. Their lips met and Adam stepped forward, pressing her back against the dresser behind her.

A thud startled them apart. They looked down at the Bible that had fallen onto the floor.

"You'd better pick it up," Adam said with a wry smile. "I'm pretty sure if I do, it will open to a verse about forgiving those who do you wrong."

Chapter 39

Dearest Amy,

    I am very happy to hear that you are praying about our future too. Since I sent my last letter to you I haven't been able to stop thinking about it. I promise that I am usually far more cautious than this, probably too cautious for my own good, but I feel so strongly about this that I can't ignore it. I know we've only been corresponding for a relatively short time and, truthfully, no one could be more surprised than me that it has happened so fast, but I believe God's hand is in all of this.

    I have been praying for so long for the right woman, God's choice for me, a wife who I will love and cherish and share the rest of a happy life with, and I believe I've finally found her in you. I can't even adequately explain how I feel and it's a bit overwhelming! Many times over the past weeks I've wondered if I was being foolish, but foolish or not I want this more than anything.

    So I'm asking, Amy, will you marry me?

    Please forgive my untidy writing, my hand is shaking! If your answer is yes and you agree, I will send a train ticket for you to come as soon as you are able. I hope you are as excited at the thought of our future together as I am!

    Yours hopefully and with kindest regards,
    Adam.

~ ~ ~

Amy's heart pattered inside her chest as she stood outside the church. Whether it was from excitement or nerves, she couldn't tell. Maybe a little of both.

Next to her, George ran his finger around the starched collar of his white shirt for the fifth time.

"Stop fidgeting with it," she said, "you'll make it dirty."

"My neck is itching."

"But you look very handsome."

There was a pause. "Well, I know that."

Amy laughed and pushed his arm.

"So," George said, shifting his feet and looking up at the cross at the top of the church, "I guess you won't be coming back to the livery."

"Why ever not?"

He waved a hand at the church door. "You're getting hitched. You're going to be a wife now, looking after your husband and having young 'uns and such."

Amy planted her hands onto her hips. "First of all, Adam's been looking after himself for years so he's perfectly able to cope with me not being home all the time. Second, whenever we have children I'll work things out then. But right now don't you even think of hiring someone to replace me. You're not getting rid of me that easily." She prodded his chest with her finger. "Is that understood?"

The corners of his mouth twitched. "Yes, Ma'am."

She nodded. "Good."

Inside the church, the multi-talented Mrs Goodwin launched into a spirited rendition of the wedding march on the slightly out of tune piano.

Feeling a sudden rush of affection for George, Amy reached up and kissed his cheek. "Thank you for agreeing to give me away. I know you aren't one for ceremonies."

His face creased into a rare smile. "Still not sure why you asked me, but I'm pleased to do it."

"I asked you because if I had a father, I'd want him to be just like you."

His mouth dropped open and, to Amy's utter surprise, his eyes began to mist over. He looked away, blinking rapidly, and cleared his throat. "Well, um, I... I'm right pleased to know that."

Not caring if anyone saw them, Amy wrapped her arms around him, laying her head against his shoulder. After a moment, he returned her embrace.

"If I had a daughter, I reckon I'd want her to be just like you too."

Drawing back, she wiped at her eyes, smiling. George offered her his arm and she slipped her hand through it

"Come on, girl," he said, "let's get you married."

To Amy's astonishment the modest church building was packed, with some people at the back even standing. After everything that had happened since she arrived four weeks ago, it seemed she and Adam were the talk of the town. Whether that was good or bad she couldn't be sure, but the faces she saw around her all seemed glad to be there. Sara, Lizzy, Louisa, Jo and Mrs Jones sat near the front, their happiness for her shining through their smiles. The front two rows on the other side were filled with Adam's family. Isaiah sat in the next row back, grinning from ear to ear.

And then there was Adam. He was wearing the grey suit, his only suit, she'd learned, that he'd worn to meet her at the station what seemed like so long ago. Somehow he looked even more handsome in it today, but maybe that was what happened when you were in love. His eyes didn't leave her the entire time she was walking up the aisle on George's arm.

Reaching the platform, George kissed Amy's hand then left her to take his seat next to a beaming Millicent Courtney who slipped her arm around his. He took her hand and returned her smile.

As they faced Pastor Jones, Adam took Amy's hand and gave it a gentle squeeze.

"Well, ladies and gentlemen," the pastor said, "I think we can all agree that Miss Watts and Mr Emerson's has been one of the more eventful courtships we've had in Green Hill Creek." He paused as laughter rippled around the gathered crowd. "But praise be to our Lord and Saviour that He worked to bring these two deserving young people together. Adam, Amy, I can honestly say that I see God's hand in everything that has happened, and I have no doubt He is going to bless your marriage with much happiness and joy. Would you face each other, please?"

There were vows and promises and at some point Amy knew she spoke the words she was meant to, but somehow all she remembered afterwards was staring into Adam's eyes through the whole ceremony and seeing everything she now knew she'd ever wanted. And a feeling of pure peace settling over her.

And then the pastor said to Adam, "You may kiss the bride."

And he did.

As if the whole town wasn't watching.

Chapter 40

Amy stood on the hill overlooking Green Hill Creek. The town stretched out before her, the line of the railroad tracks bounding it on one side and the creek itself hidden beneath a wide canopy of trees and bushes snaking towards the river in the distance. From her vantage point she could see several farms spread out over the surrounding countryside, each a cluster of barns and farmhouses at the centre of fields of crops and grazing animals. She wasn't sure, but she thought she could identify Sara and Daniel's farm far away to her right.

She raised one hand to her neck, touching the Indian-made turquoise and silver necklace at her throat, a gift from Adam on their wedding night.

Home, she thought. *This is where I belong. This is home. Thank You, Lord.*

Low grey clouds hung overhead and it would probably be raining soon. A gusting breeze sent her loose hair flapping around her face. She'd abandoned pinning it up when she and Adam were alone since sooner or later he invariably found the chance to unfasten it. It was just simpler this way.

She smiled as his arms encircled her waist from behind and his lips pressed to the side of her neck.

"Happy?" Adam said, his warm breath caressing her skin.

She leaned back into her husband's embrace with a contented sigh. "Very." She'd never imagined it was possible to feel this happy. "You have a wonderful family."

"*We* have a wonderful family. They're yours now too. You have a mother and father and brothers and sisters and aunts and uncles and nieces and nephews. Whatever happens, you won't ever be alone again." He paused. "Whenever we visit there may be times when you come to regret that."

She laughed. "Never."

He smiled against her skin and kissed her again. "I'm going to miss that bunkhouse."

Amy's cheeks heated up and she bit her lip. "It was so thoughtful of your mother to set that up for us rather than have us stay in the house."

"Ma always has been very practical."

"And it was nice how she made it all pretty and comfortable."

"And private."

"You are shameless," she said, trying to sound disapproving but failing badly.

He chuckled and nuzzled against her neck. "I can't help it if I love my wife more than any man has ever loved a woman in the whole history of the world."

She sighed again, her smile returning. "I think I must be the most blessed woman on earth."

She linked their fingers at her waist and they stood in silence, listening to the rhythmic sound of grass tearing as Stride and Clementine gave the lush, untouched grass at the top of the hill a trim.

"Are you disappointed you didn't get to your fancy hotel in San Francisco?" Adam said after a while.

Amy turned around in his arms and looked up into the blue eyes she loved so much. "Not even one tiny bit. How could I be disappointed when I have everything I've ever wanted?"

An uncertain frown creased the space between his eyebrows. "But mucking out horses and living in a tiny, three roomed house way out here instead of in luxury in the big city..."

"Is the best thing that could ever have happened to me. All I ever wanted was to be safe and happy and loved and I've got all that and so much more." She pushed up onto her toes, placed her mouth against his and whispered, "As long as I'm with you, I will never ever be disappointed."

She closed her eyes and slipped her arms around his neck and when they finally parted, Adam's frown was gone. He led her to where the horses were grazing and helped her onto Clem before mounting Stride.

Then he leaned over to take her hand and brought it to his lips with a smile. "Let's go home, Mrs Emerson."

Pure joy lifted Amy's heart into flight.

She was Adam's bride, and she didn't want it any other way.

THE END

Dear Reader

Thank you for reading No One's Bride and I hope you've enjoyed Amy and Adam's story.

Please consider leaving a review on Amazon to let others know how you felt about the book, even just a few words. Like all independent authors I rely on word of mouth to help people find my books and reviews are very important. I will be ridiculously grateful when you do!

A note about the book – I am British and can't spell any other way! Those are genuine UK English spellings and are provided free of charge for your amusement and delight. Of course, if you find an actual mistake please do let me know! I have, as far as I could, tried to make the story historically accurate while tailoring it for a modern audience, but I freely admit there might be things that I may have got wrong. If you are more knowledgeable than I am (which is highly likely) and something is making you want to tear your hair out, please do get in touch via my Facebook page or website, or at nerys@nerysleigh.com. I love to hear from readers!

No One's Bride is the first in the Escape to the West series. If the hints about what was happening to Sara, Lizzy, Louisa and Josephine have you wanting to know more, they will each be getting their own book, each of which begins with their arrival on the train. Sign up to my newsletter on my website to never miss a new release. You will receive just a handful of emails a year and absolutely no spam, ever, promise!

nerysleigh.com
facebook.com/nerysleigh

Bible Verses

These are the verses quoted, or referred to, in No One's Bride, this time from the New International Version (NIV) translation because I find it easier to understand!

Chapter 2 - Suppose a brother or a sister is without clothes and daily food. If one of you says to them, "Go in peace; keep warm and well fed," but does nothing about their physical needs, what good is it? James 2:15-16

Chapter 3 - Jesus looked at them and said, "With man this is impossible, but with God all things are possible." Matthew 19:26

Chapter 13 - If God is for us, who can be against us? He who did not spare His own Son, but gave Him up for us all—how will He not also, along with Him, graciously give us all things? Romans 8:31-32

Chapter 13 – "But if you can do anything, take pity on us and help us." " 'If you can'?" said Jesus. "Everything is possible for one who believes." Immediately the boy's father exclaimed, "I do believe; help me overcome my unbelief!" Mark 9:22-24

Chapter 13 - Trust in the Lord with all your heart and lean not on your own understanding; in all your ways submit to Him, and He will make your paths straight. Proverbs 3:5

Chapter 21 - If God is for us, who can be against us? Romans 8:31

Chapter 26 - But He said to me, "My grace is sufficient for you, for My power is made perfect in weakness." 2 Corinthians 12:9

Chapter 30 – Be kind and compassionate to one another, forgiving each other, just as in Christ God forgave you. Ephesians 4:32

Made in the USA
Middletown, DE
15 June 2017